AMBER SANDS

Madeline Dando

ISBN 978-1-78222-115-9

Book design, layout and production management by Into Print
www.intoprint.net
+44 (0)1604 832149

Printed and bound in UK and USA by Lightning Source

Foreword

Writing a book and getting it published has been a life-long ambition. Many years ago I wrote a poem called Amber Sands. I have long since thought it would provide the perfect basis for a wonderful story and at last my dream has come to fruition.

Having been work in progress for a very long time, I have come to know the characters very well. Also, some of the happenings in the book I can personally relate to in childhood and beyond. In particular the words 'It's alright for you, you can always put your hand in your pocket and find a fiver,' will stay with me forever.

Although I have read and re-written this book many times, I still find myself emotionally challenged and inspired whenever I cast my eyes over its pages.

When movie pictures were first made it was said they were intended to take people's minds away from worry and stress. They were to provide a welcome distraction from everyday life and that is what I have tried to do with this book.

TF178765

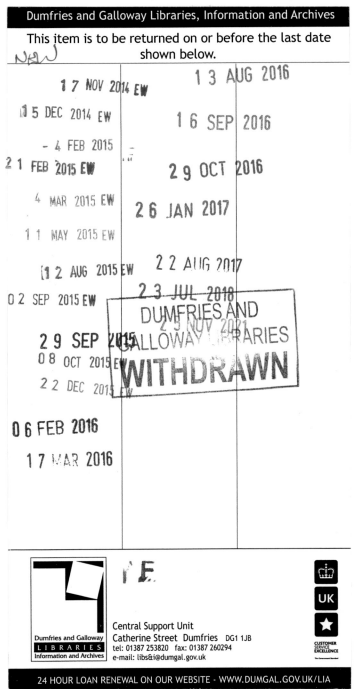

Chapter One

The early morning sunshine had disappeared and with low heavy clouds dominating the darkened sky it was gloomy for mid-morning. Rain was falling in large spots and puddles had formed on the uneven platform surface.

A little boy in a vivid green raincoat and shiny black wellington boots was irritating his father by stamping about in the water. He was dawdling and taking hold of the child with a firm grip of his left arm, he shouted 'Come on will you, we'll be left behind.'

As Amser boarded the train the heavens opened. Within seconds the rain was beating down on the railway carriages with such vigour it sounded like an army of mice in boots, scurrying about on the tin roof.

Amser looked back from her window seat as the train moved away from the station. She saw Rhonda looking smaller and smaller as she faded into the distance and waved at her friend until she was out of sight.

Now apart from having the comfort of her daughter she was alone. Amser had considered how she might feel at this time. All kinds of thoughts ran through her mind but she knew in all honesty it was something she couldn't prepare for.

She became tearful and even shivery. An uneasy feeling took hold of her body. The last moments she spent with her mum had upset her far more than she imagined. The realisation of not seeing her again had taken hold and it would have been easy to feel guilty and go back home.

Amser however wasn't going to fail at the first hurdle but she needed all her strength and determination to stay positive and focused on the time ahead. She'd taken some very difficult decisions in her life but moving from home and taking Bethan away from her grandparents were the hardest.

It was at times such as this Amser took comfort from her grandmother. Although no longer alive she had provided the girl with many words of wisdom. Amser missed their cosy chats and still looked to the old lady in her thoughts for guidance and inspiration.

The journey to Rowan in the north of the country was to take over five hours. The train consisted of four brown and cream carriages pulled by a diesel engine. It was to wind its way slowly through the hills and valleys and was known as the 'Cosy Line'. However there was nothing cosy about the journey now. The seats were old and well worn. They were uncomfortable and unnerving squeaks and creaks could be heard at every twist and turn.

Amser passed the time at first by playing games with Bethan, singing nursery rhymes and reading stories. Her favourite was about a donkey called Ned and Bethan wanted it read to her over and over again.

Despite the traumatic upheaval the little girl was contented. At such a tender age she wasn't able to understand the changes taking place in her life but she trusted her mother and always wanted to be with her.

Bethan soon became tired and the continuous sound of the carriage wheels caressing the railway track sent her into a deep sleep. The little girl's arms had turned cold and Amser warmed Bethan by tucking her favourite yellow blanket around both her body and her favourite teddy called Pinky.

Looking at her daughter Amser was determined not to let her down. During the next few hours she was to examine her life once more; to rid herself of the demons of the past and look only to the future.

Amser Edwards had been brought up in West Wales in a small, two bedroomed dwelling, in a town named Walwyn Gate. It was now a very quiet place. The houses were looking old and tired having largely been built in Victorian times. The roads were full of potholes and the pavements were cracked and uneven with weeds protruding from their crumbling surrounds. Some of the shops were closed and boarded up and everywhere you could see paint peeling, door hinges rusting and broken windows.

It was a tragedy for the local people because, many years before, Walwyn Gate had been a thriving community with a coal mine leading its industry. Although work was hard, most of the people were employed and content with their lives.

Amser's mind went back to 1969 when she was fourteen. The girl was five feet four inches tall then. She had a pretty face, an attractive slim figure and wavy, light brown hair. However, despite her good looks Amser was a quiet and sombre girl, she lacked confidence and didn't have any ambition in life.

Her father was a loud and stubborn man. He had a large body frame and his stomach always protruding from his shirt drooped over the top of his trousers. Black braces held them up and he had short grey hair which was thinning with the onset of baldness.

The man had worked for the railway as a station porter. Whilst employed he was used to having people around him. In its heyday this form of transportation not only served the coal mine, it also provided a vital link between the local communities.

The station was often busy and Mr Edwards thrived in this environment. He loved chatting to the passengers, helping them with their luggage and providing information about the trains.

He also kept the station property free from litter and in the ticket office not a speck of dust or dirt could be seen anywhere. He even made and tended the hanging flower baskets that hung from the light posts along the platforms. They provided a blaze of colour in the summer months and were loved by the passengers. Mr Edwards was respected and felt needed.

However with the demise of the pit there wasn't any coal to be moved. It used to be brought to the station yard in open trucks where it waited for collection by lorry. It was so much quieter now without these heavy vehicles rumbling up and down the road. However, people had got used to their properties shaking when they passed by and in a strange way they missed the intrusive noise.

It was a terrible time in Walwyn Gate as many people lost their jobs and some moved away. The impact of the changes was soon felt at the station. There wasn't much need for freight anymore and passenger numbers also dwindled. It was inevitable the branch line would be closed and, along with other poor souls, Mr Edwards was made redundant.

He received the news on a Friday afternoon by way of a short letter in a scruffy brown envelope. The words were cold and didn't provide any form of comfort. There wasn't any recognition of his service to the railway not even a thank-you.

The letter said 'Dear Mr Edwards it is with regret the last ever train will depart from Walwyn Gate Station at 5.15pm on the third Friday this month and from that day on your services will no longer be required.'

Mr Edwards was not a fool. He had been expecting the station to close but thought he would be offered work elsewhere. Now however, he'd been given two weeks' notice. A large part of Amser's dad died that day.

Like many people in the town he felt disillusioned and abandoned. Both the pit and the railway had been the lifeblood of the community and there wasn't a family that hadn't been affected in some way by their closures.

However, despite all the hardship very little was done by the government to help Walwyn Gate through its difficulties. The town had been forgotten and poverty had become part of everyday life.

For a few weeks Mr Edwards spent all his time at home sitting in his chair feeling sorry for himself. He didn't want to do anything or say anything; he felt his life was over. It was easy to feel pain for Mr Edwards; losing his job wasn't his fault. However, before long his lack of employment started to have an adverse effect on his family's already precarious financial situation.

Amser's parents often argued but an increasing lack of basic commodities led to an almost violent confrontation. One evening the girl watched as her mum opened the kitchen cupboards. She looked inside and all she could see was a single tin of baked beans, two Oxo cubes and some custard powder.

Turning around to her husband, she shouted at the top of her voice 'Look, will you: they're empty; can you see they're bloody empty? I can't earn enough to feed us properly let alone pay the rent and the electric. When are you going to get off your fat arse and do something?'

'You have to find a job,' she exclaimed as she slumped into a chair and cried.

Mr Edwards didn't like being chastised especially in front of his daughter. He kicked the stool in front of him and rose to his feet in a rage. Amser could see the anger he felt inside in his steely eyes and the gritting of his teeth.

She hadn't seen her parents like this before and it scared her. However her dad knew his wife was right. He calmed himself before his temper got the better of him and sat back down in his chair. Although ignoring his wife's pleas at the time this cry for help provided him with the spark he needed.

He started to search the local newspaper for work and two months later managed to get himself employed as a night security officer. It was in a textile factory in Abeglan which was only three miles away and he was able to cycle there. His job was very easy and undemanding but very different from the one he enjoyed on the railway platform and he hated it.

He didn't have contact with anyone and his only company was a small wooden-cased radio. He listened to stations far across the world to pass the time, whilst sitting in a small room for eight hours each night. Nevertheless it was a job and it provided much-needed income.

Mrs Edwards had a short tubby stature and small feet with hammered toes. She had blonde curly hair that was always untidy and wore old glasses with thick brown frames.

Amser could remember how her mother looked when she was a small child. She could recall seeing her sitting in front of her dressing table mirror, brushing her hair for ages at a time. She looked beautiful then and Amser was very proud of her.

However, just like her dad, her mum was disenchanted with all that had happened around her. She didn't have the time, money or inclination to make herself up now and had lost her self-respect.

Mr and Mrs Edwards had never been well off but they'd always paid their way and had never got into debt. To add to the family's income Mrs Edwards was employed as a day carer in the town. The work was hard as she was on her feet all day.

Sometimes she would be running between patients' homes to get her jobs done. She often had to lift disabled people in and out of wheelchairs and on and off beds. For some patients she cleaned, cooked and did their washing and ironing.

There was never enough time to provide the level of care needed. Some people however were always moaning if she arrived at their homes a minute late or forgot an item of shopping. On occasions they were rude and selfish. It was very unusual for anyone to thank Mrs Edwards for the help she was providing. They believed it was their right to be nursed and treated her like dirt.

However, because she often worked in squalid conditions, in dirty smelly rooms or homes where electricity had been cut off, she never complained about her life. Mrs Edwards realised that many of her patients had problems worse than her own.

Amser's parents, working long hours, didn't have time for themselves or Amser who was their only child. They lurched from one day to the next and tried to get through each one as best they could. They were always tired in the evenings and even the weekends were absorbed by the need for them to look after Amser's grandmother Bethan.

This was Amser's only surviving grandparent and her mother's mum. The lady, although only sixty two, was unable to do things for herself. She had a stroke some years earlier and had been left with a paralysed left arm and found it difficult to walk.

Her husband Dilwyn had died in the Second World War on a merchant ship sunk by a German submarine in the English Channel. They'd been childhood sweethearts since infant school.

Now having to spend most of her time in her wheelchair she was comforted by his photo which she kept on her lap. It was housed in a brown wooden frame and at night she placed it beside her bed in the centre of a small teak table draped with a shiny red cloth.

Despite her misfortune the lady never complained. Her incapacity irritated her and whilst alone she often shed a tear or two. However, she was a proud woman and when in the company of others she masked her grief. Any mention of Dilwyn was a comfort to her.

Amser's granny lived at the far end of the village in Rose Cottage. It was situated next to an old wooden footbridge that spanned a river. It was a quiet place except for the sound of rushing water fed by a small waterfall up stream.

Her house had a dark brown thatched roof and a wide wooden gate guarded a stone path leading up to its scarlet red door. Surrounding the entrance were two rambling roses that produced masses of bright pink blooms in the summer months; they were beautiful.

Mr and Mrs Edwards spent Saturdays there until late in the evening and returned again on Sunday after attending church in the morning. During the week Mrs Edwards also visited her mother at 8am each day, at lunch time around 1pm and again to put her to bed in the evening at 9pm. With these pressures always upon her she was exhausted but carried on regardless.

Life was also very hard on Amser. Because of their domestic situation her parents expected their daughter to cook, clean, shop and keep the house tidy. She was treated more like a hired help than a teenage child and they moaned at her if she forgot the slightest thing. Amser, although longing for love and attention, never complained. She knew how difficult things were for her mum and dad.

Amser too went to see her granny whenever she could. She loved the old lady who always made her feel warm inside with cuddles and words of re-assurance.

She used to say to the girl 'In my crystal ball I can see a wonderful future for you.'

Amser didn't believe it. She knew her granny didn't have such an object, and believed the lady was only trying to comfort her.

'Who has a wonderful future in Walwyn Gate?' she chuckled to herself.

However, every time she saw her granny she was given the same message and these words became entrenched in her mind.

Whilst in bed one night Amser listened to her parents arguing.

Her father shouted out 'I can't earn any more money.'

Then she heard her mother crying. The girl was used to the

angry voices coming from downstairs. There used to be disagreements that happened from time to time but lately they had become more frequent and intense. How she wished things could be different.

Amser's clothes were all second hand from her mum's friends' children. Sometimes, the family couldn't afford to buy toothpaste and they had to use soap. Even toilet paper would run out occasionally and they had to manage with paper bags or newspaper.

However, despite all the family's problems Amser knew there were many people worse off than her. She was thankful that, although on some days there was little more to eat than bread and potatoes, she never went hungry.

As Amser listened to the raised voices she looked around her room. It was draughty and damp and lit by a single bulb peering down from the ceiling above. The room was small and the door opened onto a cupboard containing her clothes. She had to shut the door behind her before she could open it.

There was just enough room for her single bed and a small table and chair. It was there she sat to do her homework and comb her hair in front of a mirror that was fixed to the wall. The room had a small window draped with brown-stained curtains and through the pane all Amser was able to see was an old watermill.

It was whilst she was lying in bed that night feeling sad and tearful that words expressing her feelings started going round and round inside her head. Amser kept thinking about the same words and couldn't get them out of her mind. She got up and took an exercise book out of her school bag. Turning to the inside of the back page she started writing:-

I'm sitting in my room I'm crying again
Such a steady stream it's almost rain
Nobody cares it's only me
Please love me

The more she wrote the sadder she became and the sadder she felt the more she wrote.

Please love me, please want me, I need you
How many times I've called from my door
Just a little love that's all I need, nothing more
I'm so sad and lonely, I'm so sad and blue
I must have dreamt a thousand dreams
But none of them come true.

Amser longed for a better life and like on so many evenings she cried herself to sleep.

Chapter Two

A few weeks later whilst she was at school Amser was asked by her English teacher, Mrs Reece, to wait behind after lessons had finished.

The school was housed in an old three-storey building which was erected at the end of the 19ᵗʰ century. The rooms had small windows and high ceilings. When the lights weren't on they seemed a little dark and even when heated they always felt cold.

Desks were arranged in lines of six in neat rows facing the front where the teacher sat with a large blackboard on the wall behind. The classrooms were intimidating places for the children but they breathed authority and commanded respect. The corridors were long and narrow and every footstep could be heard on the surface of the brown-stained stone floor.

Amser didn't believe she'd done anything wrong as she always did what she was told. However, she knew her teacher must have a reason and became more concerned as the end of the day approached.

Mrs Reece was tall and supported a heavy body frame. She had long grey hair tied back in a ponytail with a velvet bow and wore thick blue-framed glasses. The teacher was always dressed in a black skirt, white blouse and shiny, closed, black shoes. She was obsessed with cleanliness and throughout the day could be seen wiping her desk with a duster or removing the slightest suspicion of dirt from under her fingernails.

Mrs Reece was very strict. She insisted on having the full attention of her children for every moment during her lessons.

Amser remembered the first minute of her first day in the teacher's room. The lady stood with her hands on her hips by the door as the girl and her classmates entered.

'Just find a desk anywhere you like,' instructed Mrs Reece.

Then she watched everybody, like a hawk as they passed by her. One boy was stopped and told to do his top shirt button up and a girl was told to tie her hair back.

Then as the children were selecting their desks a boy sat down straight away.

Mrs Reece bellowed at him 'Stand up boy.'

When all the children were settled they were asked to sit down. Then the teacher closed the door and walked across the room until she was behind her desk. There, standing with her arms folded, she gazed at her pupils in silence and all eyes were fixed on her.

Then she started to lay down her rules.

She said 'Whilst you're in my class you will not speak to one another.'

At this moment an unpleasant girl called Pauline Reynolds whispered something to her friend. They were sitting together at the back of the room but Mrs Reece spotted the misdemeanour and moved towards her.

Being a tall lady her leg stride was wide and in less than a moment she was pulling the girl out of her desk chair. Clutching Pauline by her arm with a firm hand she dragged her to the front of the class. Pauline was very cocky and a bit of a bully but at this moment her hands were shaking.

'Now face the class girl,' Mrs Reece bellowed as she turned her around.

'Do you want your pals to have extra homework because of you?'

Before Pauline could utter a single word the teacher gave her a gentle push and told her to go back to her desk and sit down.

Mrs Reece walked across the front line of desks and gazed around the class. She focused her eyes on all of the children one by one. The room was silent and a few seconds passed whilst the teacher's attention was drawn to something or someone outside.

Then without warning she turned around as quick as a spinning top and shouted 'That's the last time I will be disobeyed. Do you all understand?'

Most of the children mumbled the word yes. The teacher became more agitated and banged her right hand hard on her desk causing two pencils to fly in the air and land on the floor beside her.

'I said do you understand class?' she bellowed.

The children immediately replied 'Yes Mrs Reece.'

Now as quiet as mice they listened as she continued 'If you want to speak to me you will put up your hand. You will not leave your desk without permission and above everything else you will keep your eyes fixed on me or your work.'

From that day on the girl had always been a little scared of this lady and her eyes were focused on Amser as the other children left the class.

The last person to leave closed the door and as soon as it was shut the teacher called out to Amser 'Come here girl.'

Amser got up and started walking towards her.

'Don't dawdle Amser, I haven't got all day,' she shouted.

The girl quickened her step until she was standing right in front of the teacher's desk. Mrs Reece never smiled and she made Amser feel very nervous.

Then Amser watched as she took an exercise book from the top drawer under her desk. She could see the book was hers but still didn't know what she'd done that was so awful.

Mrs Reece looked over the top of her glasses, raised her eyebrows and asked 'Why has your school material been misused?'

Amser looked perplexed; she didn't have any idea what the teacher was referring to and didn't know what to say. Mrs Reece opened the book to the offending page. Then she slapped it on the desk in front of Amser.

'There girl,' she said, pointing to Amser's writing and prodding the page with her fingers.

'Look at it, what were you thinking of? Aren't you aware that writing whatever you like in school books isn't allowed?'

Amser nodded.

'Answer me,' Mrs Reece shouted.

Amser very sheepishly said 'Yes I did, I'm sorry.'

'I should think so,' replied the teacher.

At this point Amser felt as though the whole world was against her and broke down in tears. She knew she shouldn't have done it, but it wasn't as if it was anything life-threatening or illegal. Her only crime was to write in an English exercise book.

Amser was embarrassed to cry in front of Mrs Reece but not only was she upset, she was also annoyed. Mrs Reece in seeing this emotion felt perhaps she hadn't measured her response correctly and had been a little too hard on the girl.

As Amser was walking out of the classroom with her head bowed Mrs Reece called her back to her desk.

She said 'Look Amser, I can't have you writing whatever you like in your books.'

The girl responded 'I know Mrs Reece I am really sorry it won't happen again.'

Then to Amser's surprise the teacher's tone changed and the harshness in her face disappeared.

After hesitating she said in a soft voice 'But I did happen to show your poem to another teacher, Mr Williams; we both liked it very much.'

Mr Williams taught English Literature.

Then Mrs Reece asked Amser how she felt about poetry.

'I haven't thought about it before. I do like reading beautiful stories and I know that sadness inspires me to look at things in different ways. I don't know why but it's amazing the things that go through my mind sometimes, which is why I wrote the poetry.'

Mrs Reece, now much more relaxed in her approach, invited Amser to sit down on a chair beside her.

She enquired 'Why are you so sad?'

'It's difficult,' said Amser.

'What do you mean difficult?' she enquired.

'My mum and dad are busy all the time. They work very hard and for them life seems to be such a struggle. You know how it is in Walwyn Gate now.'

The teacher did know, she'd lived close by for over twenty years and watched the town decline but had never considered the effects it had on the children.

Mrs Reece opened up her desk again and produced a poetry book called 'Collected Poems' by R S Thomas.

Looking up at the girl she said 'Perhaps you'd like to borrow this Amser?'

Amser took the book from her teacher and examined it. On opening the front cover she saw it had been inscribed with the words 'To Angela with love from John'.

Mrs Reece didn't say a word but Amser guessed it had been a present that must have meant something special to her teacher in the past.

She replied 'Thank you so much. I'll look after it I promise.'

'I know you will, please let me have it back whenever you like. Please don't write in it Amser,' said the teacher.

At that moment Mrs Reece almost smiled and the girl left the classroom.

She'd never liked her teacher but from that day she saw her in a different light. She hadn't seen Mrs Reece show any compassion before or notice her help anyone. Now Amser knew hidden in Mrs Reece's makeup was a thoughtful, caring lady and she wasn't to be intimidated by her again.

It was the first time in Amser's life she'd received praise from anyone and she'd also been trusted with a prized possession. She bounced out of the classroom with an air of confidence and had a warm glow inside her she hoped would last forever.

Amser's classmates had all gone home except for her best friend Rhonda. She had waited for over half an hour sitting on a low wall outside the school gates.

Rhonda lived a short distance away from Amser. Her family was a little better off and lived in a three-bedroomed semi-detached house in a tree-lined avenue.

She was always dressed in clean, bright, ironed clothes, had black wavy hair down to her shoulders and a slim figure. She was very bubbly albeit a little mischievous and everybody loved her.

Rhonda liked Amser more than her other friends because she was honest, caring and reliable. She was concerned about Amser as well as a little nosy. She couldn't wait to find out why Mrs Reece wanted to see her. Then Amser came out of the school and immediately Rhonda noticed the spring in her step and the wide smile on her face.

'What an earth could have happened,' she thought.

Amser told her friend everything that was said but no matter how hard she tried Rhonda would not be convinced Mrs Reece was a very caring person.

'Goodness Ams you'll be telling me next the old witch has invited you to her home for tea,' she said.

'Don't be silly,' came the reply.

'The strange thing is she told me off and then she helped me. I know it's hard to believe.'

Then taking the book of poems out of her bag she said 'Look Rhon, look what she's lent me.'

When Amser drew Rhonda's attention to the inscription they both started to consider what John might have been like. All sorts of ideas were put forward and the girls were laughing out loud.

Then Rhonda said 'Do you think they used to do it?'

'Do what?' enquired Amser.

'You know Ams, do it, sex and all that.'

There was more laughter as the girls couldn't imagine Mrs Reece doing anything sexual. They both thought about their teacher and tried to imagine the mysterious inscriber. They were now becoming hysterical as they continued to swap rude remarks about Mrs Reece being with a man.

Then Amser started to feel guilty and became a little sad. It had only been a short while since she left her teacher's room and she felt ashamed. The girls both knew Mrs Reece was a widow but they didn't know if John had been her husband. They didn't know anything about their teacher's life and yet as a result of the lady's act of kindness they were being disrespectful.

'I feel awful talking about her like this,' she said.

Rhonda however, wasn't concerned at all.

'Well, whoever he was he would have deserved a medal if he was a friend of the old bat,' she replied.

Amser said 'It must have been a long time ago. I don't think she would have lent me the book if John was still around.'

Whilst making their way home Rhonda asked more and more questions but Amser wasn't listening. She kept thinking about Mrs Reece and her kindness. In just a few minutes her outlook on life had changed and for once she was already looking forward to attending class the next morning. Amser realised what a positive affect her teacher had on her and for the first time she considered the possibility of becoming a teacher of English Literature.

As the girls continued their walk home, Rhonda unwittingly stepped on a broken paving stone. It collapsed into a hole beneath and she slipped over. The girl landed on her bottom on the kerb, giving two lads who were standing close by a glimpse of her red knickers.

However, Rhonda (being Rhonda) wasn't concerned and flirted with them as they joked about the colour. Amser was used to Rhonda, but appalled by her behaviour.

'Come on Rhon we'll never get home,' said Amser as she helped her friend to her feet.

The boys continued hounding Rhonda by whistling and making suggestive remarks. To Amser's horror Rhonda responded with smiles and laughter.

Taking hold of her arm she almost had to drag her friend away and said 'Honestly Rhon have you no shame at all?'

Rhonda always thought Amser was far too serious and her friend's remarks made her giggle all the more. When she fell she was able to cushion her body with her hands and there didn't seem to be any harm to the girl apart from her obtaining a few bruises which would become more apparent the following morning.

However, as she got back on her feet she noticed the strap had broken on one of her shoes. Rhonda adored shoes more than any other item of clothing, she was obsessed by them and at home they covered one side of her bedroom floor.

Taking it off to examine the damage she moaned 'Look at that Ams I can't wear it now. I only bought the shoes last week.'

Amser was sympathetic but to her surprise Rhonda decided she was going to take the shoes back to the place where she bought them for replacement. The shop aptly named 'Walkers' was situated around the corner from where they were.

Amser said 'You can't do that. It's not their fault.'

'I don't think the shoes have been made very well,' she replied.

Then whilst giggling she added 'Anyway I have a plan.'

On walking into the shop the girls could see it was very busy. All the shop assistants were dealing with customers.

Amser was already feeling uncomfortable and said 'Come on Rhon we'll be ages in here we might as well go.'

However, Rhonda was a stubborn girl and once she made up her mind she was going to do something, nothing would change it.

'It won't take long,' she said.

Being late in the day it was not very tidy in the shop and odd shoes had been left lying around on the carpet in various places. Rhonda started eyeing all the goods on the shelves. Amser could see her friend was looking for something particular and saw her pick up a shoe that was the same style and colour as the one she was wearing.

Then Rhonda sat down and took off her damaged shoe and tried on the new one. To Amser's surprise and horror her friend then placed her own shoe back on the shelf.

'You can't do that Rhon,' whispered Amser.

'I've done it,' she replied with a cheeky grin.

Amser was worried and looked all around the shop to see if anybody had noticed. At that time however, all the staff were occupied with other customers. Rhonda's action didn't seem to have been witnessed.

'Come on let's go Rhon,' pleaded Amser.

'Just a few more minutes,' she replied.

Almost dreading Rhonda's response she enquired 'Why can't we go now?'

'Because the shoe I put on doesn't fit. I'm a size five and the shoe I took from the shelf is a four. It's too small so I need to change it.'

'Change it?' said Amser.

'How can you do that?'

'Just watch me,' said Rhonda.

Then she attracted the attention of a male assistant who'd become free after serving another customer.

'I hope you can help me. I purchased these shoes last week and have found the right one to be a little tight.'

She went on 'Looking inside I noticed it's a size four and not a size five like the left one.'

The assistant listened to Rhonda explain the situation.

He replied 'I think we must have odd shoes left in the shop. I've never known this to happen before. I'll go and look for you.'

The assistant disappeared into the stock room at the back of the premises and left the girls muttering about the situation. He was away for some time and Rhonda decided to have a good look at other shoes in the shop.

Holding up a pair of red sandals she said 'These look nice don't they Ams?'

Amser felt embarrassed. She wanted to leave and pretended not to hear but her friend wasn't to be put off.

'Look Ams what do you think?' she said.

Then the assistant returned to say 'I can only find an odd size four in a box but not a five.'

Rhonda became agitated.

She said 'Well something has to be done. I can't keep wearing this shoe it's too small. I will damage my foot.'

Amser sat silently watching her friend impose her personality on the male assistant as only she could.

Rhonda fluttered her eyes at him, lifted her long hair with her fingers and said 'You wouldn't want me to hurt my pretty little foot would you?'

'Certainly not,' came a mumbled reply.

Then he said 'Wait a moment I think I may have the answer.'

Both girls cringed as the man walked over to the shelf and searched for the same style of shoe. He picked up the size five that Rhonda had deposited and started examining it as he brought it to them.

'I think I've found a size five but it has a broken strap.'

'Well that's no good to me, what are you going to do about it?' enquired Rhonda.

The assistant spoke to his manager before returning and asking to see the girl's receipt.

Rhonda smiled and said 'I'm sure I have it here,' placing her bag on a large table.

Rhonda carried everything you can imagine in her handbag. She searched it with her hand but was unable to find the item and tipped it upside down.

Amongst her belongings were five lipsticks, a box of tissues, a mirror, a comb, a pair of blue knickers and some hygiene items. The assistant was very embarrassed as was Amser but Rhonda handled the situation with ease.

She giggled and said 'Oh sorry I think I put it in my purse.'

Amser was sure her friend had done this on purpose. She watched Rhonda refill her handbag before calmly unzipping a small compartment, taking the receipt from her purse and handing it to the assistant. He passed it to the manager who was now close by.

He examined it to make sure it related to the purchase before agreeing to give her a credit note.

Rhonda wasted no time in purchasing the sandals she'd eyed in the shop and to Amser's amazement the assistant gave her a free shoe cleaner and an apology for selling her odd shoes. On leaving the shop the girls burst out laughing.

Amser said 'You're unbelievable, I could never do anything like that. I don't know how they fell for it. You've dirt on your face and mud on your clothes. They could easily see you had fallen over.'

'Oh yes,' replied Rhonda.

'I hadn't thought of that.'

'The state of that shoe you put on the shelf. When the man picked it up I thought you were dead,' giggled Amser.

The girls started to laugh again and continued their walk home.

Chapter Three

Amser was very happy at this time. Despite her anxiety in the shoe shop she was still living on the most extraordinary and yet uplifting conversation she had with her teacher. However this feeling of ecstasy was lost on arriving home. As soon as she opened the front door her mother shouted at her for being late.

'Where on earth have you been, school closed two hours ago?' she bellowed.

Amser didn't get a chance to reply and listened to her mother as she reminded her of the house chores that needed doing. Mrs Edwards became animated when she was annoyed. She had the habit of rubbing the tip of her nose with the fourth finger on her right hand and her voice became high-pitched.

Life had returned to normal with a bump but Amser took the criticism in her stride. Without saying a word she carried out her mother's wishes. It had been quite a day and she was determined nothing was going to spoil it. The little bit of attention she received meant everything and for once she hadn't felt so ashamed in the company of her friend.

When she arrived at school the following morning, Amser's school pals were waiting for her in the playground. They too were intrigued by the need for her to stay behind the previous afternoon.

'Look there she is,' shouted one of her classmates.

After running towards her the crowd of children encircled Amser like a circus cage. She couldn't escape their questions and no matter how hard she tried to convince them, like Rhonda they refused to change their opinion of Mrs Reece.

One girl remarked 'You can't tell me the old bag was actually nice.'

Another said 'You're having a laugh aren't you.'

'Tell us honestly will you, have you got lines, detention, extra homework or what then?'

Amser laughed and said 'I got a book of poems to read that's all.'

At that moment the school bell rang and the children made their way to the classroom. Some of the girls were still making comments about Mrs Reece and were taunting Amser as they walked down the corridor.

'Teacher's pet now then are you?' one girl enquired.

'Mrs Reece doesn't have pet's only slaves,' remarked one of the boys.

However, Amser didn't care what they believed. It was what really happened that was important.

From that day Amser's outlook changed. There was something different about her. She now had a purpose in life and from being an average scholar; over the months ahead she was to become a high achiever.

Continuing to use Mrs Reece's words for encouragement and the book of poems for her inspiration, there now seemed nothing the girl couldn't achieve. There was enthusiasm in all her activities, she was more confident and now even her dreary old clothes seemed to have a sparkle about them.

Having given her future a great deal of thought Amser was now desperate to get to university to do a teaching degree but there were many hurdles in front of her which needed to be overcome. Predictably, her parents were adamant she was going to leave school at sixteen and get a job.

Amser pleaded with them but her father said 'It's impossible we'll be better off if you're at work.'

'Your dad's right, I'm sorry but we need the money so you'll have to get a job,' said her mum.

Amser realised money was tight but even if she did leave school both she and her parents knew there were few work opportunities in Walwyn Gate. The girl wasn't going to give up on her dream but she needed help and decided to go and see her grandmother.

Granny saw Amser walking up her garden path whilst she was sitting in her front room. It was the lightest place in her cottage and she would peer out of the window watching the birds feeding on fat balls and nuts hanging from a tree. She could see from the quickness in her step there was something important on her mind.

The lady always had time for Amser who was her only grand-child and was ready to open the door as soon as Amser knocked. As usual she was greeted with a warm kiss but the usual smile was absent and the girl looked at her granny and burst into tears.

'Now, now whatever is the matter?' enquired the old lady.

'I've got to leave school this year and get a job,' the girl mumbled in reply.

There were more tears and the lady was anxious for Amser to calm down.

'Sit down in there, I'm going to make us a drink,' she said pointing to the room she had been occupying.

She returned with two cups of tea and two large scones on a small trolley she was able to wheel into the room. The lady was aware from previous conversations what Amser wanted to do with her life and whilst holding her hands she listened to her sob story.

'I don't know what I'm going to do. I have to stay at school after my GCEs, I really have to,' she said.

Amser's granny had never known anybody who went to university, not even outside of her circle of friends and family. The prospect of her granddaughter studying to be a teacher excited her and she was determined to help.

She placed her hands on Amser's shoulders and said 'You leave everything to me. I'll talk to your mum and dad; I promise you everything will be alright.'

The following weekend the lady spoke to her daughter and son in law when they made their usual visit. She had to be very blunt with them to overcome the obstacles they put in the way and had something up her sleeve.

'This is the deal,' she said.

'You say you can't afford for Amser to stay in education and I understand why. However, Amser is a bright girl and she must continue with her schooling.'

Mr Edwards tried to interrupt but granny replied 'Be quiet will you I'm not going to beat around the bush, you know I have some money. I will pay you so Amser can go on with her studies.'

'I can't let you do that,' said Mrs Edwards.

'She's going to go to work,' added Amser's dad.

However, Amser's granny wasn't going to be silenced and decided to get something off her chest that had tormented her for a long time. It was something she never intended to say but she was determined Amser was going to stay at school.

'I don't know why you're worried about me paying you some money,' she remarked.

'I know you stole two small pretty vases from my bedroom upstairs a while ago. They disappeared from my glass cabinet so I know you took them. I assume they were sold?'

Amser's parents looked at one another. They'd taken the vases when Mr Edwards was out of work and they were desperate for money. They fetched £20 each at an auction and to this day the couple didn't have any idea she had noticed.

How they'd both misjudged her. Mrs Edwards in particular was distraught they'd been found out. Standing in front of her mother she was shaking and her face was bright red.

Before either of them could speak, granny said with firmness in her voice 'Please don't deny it; don't say a word. Let me do this will you, it's not for you it's for your daughter.'

In the circumstances Mr and Mrs Edwards couldn't refuse but when they got home they took out their guilt on Amser. She was coming down the stairs when they opened the front door.

'Here's our sneaky daughter,' said her father.

'How dare you go behind our backs?' he shouted.

'Most of your classmates will be leaving school, isn't work good enough for you then?'

'I want to make something of my life,' she replied whilst putting on her coat.

'Where do you think you're going?' he asked.

'She's going to see my mother, that's where she's going,' said Mrs Edwards.

'Go on then I'm sure she's expecting you,' ranted her father.

Amser couldn't get out of the house quickly enough. She didn't care what her parents thought. As she ran down the road for once she was thinking about herself. By the time she reached the cottage she was out of breath but when her granny opened the door it didn't stop Amser clasping her arms around the old lady and hugging and kissing her.

'Goodness Amser let me go will you.'

'Thank you, thank you so much,' said the girl still breathing heavily.

Granny replied 'Remember what I said Amser the future is bright for you. You can do anything you like in this world if you want it enough. All you have to do is work hard and have courage and determination. You'd better go now before your mum moans at you for not doing your chores and we wouldn't want that would we?'

'Yes granny, no granny, thank you granny,' said Amser as she smiled, hugged and kissed her again before running home.

Despite the financial agreement life was still hard for Amser. She'd house work to do as well as home work. Because she was so busy the days and months seemed to get shorter and shorter and the exams were worrying her.

However, Amser was a different child now. She had caring teachers, the love of her beloved grandmother and a burning desire to succeed. As the exam dates approached she worked late at night and got up at 6am each morning so she could juggle all her responsibilities.

She was exhausted but somehow found the strength to get everything done. It was a Thursday afternoon at 3pm when she put down her pen on her last exam and a great burden was lifted from her shoulders.

That summer it was hot almost every day and when Amser wasn't at home she spent time with Rhonda relaxing in the local park. Her friend had a black labrador called Bonnie and they walked for miles around a large lake watching windsurfers and rowers. They strolled along the tree-lined paths under the leaves and branches protecting them from the sun.

There was one particular oak tree where they always stopped for a breather. They sat down on the large protruding roots that spread out around the trunk and ate the sandwiches they brought with them. Amser's were always either jam or fish paste whilst Rhonda would bring ham, chicken or cheese but the girls just shared them.

This tree became very special. It was a little off the beaten track and other people tended to walk on the main footpaths. The girls came to regard it as their tree and on one occasion they etched their names on it with a small knife that Rhonda had brought with her.

August soon came and Amser waited at home on the day the exam results were due to be received. She was feeling anxious and couldn't keep still as time passed by. The postman made his deliveries in the street at around 8.30am but on this particular day he was late. Amser kept opening the front door to see if he was coming.

It wasn't until 9.20am that she saw the man on his bike in the distance. The girl had been very happy with her exams but doubts about her success began to creep into her head. She started to review all her work in her mind as best she could and began to contemplate failure.

If she didn't get the GCE passes she needed she couldn't stay on at school and if she couldn't stay on at school she couldn't do her A Levels. She'd have to start work and the thought of going to university would soon become a distant memory.

Standing by the front door with these thoughts in her mind the letter box opened. A small brown envelope was pushed through and dropped on the wooden floor below. It was the only posting that day and Amser stared at it knowing her future would be decided by its contents.

The girl picked up the item, took it into the kitchen and laid it on the table. For some reason she lined it up exactly with the table edge and was frightened to open it.

Then she remembered her grandmother's words. She was told she could do anything with courage and determination and this was the first test. She had worked hard and this was to be her reward.

Without further ado she picked up the envelope and sliced

open the top with her fingers. Inside was one piece of paper folded in half. As she removed it she held her breath and looked inside.

Her anxiety turned to glee as she eyed her results. She had good passes in Mathematics, Geography, History and Science but in Welsh Language, English Language and most importantly English Literature she had 'A' passes. This was a remarkable achievement for a girl in this community with so many other demands on her life.

Her parents were stunned and refused to believe they had such a clever daughter. Her grandmother however was lifted by Amser's success.

When given the good news she said 'Oh my dear Amser.'

For a moment she looked at her husband's photo and then added 'You know your granddad would have been as proud of you as I am. There didn't I tell you, this is the start of a long journey, who knows where life might take you.'

They hugged and there were tears of joy and then granny drew Amser's attention to a long slim box on the table beside her.

'Open it Amser,' she said.

On lifting the lid the girl saw a beautiful two-string pearl necklace.

'Take it out of the box Amser and try it on.'

Amser did as she was told and stood in front of the lady.

Granny smiled and nodded in approval but then sighed a little before saying 'I feel a little sad as I'd always intended giving it to your mother but you know how things are between us. I want you to have it Amser I know you'll look after it. Perhaps one day you will have a daughter to be proud of to pass it on to.'

The girl couldn't find the words to express her thanks; putting her arms around her granny again she said 'I love you so much I will always treasure it.'

Chapter Four

Amser was now sixteen and one of fifteen children who'd stayed on at school for a further two years. She was pleased Rhonda was also there having got excellent results and they continued to share much of their spare time together.

At home however, despite granny's insistence on helping her mother and son-in-law financially, Amser was still treated badly. She had increased learning responsibilities but was made to undertake more and more chores.

As the weeks went by it was becoming more difficult for Amser to keep up with her homework but somehow she managed to cope. Things improved during the school holidays the following summer but when the next academic year started, leading up to her A Levels the heavy demands of balancing school work and house chores returned.

Amser had never rebelled before but she was now almost an adult and had enough of being told what to do and when to do it. She made up her mind that for once she was going to do something for herself.

When the weekend arrived and after her parents left home to look after her grandmother, Amser went to her bedroom to get ready. She decided to take the 9.10am bus to Amber Sands which was four miles away. It was now late September but there was still some warmth in the air.

She dressed herself in her favourite light blue top and white shorts and set off down the road that led through the town. She was very nervous. In Walwyn Gate everybody knew everybody else and people were staring as it was unusual to see Amser arrive at the bus stop. There were faces she recognised and she gave the odd smile and nod of the head. She could hear people muttering about her and she was feeling a little intimidated.

Then when she'd almost decided to go back home the bus appeared in the distance coming down the steep hill known as Warren Mount. As it approached, Amser could see it was blue and white and displayed a large sign at the front saying 'No 4 Amber Sands'.

The bus screeched to a halt in front of where Amser was standing. She took a deep breath, moved forward and stepped on to the vehicle. Having paid her fare Amser moved down the aisle and sat on the left side at the back.

She looked down and noticed the fabric was torn on the front edge of her seat and could see old chewing gum lying all over the floor that had been flattened by shoes. The window beside her was dirty and the whole bus looked old and dingy. However, the girl wasn't worried about such things and sat there watching other people boarding the vehicle.

She didn't want to converse with anybody and became agitated as the seats were filling up towards where she was sitting. She could feel her hands shaking in her pockets.

Then she cringed as a man with a very large body frame eased his way down the vehicle, just managing to push past people that were seated. He was wearing an unbuttoned black collared shirt revealing unsightly flabby skin and he planted himself right next to Amser. As he sat down his large exterior intruded into her space and he smelt of body odour and cigarette ash. It wasn't pleasant and the girl looked away from him and out of the window.

Amser hadn't been to Amber Sands for some years. Her mum and dad used to take her there and to other places before the railway closed and her grandmother became ill. She missed these outings as they provided an escape from her dreary life and she remembered how happy her parents once were.

When everybody was settled, the driver closed the door. It had to be shut forcibly to stay in its groove and everything shook as it was slammed tight. Then the engine was started and the vehicle made its way out of Walwyn Gate.

The ride was uncomfortable with the wheels on the old bus running over the bumpy road and the brakes squeaking at every twist and turn. The rather ghastly man next to her burped and broke wind at regular intervals but Amser was oblivious to it all. Her nerves had gone and nothing was going to spoil her day.

As the vehicle got closer to its destination she knew before long she would see the sea lapping on the beach. Amber Sands was a lovely place that looked out west over the Irish Sea. All around there were rolling hills, pretty houses, gardens and fields with animals and flowers. It was like a paradise compared to where she lived and yet it was only a short distance away.

Amser recalled the journey as if it was yesterday. She remembered a steep hill with an old church ruin near the top and knew as soon as the bus passed it, the sea would be in sight. Looking down inside the vehicle and out through the driver's windscreen the girl saw the road starting to rise.

She was like a small child again remembering her mum saying 'Who's going to see the sea first?'

It made Amser sad thinking about how things used to be but then seconds later she became excited when she could see the old ruin in the distance. Nothing had changed, she had the same feeling of joyful anticipation she had all those years before. In seconds the vehicle reached the summit and the sight of the sea was in her eyes.

Amser looked out across the silky sand and over the gleaming water. Before long the bus was gliding along the sea front. The tide was a little way out and the beach was already packed with families enjoying themselves. Children were swimming in the water, playing games and digging in the sand.

It was a beautiful, calm, clear, sunny day and Amser was determined to make the most of it. Her parents having struggled for money for many years were unable to give her nice things and she'd been brought up not to take anything for granted. She was a kind, warm-hearted girl and got pleasure out of seeing other children enjoying themselves but this was her day and Amser knew how she wanted to spend it.

As soon as the bus stopped in Amber Sands Town Amser couldn't wait to get off. Unfortunately being seated at the back it took a little while as there were many people in front of her. Pushchairs and trolleys had to be collected and one gentleman had two fishing rods and a rather large dirty bucket.

Another man had a cloth sack which he picked up and put over his shoulder. It was tied at the top and from the movement coming from within people could see something was alive inside. They started muttering as they were intrigued and concerned what the contents might be.

A lady said to her friend 'Do you think it's a cat?'

She replied 'No I think it's a snake, I'm sure I heard it hiss.'

On hearing this there were screams from some of the passengers and they started to push forward to quicken their exit. The man was given space both in front and behind but he ignored the obvious interest and the animal's identity wasn't revealed.

Amser reached the door and after thanking the driver she strode towards the beach. It was about five hundred yards away and she hadn't seen it for over six years.

She remembered a puppet theatre built on wooden pillars in the sand. When the tide was out chairs were arranged in lines where children sat to watch the shows. Amser's favourite was Punch and Judy which drew large audiences although the appearance of a large crocodile scared her.

Now older, Amser was only interested in the pier and she recalled an imposing green arched entrance. She chuckled to herself as she remembered a plump, elderly man in a royal blue uniform with a bright yellow hat giving out penny tickets.

Amser joined a long queue but as she got closer to the front she could see a large red sign indicating the entrance fee was now 12 pence. Amser's heart sunk. Apart from a small lunch she'd prepared for herself at home, the girl had brought little more with her than enough money for the bus journey.

There was no sign of the old man either and the joyful anticipation of a wonderful day was in tatters. Amser felt sorry for herself. She wasn't selfish and never asked for anything but for once life could have been a little kinder to her.

She moved out of the queue and the young lady ticket attendant made things worse by scolding her.

'Why did you queue up if you didn't want to go on the pier?' she enquired in a rather loud voice.

Amser didn't reply; she sat down on a bench beside the line of people and burst into tears. She was devastated and held her head in her hands. Whilst she was hiding her face a young man sat down beside her.

'Whatever it is, it can't be that bad,' he said.

It startled Amser and she looked at him but didn't know what to say. 'Who is this person? What does he want?' she thought.

The boy smiled, took a tissue from his bag and began to mop the tears from her eyes and around her face. Amser still hadn't said a word; she was nervous of boys. She wasn't often in their company and they worried her. But here she was with a handsome young man with long yellowish hair and clear blue eyes. He was looking straight at her from only a few feet away.

'Are you going to tell me your name then?' he asked.

Amser paused for a moment and then shook her head, she couldn't speak.

'Why were you crying?' he said.

Still Amser stayed silent.

The boy said 'Oh come on please talk to me'.

Amser at last found the courage to look at him. She was feeling a little more confident and her tears were behind her. She gazed straight at him with her attractive large brown eyes and when she smiled the boy could see how beautiful she was.

'My name is Amser,' she said.

The boy looked puzzled.

'Amser did you say? I've never heard it before.'

'I know it's a horrible name, I've never liked it,' said the girl.

'Oh no!' exclaimed the boy.

'It's truly a beautiful name I like it very much but where does it come from?'

'It's an old Welsh name, I think it means time,' said Amser.

'Amser, Amser,' repeated the boy.

'Yes, it suits you very well.'

Amser had been charmed by his kindness and the softness of his voice. She wanted to know more about him.

'What's your name?' she enquired.

'Richard,' he replied.

'I'm from Norfolk in England but I'm staying in Amber Sands with my sister.'

There was an instant attraction between Amser and Richard and they started to ask all sorts of questions of one another. However, they'd both intended to go on the pier and time was passing by. Amser had to admit she was embarrassed because she didn't have enough money for the entrance fee.

'So that's the reason why you were crying,' said the boy.

Richard was armed with a large rucksack and two fishing rods and he offered to pay for Amser's admittance.

'I can't accept money from a stranger,' she said.

'I only met you a few minutes ago, it wouldn't be right,' she remarked.

Richard said 'Listen here, you let me comfort you when you were crying. You've told me your name and what it means and you've let me sit with you and watch your face light up with an amazing smile.'

He added 'I think I can manage to pay 12 pence for you to enter the pier. After all, who am I going to talk to whilst I'm fishing if you don't come with me?'

Amser was speechless again. It was only an invitation to sit with a boy at the end of the pier but she felt nervous. However she did like Richard and after all, what harm could come of it with people passing by all the time.

She reasoned 'Well I was going to sit and read my book in the sun anyway. If I don't let him help I won't be going on the pier.'

With those thoughts in her mind she agreed and they both made their way towards the entrance.

The ticket lady looked at Amser and muttered under her breath 'Some girls will pick up anybody' as Richard paid the admission fees.

Having pushed through the heavy turnstile the couple walked over old rickety wooden boards that squeaked and creaked on every step. Looking through the gaps between them Amser was a little frightened by the sight of the sea thrashing around the supports of the construction. However, she'd embarrassed herself enough for one day and wasn't about to share her further anxiety with her new found friend.

The sun was still shining and Amser and Richard both stayed silent as they continued to walk whilst tossing their private thoughts around in their heads. The girl had only come to Amber Sands to read a book and the boy had only intended to fish, yet on this day something special had happened to both of them. They were excited at the notion of sharing each other's company.

As they approached the end of the pier they could see two men fishing. One stood over six feet six inches tall and wore a red baseball cap, a thick, black, woollen jumper and black jeans. The other was seated next to him in a brown leather hooded coat and for some reason was wearing knee length wellington boots.

Amser and Richard were looking at the equipment they'd brought with them when the tall man got a bite on his line. He started to reel in his catch but it was causing him anxiety.

The fish didn't want to be caught and was pulling hard from the hook in its mouth, trying to make its escape. Such was the strength of the creature his friend had to help him and put his arms around his waist.

The fish was pulling harder and harder until the line snapped and the men fell over backwards landing on top of one another. Amser and Richard somehow managed not to laugh until they noticed the man in the wellington boots had knocked over a large bucket. The water inside had saturated his trousers and two large fish that had been caught had been flattened by the weight of his body.

Amser couldn't contain herself and giggled out loud but this outburst caused Richard embarrassment. He ushered her away and she realised laughing at a fellow fisherman in distress wasn't done.

On the other side of the pier they found a vacant seat and Amser sat down facing out to sea. Richard opened his rucksack and took out a large bag which converted into a chair and placed it beside her. Then Amser watched him assemble his fishing rods and in a few seconds they were complete.

Boy and girl both sat there. Amser kept staring at the same page in her book and Richard didn't bother to recast his lines. They spent their time thinking about each other and the chance meeting that had brought them together. Richard didn't have any lunch with him so Amser shared hers. They began to chat and found out a little more about each other.

Time passed quickly and people started to leave the pier. Looking towards the beach the couple could see it was becoming deserted. Neither of them wanted the day to end but they packed up their things and made their way to the exit.

On returning to the shore Amser said 'I'm sorry I must go home now.'

Richard didn't want her to leave and said 'Please, won't you stay for a little while longer?'

The girl didn't need much persuading. She didn't want to go as she was only going back to an empty house.

'For just a little longer then,' she said.

Richard expressed his delight by putting an arm around Amser's waist and pulling her body towards him. A broad smile took over his face and they walked along together.

How surprised Amser's friends would have been to see her like this. She didn't have a care in the world as she waited for Richard whilst he queued up at a little café selling hot takeaway meals. He bought them both a pizza and they leaned on the sea wall at the end of the promenade eating their food.

Pretty lights shining from lanterns above got brighter and brighter as darkness fell and a beautiful sunset imposed itself over the water. Side by side with one arm around each other Amser and Richard watched the sun disappear. It was a magical moment neither of them wanted to end.

Then without warning Amser took off her shoes and socks and jumped down from the wall. Before Richard realised what was happening she was off in the distance, running towards the sea.

'Come on,' Amser called out.

'Come on Richard,' she shouted.

Richard jumped on to the sand and started to follow her as fast as he could.

Amser taunted Richard 'You can't catch me, can you?'

The girl was laughing and giggling as she ran and the lad was unable to get to her before she reached the sea. Amser rushed into the water but its coldness caused her to retreat in haste. She raced back onto the beach towards Richard and he lifted her up in his arms. Carefully he carried her over the sand and lowered her down by a dune.

Amser shivered and Richard removed his thick woollen jumper and wrapped it around her. Then he took a cloth from his rucksack and dried her feet. Richard, resting on his knees, looked down upon her as the moon danced across the sky in and out of the clouds. The intermittent brightness lit up her eyes and her face shone out of the darkness.

Amser laid still and silent as Richard started to touch her hair with the back of his hands. He ran his fingers through the strands down to her shoulders over and over again. He couldn't take his eyes off her and she remained silent as he brought his whole body closer to hers.

'Amser you're so beautiful,' he said as he lent forward to kiss her on the eyebrows and forehead.

Richard's body had been taken over by a strange force and he seemed powerless to stop it. It felt like all his actions were now in the hands of someone else as his fingers were continuing to play with her hair and his lips were now caressing her ears.

Amser too had strange feelings inside her as she looked up at him, waiting excitedly for his every move.

'Kiss me Richard, please kiss me, kiss me now,' she demanded.

Richard needed no encouragement and with her eyes closed he put his mouth on hers but as soon as their lips touched she moved her face to one side. She was frightened and Richard sensing her anxiety moved his hands and face away from her.

'Are you OK?' he enquired.

'Yes but I haven't done anything with a boy before,' she replied.

Richard laughed and asked 'What not even kissed?'

Amser was in tears again in Richard's presence.

'Please don't laugh. I want to but I don't know how.'

Richard put his arms around her and hugged her.

He said 'Please don't be afraid. We don't have to kiss if you don't want to.'

But Amser did want to and without another word she pulled his face towards hers. This time when their lips met Amser kept pushing her face forward. All the tension she had built up came flooding out but it wasn't a kiss to be enjoyed until she felt Richard's tongue feeling its way inside her mouth.

As she started to hold back he imposed his lips on her a little more and then Amser dared to venture with her tongue. The girl now a little more self-assured opened her eyes as she continued to play with Richard's mouth. They couldn't stop looking at one another as every touch of their bodies excited them.

The couple were struggling to come to terms with their feelings and emotions and for Amser everything seemed so natural now. Their hands wandered indiscriminately over each other. They rolled between the dunes and ignoring the coolness of the sea breeze items of clothing were frantically removed. Then lying naked with Richard kissing every inch of her body Amser was helpless.

She gasped as he moved his flesh even closer and now there wasn't a grain of sand between them. They were sliding their legs against each other, grasping one another's hands and kissing ferociously. There were no smiles just a feeling of excitement and expectancy.

Amser and Richard were both breathing fast and for two minutes they looked into each other's eyes without a word being spoken. They knew where they were going in body and mind and nothing could stop them.

They'd only met a few hours before but this was so much more than sex. It wasn't dirty or contrived in any way. It was an act of passion brought out of love at first sight that many would not understand.

In seven minutes it was all over and as the couple lay back on the beach Amser burst into tears. She knew she shouldn't have done it and felt guilty and tarnished but in all her life she'd never been so happy.

Richard was concerned for her. It had never been his intention to make love but it had happened and like when he first saw her he wanted to comfort her.

As they looked up above they could see thousands of stars. Some were shining as if they were brand new whilst others flickered dimly as if they were about to go out forever. It was so quiet apart from the gentle rush of the sea and with the strengthening breeze it was getting a little cold.

Amser started to shiver and Richard held her in his arms as a star raced across the sky and disappeared.

'I've never seen a shooting star before,' remarked Amser.

'Neither have I,' replied Richard.

'It was so beautiful like you.'

'If it fell out of the sky I would catch it and put it in a bottle for you to keep for ever.'

Amser's eyes had dried and she was clinging to Richard wishing these special moments would last for eternity.

Then she looked at her watch.

'Oh my goodness the last bus leaves from the town in thirty minutes,' said Amser.

They both dressed and made their way back to the pier. From there it was a short distance to the bus stop and Richard waited with Amser for the vehicle to arrive. They had so much fun but making love had changed everything. Although she tried to hide it, it was impossible. Amser felt cheap and Richard was worried she might think he'd planned it all. Then the bus came and in their sadness they hadn't arranged to see each other again.

As Amser sat down, Richard realised their mistake. He started waving his arms and called out 'Come next week, the pier at eleven o'clock.'

Amser seeing him thorough the bus window looked perplexed. She didn't understand what he was saying.

Then Richard pointed to his watch and repeated 'eleven o'clock next Saturday at the pier.'

Still Amser didn't hear and the bus driver was getting fidgety as he wanted to start his journey.

There was more shouting until the driver lost his patience and called out to Amser 'At the pier, eleven in the morning, next Saturday.'

Amser was embarrassed as the other customers were laughing but she smiled and nodded that she would be there. Then the bus pulled away leaving Richard standing alone on the pavement.

As Amser journeyed home she re-lived every moment of the day in her mind. It seemed inconceivable but she'd met the most wonderful boy. He was kind, gentle and extremely handsome; for a moment she thought she must have been dreaming.

She considered how different things might have been if she'd taken a little more money with her that morning and had entered the pier unaided. She thought about the conversations they had, the laughs they shared, eating pizza, running into the sea and of course the dunes.

What they did on the sand still worried her. She felt a little sore which she thought was her punishment but nothing could stop her thinking about Richard.

Chapter Five

Amser got home at 9.15pm. It had been dark for a while and she could see a light on in her home. She was worried the house might be being burgled and wasn't sure what to do. As she got closer she could see the front door was still shut and the windows looked intact.

She decided to inspect the rear of the property and made her way down an alley that was two houses along. Amser rarely ventured along this path at night as there weren't any street lights and she felt it was a little scary. As she walked a cat jumped off a brick wall and landed on a bucket. It made a loud noise and she screamed.

On arriving at her house she examined the back door. It was locked and although she could still see the light inside there was no sign of a break-in anywhere. Walking around to the front again Amser made up her mind the light must have been on when she left home in the morning. However, on entry, much to her surprise, she found her parents waiting for her in the living room. They'd come home earlier than usual and were shocked to find the house empty on their return.

Mr Edwards was furious. He'd been pacing up and down the living room waiting for his daughter and had become very annoyed. Mrs Edwards was seated and was worried where her daughter might be. She hadn't seen her husband so upset since he lost his job and was concerned he might raise a hand to her.

Amser was used to being scolded for not doing chores but as soon as she entered Mr Edwards shouted at the girl so loudly he scared her.

Standing in front of his daughter he bellowed 'Where have you been? Do you always go out when we aren't here?'

Question followed question and the girl wasn't given time to answer any of them. Amser's mother burst into tears. She was desperate to calm him down and intervened.

She said 'We were worried about you Amser.'

However, the girl knew she was more worried about the jobs that hadn't been done.

With her father still at boiling point Amser summoned up all her courage and enquired 'Why have you come home early?'

Her mother replied 'Mrs Roberts, a friend of your granny who lives in Lea Hall Road telephoned to say you were at the bus stop this morning.'

Amser thought to herself 'nosy old cow' but that's what it was like in the town, people talking about one another all the time.

Mrs Edwards said 'I didn't believe her at first because you're always here but she was so insistent I knew it must be true.'

'We've been wondering all day where you've been.'

Her father was now seated and ready to mellow his approach.

'Where did you go Amser?' he enquired.

'I wanted to see Amber Sands,' she replied.

'Amber Sands, why would you want to go there?' he demanded to know.

'You used to take me there when I was younger and I loved it so much; I wanted to see if everything was the same,' she replied.

Amser's parents looked at one another. They realised for the first time in a long while their daughter had few pleasures in life and nothing to look forward to, unlike other children.

'Go to bed,' said her mother.

Little did they know what kind of a day she had experienced and she wasn't about to tell them.

As Amser lay in her room she thought about Richard. She couldn't get him out of her mind. When she closed her eyes she could see his face and hear his loving voice. She'd never experienced such a feeling of warmth and tenderness and couldn't wait to see him again.

Amser drifted into a deep sleep and didn't awake until eight o'clock the following morning. It was another beautiful day and with Richard on her mind when she opened her curtains even the old water mill looked attractive in the sunlight.

The week ahead seemed to pass at a snail's pace as Richard

continued to occupy Amser's thoughts. She'd become obsessed with him after sharing his company for only a few hours. She couldn't concentrate on anything in school or at home.

Her only comfort was the book given to her by Mrs Reece. The poems about life and history provided some contentment. They helped her stop feeling sorry for herself and cope with day to day pressures. However, when the weekend approached Amser's parents had a shock in store for her.

Whilst sitting down for their evening meal on Friday her mum said 'Your father and I have been thinking; we feel it would be a good idea if you come to granny's with us in future on Saturdays.'

Amser's face dropped and tears filled her eyes.

'So you don't trust me,' she said.

Her mother didn't answer.

'What about the jobs I do when you're away?' Amser enquired.

'I don't think it will matter. After all you didn't do the house-work last Saturday did you? No, you can do your homework at your gran's tomorrow and your jobs at home on Sunday after church,' she replied.

Amser broke down in tears. She sobbed and sobbed and her parents couldn't understand why she was so distressed. They expected her to be a little annoyed but her emotional response took them by surprise.

The girl was uncontrollable prompting her mother to remark 'It's no good you turning on the water works, you're coming to gran's and that's that.'

Amser's heart was broken. She'd been looking forward to seeing Richard again so much but now had to face the fact she would never set her eyes on him again. The girl didn't have any idea where he lived and was concerned he would be waiting for her.

'What will he do when I don't turn up? What will he think of me?' Amser thought.

She'd only known him for a short while but he was now more important than anyone or anything in her life. Saturday morning arrived and as usual mum and dad were both getting ready for their granny visit.

'Are you up yet?' Amser's mum called out.

'We don't want to be late. If you want any breakfast you'd better hurry up girl.'

However, all Amser could think about was Richard waiting for her by the pier. She was worried and frustrated but there was nothing she could do about it.

Five weeks later on another Saturday morning Amser felt sick as soon as she got up. After a few spoonfuls of breakfast cereal she rushed to the bathroom and was very ill.

Amser's mum was used to her daughter trying to make excuses. It wasn't because the girl didn't want to see her granny. She visited Rose Cottage during the week and Saturday was when she used to have time on her own.

Mrs Edwards dismissed her daughter's plea to stay at home and said 'You're coming with us and that's that.'

However whilst at her granny's and in a quiet moment the old lady once again said 'I promise life will get much better for you.'

Amser wanted more information but all her granny would say was 'Don't be impatient dear all good things come to those who wait.'

As the days went by Amser didn't feel any better. She was sick every morning after her parents went out to work and always looked ill at school. This continued until one day she was spoken to during the lunch break by Mrs Reece.

The teacher said 'You don't look well Amser, is there anything I should know?'

The girl knew what Mrs Reece was implying. She had unprotected sex and her period was very late. She tried to convince herself it couldn't happen the first time and just wanted the problem to go away.

'What would her parents think? How could she tell them? How would she cope?'

All these things had been going around in her head and now she had a teacher standing in front of her asking if she could be having a baby.

In the absence of a response Mrs Reece didn't beat about the bush and enquired 'Are you pregnant?'

Amser looked at her and gave the only answer she could 'I don't know, I really don't know.'

The teacher looked at her with a hint of sadness in her eyes.

Now speaking softly she said 'Oh Amser, you silly girl, you silly, silly girl. I'm disappointed in you. I think you'd better go and talk to your doctor.'

With Mrs Reece's blessing the girl went to the surgery the following morning. Given the circumstances this was a very daunting prospect and she'd have liked her mum by her side. However, her parents had no idea what she was going through and she didn't want to tell them in the hope it was a false alarm.

Waiting for the doctor was always a stressful experience. There was no appointment system and patients took their turn after they arrived. Sometimes the wait was made longer because the doctor had to go out on an emergency home visit.

The surgery was a dull place. It was clean but the walls painted cream and brown were bare and people sat close together in lines on brown wooden chairs.

Many of the attendees would be coughing, sneezing and fidgeting. It was easy for the patients to come out of the surgery in a more unhealthy state than when they went in.

Amser was nervous as she expected to see some familiar faces but when she opened the door there was nobody she knew in sight. Her stomach was churning as she sat at the end of the back row. Her chair was a little wobbly and she couldn't keep still.

One by one the patients in front of Amser were seen until it was her turn. Her GP's name was Dr Brown and the girl didn't like him very much. He always made her feel she was wasting his time.

Without looking at the girl he said 'Come and sit down.'

Amser did as she was told and the doctor looked at her waiting for her to speak. Her hands were trembling and he could see her anxiety.

'Are you going to tell me what's wrong or do you want me to guess?' he enquired.

Amser looked at him and burst into tears; it was all too much for her. Dr Brown sat back in his chair and folded his arms.

He said 'Whatever is the matter? Crying won't help, please tell me what the problem is will you.'

Amser was appalled by the doctor's attitude.

Getting to her feet in readiness to leave the room she said angrily 'My period is late, I'm being sick every morning and I don't feel well. I think I might be pregnant but you don't care do you.'

Amser was about to open the door when the doctor said 'Stop right there young lady, come back and sit down.'

There was an authority in his voice and she did as she was told. To her surprise Dr Brown became very attentive.

He listened as Amser explained what had happened and said 'Well, we'd better find out if you're expecting hadn't we?'

The tests were completed and when Amser telephoned the surgery in her school lunch hour her worst fears were confirmed. She faced the prospect of having to tell her parents but first she had to see Mrs Reece.

The teacher comforted the girl. It was the worst moment in the child's life. She'd been punished hard for her mistake and couldn't imagine how she'd cope with a baby.

Mrs Reece said 'Look my girl, I'm not going to lie, a baby brings enormous responsibility and life will never be quite the same for you.'

Then after lifting Amser's bowed head with her hands she added 'But remember this girl, things happen for a reason, everything in life has a meaning. As human beings we are constantly being tested.'

Amser replied 'My granny is always saying things like that.'

'And she's right,' said the teacher.

'The question you must ask yourself is can you rise to the challenge because in a few months' time a tiny bundle of joy is going to enter the world. A brand new boy or girl is going to rely on you for his or her every need.'

Amser wasn't sure how to answer but after a few minutes she was able to compose herself and was ready to go home. Getting to her feet she was still unable to speak but looked at Mrs Reece and smiled.

The teacher said 'It will be alright Amser I promise you. It's just another test; you can pass it with flying colours.'

Chapter Six

It was a Friday again and Amser was allowed to go home early. Her mother was at work and her father, having slept in the morning after working overnight, was out helping a friend repair his roof.

Whilst alone she tried to imagine how she would tell them. She always felt better later in the day and to occupy her mind she got on with her chores. She cleaned the house from top to bottom and made sure there was nothing for her parents to complain about.

Her dad arrived home within an hour and sat himself down on a kitchen chair with his newspaper. Amser made sure she didn't disturb him and decided to wait for her mother before spilling the news. It was such a hard thing for her to do and as the minutes passed she became more and more nervous and fearful of their reaction.

Just after six o'clock the waiting was over. Amser heard a key turn in the lock.

Her mum entered and after closing the door she said 'You'll never believe what's happened today.'

She had a beaming smile on her face and Amser couldn't remember the last time she'd seen her mum so happy. She was used to her being tired having been on her feet all day looking after old people.

Mrs Edwards had been given some wonderful news. A male patient in her care had been incorrectly diagnosed with an aggressive form of prostate cancer the previous week. However, having been given a life expectancy of no more than a year, it now transpired the test results had been misinterpreted. The cancer was only thought to be growing at a very slow pace and he was now expected to live for a long time.

Good news like this was hard to come by in Walwyn Gate and Amser's mum was overjoyed. How the girl wished her doctor would knock on the door at this moment and tell her a mistake had been made and she wasn't having a baby.

The girl didn't know whether the patient's news had made her job easier or harder. In any event she knew she couldn't carry the burden any longer and asked both her parents to sit down.

'There is something I need to tell you,' she said.

At first they were dismissive of Amser's request. Being so wrapped up in their own lives they didn't value things Amser might have to say.

'Please mum, please dad, sit down will you,' she pleaded.

Her parents didn't have any idea what might be the matter. They'd noticed Amser hadn't looked well for a while but they'd put it down to a tummy bug going around her school and the usual homework pressures. However, they could see their daughter was stressed about something and did as they were asked.

Staying silent they sat there watching Amser fidgeting with the buttons on her jumper as she tried to pluck up the courage to deliver the most awful news they could ever want to hear. Walwyn Gate wasn't in the dark ages but nevertheless, it was a very close-knit community. Everybody knew everybody else's business and Amser knew this news would cause them great anxiety and provide them with much embarrassment.

As she sat down opposite her mum and dad she was sweating and her face went red.

She took a deep breath and said 'It's difficult for me to say this to you both. I'm so sorry but I'm pregnant.'

Her parents were devastated. They looked at one another and then looked at their daughter, not quite believing what had been said.

Amser repeated 'I'm so sorry I never meant it to happen.'

Her mum broke down in tears whilst her dad continued to sit in silence.

Then as Amser tried to comfort her mum, her dad said 'Amser go to your room, go now before I say something I might regret.'

'But dad I want to cuddle my mum,' replied Amser.

'Go to your room,' Amser's dad shouted.

'Go now,' he bellowed.

'Go Amser, will you,' said her mum and then she bowed her head in her hands as her daughter went upstairs.

Amser was sobbing and whilst lying on her bed listened to her parents trying to come to terms with the situation. She could hear every word through the wafer thin walls in the house. Her dad was demanding to know who the father was and when it happened.

'She must tell us,' he exclaimed.

'Wait till I get my hands on him,' he shouted.

Her mother although devastated was for once a little concerned about their daughter.

'I wonder how it happened. I wonder how she feels and how long she's known,' she remarked as she sobbed.

'She must feel so alone, so sad and so worried about the future.'

'The future!' her dad replied.

'I know what the future holds,' he said.

'You're taking her to the hospital on Monday and she's going to get rid of it. It's best for everybody. How would we cope with a baby in the house and how will Amser do her jobs and keep up with her precious schooling?'

'You're more worried about the shame of it all than you are about our girl,' said Amser's mum.

'Well, just think of it, can you imagine what people will say, she's only seventeen, for God's sake,' shouted her dad.

Amser was upset, confused and frightened but with all the anxiety she had suffered during these last few days, not once had she considered having an abortion. It's true she didn't want a baby. She was concerned about looking after a child, but to have it taken from her body was something she wasn't prepared to contemplate.

Then, listening further to her parents talking below she was astounded by what she heard.

Her dad said 'Look dear, you know how hard it is to bring up a child. Have you forgotten we made the same mistake?'

He added 'You know what we have been through with Amser. I should never have listened to your mother.'

He continued 'Without her we would have had more money in our pockets and life would have been easier for us.'

Amser couldn't believe it and then to her amazement she heard her mum say 'Yes I know you're right, life would have been better without her.'

Amser was overwhelmed with grief and lay silent. She was stunned by these admissions. Not only was she an unwanted child but also her parents both agreed she should never have been born. The girl juggled these thoughts in her mind as she tried to make sense of it all.

As the minutes passed by she started to think of Richard. She knew she wouldn't see him again but thought about how they first met, the pier, the sea, the sand and of course what they did together. She never wanted to forget that wonderful day and decided to write down her thoughts.

Once again words came easy to Amser when she was sad and she wrote:-

Sea shells on a silent beach
Dark skies almost in reach
Warm winds on a rushing tide
You lying by my side
Young hearts so wild and free
Embracing so tenderly
I felt the life love inside of me
Oh, how I wanted you.

Amser put her pen down and lay back on her bed. Still in her school clothes with her face wet with tears she was exhausted and fell into a deep sleep.

When she awoke next morning, for a moment Amser was content. You know sometimes, for a second or two you can forget the present when you wake up. However, all too quickly she remembered she was pregnant and recalled the things she'd heard her parents say the previous evening.

It was Saturday again so Amser got up and took off her school clothes.

She'd started washing herself when her mother called up to her 'We'll be going soon Amser, we don't want to be late.'

It was as if nothing had happened. There wasn't any kindness in her mum's voice only the usual blunt command for her to hurry up. Amser was feeling sick again and asked if she could stay behind but her parents wouldn't allow it.

'No,' said her mum.

'You're coming and that's final.'

Chapter Seven

When they got to granny's, Amser's mum called out and usually the lady came to the door. It took her a little while because of her incapacity as she had to manoeuvre her wheelchair out of her sitting room and down the hall.

Normally they would hear her say 'I won't be a minute,' but on this Saturday the cottage was silent.

The family waited after Amser's mum called out again but granny's voice wasn't heard and there was no movement inside. Mrs Edwards bent down, opened the letter box and shouted out for her mother but not a sound could be heard.

Amser's mum had a spare key and on entry they found her lying in bed. Mrs Edwards had called in to see her the previous evening and she was OK so it seemed she must have died overnight. What a terrible week it had been for the family and for a few days granny's death overshadowed Amser's pregnancy.

The following weekend whilst helping her mother clear out granny's belongings Amser came across a large sealed envelope under a cushion on her chair. There wasn't any writing on the outside and she gave it to her mother.

Mrs Edwards didn't want to open it without her husband being present but she was anxious to find out what it contained. Taking a knife from the kitchen drawer she slit the top of the envelope and looked inside.

Straightaway, Amser's mum could see it was a will. She unfolded it and studied the contents. She kept looking at the document and reading it over and over again as if she couldn't believe what had been written.

Amser could see it was causing her mum distress.

'What is it mum? What's the matter?' she uttered.

Mrs Edwards tried to ignore Amser's curiosity and didn't answer. After putting the will back in the envelope and placing it on a table she started to look at other things around the house.

Amser watched her mother. Her behaviour had changed. She became agitated when a drawer didn't open. She looked at items she had already browsed and dropped a candlestick holder on the carpet. Amser could tell there was something not quite right and questioned her mother again.

'Please mum what's in the envelope that's upset you so much? Tell me will you?'

Mrs Edwards stopped what she was doing. She now seemed to be a little shaky and had to steady herself against a chair. Staring at the envelope it was as if she'd seen a ghost.

'Alright I'll tell you, you will find out soon enough anyway. It seems your granny has been very kind to you, very kind indeed,' she said loudly.

'What do you mean, kind to me?' Amser enquired.

'She's left you her cottage, her money and her jewellery, is that clear enough for you.'

'But she can't have done, why would she do that?' enquired Amser.

'Because, you were her favourite grandchild,' came the sharp reply in a raised voice.

Amser remarked 'I was her only grandchild mum.'

Mrs Edwards was in no mood to be corrected but in the knowledge her granny was the only reason she was alive the girl couldn't resist saying it.

Amser wasn't deterred by her mother shouting and enquired further 'Has your mum left you anything at all?'

Mrs Edwards had also read a letter that accompanied the will.

'It seems your dad and I are to be pleased you're having granny's assets. She says she wants you to enjoy your life and not struggle like we have done all these past years and it will be a comfort to us.'

Amser's mum went on 'Don't think you're getting your hands on the money now my girl.'

Amser felt she was being scolded for something she hadn't done.

'Perhaps mum thinks I've known about this for a long time,' she thought.

The girl continued to listen as her mother added 'To make sure you don't fritter your legacy away too easily granny's assets are to be held in trust until you are twenty one years old. Solicitors Messrs Jones, Jones and Hughes are to hold the funds in a bank account for you. Aren't you the lucky one?'

Amser's mum didn't say another word except 'I've had enough today, we'd better go home and tell your father the exciting news. Goodness knows what he'll make of it.'

Amser went straight to her room and within seconds she knew her father had been told as his loud voice could be heard bellowing from below.

To her horror she heard him say 'You mean to tell me we've been nursing your mother all this time for her to leave almost everything to our daughter. If I'd known I would have stopped going to see her a long time ago.'

The girl couldn't believe her ears. 'So my parents were only after granny's money and hadn't been concerned at all about her well-being,' she thought.

Amser was now even more disenchanted with her mum and dad, but now for the first time granny saying life one day would be good to her was making sense. 'She must have had this planned all along,' reasoned Amser.

The funeral was arranged at their local church of St Mary The Virgin where the Edwards family attended on a Sunday morning. It was situated a short walk away from the old lady's cottage.

The building was erected in the sixteenth century and was built almost entirely of wood although the construction supported an imposing thatched roof. It occupied a wonderful position on the edge of a water meadow that was a haven for wild life and wild flowers.

The church was a popular place for weddings because of the sumptuous views from its grounds. It also provided comfort to the bereaved because its small graveyard was very quiet and the only sounds to be heard came from the birds.

It's always sad when someone passes away and for some unknown reason funerals are associated with cold wet days. This mournful occasion was no exception and a biting wind added to the trauma.

Granny didn't have any relatives apart from the Edwards family. The chapel congregation was completed by her friend Mrs Erwin Emmanuel who worked in the Post Office, Miss Wade from the book club where she attended before she had her stroke and other people from the local community who wanted to pay their respects.

The Vicar was Reverend Glen Bevan. He made it his business to know everyone and was always ready to lend a helping hand in times of need. During the recession in the village he worked hard to bring people together and encouraged community-based activities.

He was very good to the children and organised all sorts of games for them in the school holidays. However kids can be very cruel. The vicar had two large protruding teeth and behind his back they called him Bugs Bunny.

Reverend Glen Bevan liked the grandmother. She'd been unable to attend church for many years so he made visits to her cottage. He paid tribute to her courage having lost her husband at such a young age and having to cope with her invalidity.

It wasn't known what information the Vicar may have gleaned from Bethan about the Edwards family but he showed little compassion towards Amser's mum and dad. However, turning towards Amser he took a moment to come down from the pulpit to where she was sitting in the front pew.

Taking hold of her hands he said 'My dear girl, your grand-mother loved you very much. You lit up her life with your visits. She was always talking about you and the life you have in front of you.'

Then he added 'I know you'll miss her but in time all the wonderful memories you have will become a comfort to you. Now she's looking down keeping watch over you.'

Amser couldn't speak, with her eyes swollen with grief she just nodded and then sobbed with her head bowed.

After the service the small funeral party made its way to where the coffin was to be placed in the ground. The cemetery was narrow and the resting place was at the farthest point from the church. As they walked along the muddy path they gazed at the many tombstones either side. Some were very old and the inscriptions had faded and were now unreadable.

Much of the graveyard was overgrown with weeds and covered with twigs, fallen branches and leaves. Amser thought it was wrong for the dead to be ignored in this way. However, the area being used for the most recent burials was much tidier and flowers could be seen around the graves.

As Amser's granny was laid to rest, prayers were said over the grave but she didn't see either her mum or her dad show any emotion. However, Amser was still overwhelmed with sadness. She cried her heart out whilst being comforted by the vicar and threw a handkerchief into the grave.

The previous Christmas granny had given her a present of two such items she'd embroidered with Amser's name. Parting with one of these two small gifts was her way of ensuring they would never be apart. However, as the rain continued to lash down on the wind, the girl felt empty and alone.

It didn't seem fair but in a small space of time the two people she cared about most had been taken from her. Amser was to miss her granny more than she could have imagined and Richard was becoming a distant memory.

The following day a visit had been arranged to the offices of Solicitors Messrs Jones, Jones and Hughes for the will to be read officially. In particular they were to discuss the value of granny's assets and her wishes.

The family met Mr Hughes in the reception area. He spotted them through his office window and came out to greet them. The man was short and stocky and had a mass of grey curly hair. He spoke in a soft voice and with a lisp.

Having been escorted into a small lounge, they were invited to take a seat. They made themselves comfortable on cosy chairs and their bodies moulded into the softness of the light brown fabric. Amser had never seen anything like it before and kept running her hands over the surface.

Mr Hughes waited until they were settled and then started the meeting by expressing his heartfelt sympathy for the family's sad loss and by offering refreshments. Then taking the will in his hand he read the contents whilst the family sat in silence.

When he finished he said 'I know you've already seen the will but I always find a reading at this stage to prove most beneficial.'

Then looking at Amser Mr Hughes enquired 'Would you like the cottage sold, would you like to live in it or just have it maintained?'

The property was in better condition than the house the family resided in and Mr and Mrs Edwards took it for granted they'd be moving. However, mindful, of what she'd heard from her bedroom, Amser had other ideas. She wasn't about to let her parents occupy the cottage.

Taking a deep breath the girl said 'I think I'd like you to sell it please Mr Hughes.'

'Sell it!' exclaimed her dad at the top of his voice whilst leaning forward to the edge of his chair.

'Why would you want to do that?' he enquired with his face going red with anger.

Amser's response also took the solicitor by surprise. He too expected the property to be occupied and waited for her to speak. Amser felt a little nervous with all eyes on her. She realised she needed a credible excuse and had to think on her feet.

'I can't live in granny's cottage now she isn't there anymore; it's too upsetting for me. I don't think I could ever go in the cottage again,' she replied.

Keeping her eyes fixed on Mr Hughes she added 'No please sell it and keep the money for me will you.'

Mr and Mrs Edwards were astounded and even more so when the solicitor revealed there was over £200,000 in a banking account which was also now Amser's.

'What about all the things in the house?' enquired Amser's mum.

Amser's mum hadn't read the will in detail or listened to the reading.

Mr Hughes replied 'As I said earlier Mrs Edwards, you're welcome to all the contents except the jewellery. As soon as the legal formalities have been completed I'll arrange for an estate agent to visit the property with you, when you wish to take things away.'

'When she wishes to take things away,' shouted Mr Edwards.

Raising his voice with his eyes fixed on his daughter he was frightening her. Amser had seen her father in a temper before but she'd never seen him so angry. None of this was her fault but with a bit more love and affection in the past from Mr and Mrs Edwards towards her granny things might have been different.

'Will you please calm down,' said Mr Hughes.

Mr Edwards was in no mood to be told what to do.

'So you don't even trust my wife and me to take what belongs to us,' he bellowed.

'It's not a matter of trust it's a matter of procedure,' replied the solicitor.

At this point the solicitor antagonised Mr Edwards further by asking for the house keys and Mr Edwards reacted violently by banging his fist on the desk in front of him.

Then getting to his feet he shouted even louder 'No it's too much, you can't have them. It's my wife's mother's cottage for heaven's sake.'

'It's just procedure,' the solicitor repeated.

'I've already said most of the contents belong to Mrs Edwards.'

'She can collect them as long as she makes the appropriate arrangements to do so.'

Mrs Edwards did her best to calm her husband down as Amser looked on in silence. She took the keys from her purse and against her husband's wishes handed them over.

Then the solicitor addressed Amser once more.

He said 'Amser my dear, although your granny wanted you to wait until you're twenty one before you inherit her assets, she's made a further provision for you. You may draw out sufficient funds when required to assist you in the completion of your A levels and your teaching degree. All you need to do is make your requests to the trustees in writing and, providing they are deemed reasonable, they'll be met.'

Mr and Mrs Edwards couldn't believe their ears. They didn't have any idea their daughter wanted to be a teacher.

'Why didn't you tell us you wanted to teach?' her mum enquired.

'Because you never listen to what I say and never take any interest in me at all,' she replied.

Amser's mum was upset. She hadn't realised how much she'd neglected her daughter.

She remarked 'Oh Amser you must despise us.'

Mrs Edwards didn't want a reply and her daughter obliged by not saying a word. Then the family left the solicitor's office with Amser's dad still moaning about the will.

From that day on the girl was to enjoy much more care and attention. Amser knew her mum and dad were only being kind because they wanted a share of granny's money but now she was given time to rest and do her homework. Also the question of an abortion wasn't mentioned again.

Chapter Eight

Outside their home, tongues were wagging as one by one the family's acquaintances began to find out about the baby. The following Sunday was very daunting for the Edwards family when they attended church. People looked and stared as Amser made her way into God's House and the noise of conversation before the service was much louder than usual with the baby being the only topic of interest.

On this day the usual warm greetings were no more than polite gestures but despite all the hurt, embarrassment and anxiety Mrs Edwards was determined her family wasn't going to be shunned by her own church.

Then Reverend Glen Bevan entered the arena from a door adjacent to the altar and the congregational chatter stopped. Each week the service commenced with a hymn but on this day the tradition was broken.

Of course the church didn't condone what Amser had done and neither did the vicar, but through her grandmother he knew her very well. She was an honest girl who'd made a mistake and God would still love her. His sermon was carefully balanced to deal with responsibility, kindness and forgiveness. The worshipers listened as he spoke with authority about family life and good neighbours.

Then the vicar interrupted himself and said 'Look you all know what I've been talking about. I've heard the gossiping and seen the disapproving faces but there isn't one person before me that hasn't made a mistake.'

He added 'Think of the secrets I know about some of you. Are you really any better because they aren't in the public domain? Sometimes things happen we don't plan for. Now either we're a community in which people support one another or we're not.'

Mrs Edwards found the situation hard to deal with. She got up and ran out of the church crying. Mr Edwards and Amser followed and they went straight home.

The girl tried to imagine what the situation was like for her mother and when her dad was out she took time to comfort her. However, because of the things that had been said it was an empty gesture and more out of pity. It was too late now for her mother or father to make amends as Amser was already beginning to gather her thoughts for the future.

At school Amser's classmates were astounded by the news.

'I don't believe it,' said Rhonda.

'You never talk to boys let alone do anything with them,' remarked another school pal.

'What's his name?' asked Rhonda.

'Richard,' she answered with a wide smile on her face. She loved saying his name.

They wanted to know all about him but Amser was reluctant to tell them.

Sitting on a window ledge by the classroom entrance with her school chums gathered around her, all Amser would say was 'I haven't seen him since it happened. He doesn't know I'm having his baby and I don't know where he is.'

The girl couldn't contain her tears. She'd done so much crying but talking about Richard caused her to break down again. She was sobbing and her school mates could see how much she was hurting. From that day on they were to provide her with all the comfort and support she needed.

Time, as they say, is a great healer and as the days went by the frowns of local people turned to concern and words of encouragement. Small towns love to gossip but deep down the residents of Walwyn Gate were decent beings and it seemed now everybody was looking forward to the birth.

People were enquiring of Mr and Mrs Edwards about their daughter's health. Amser was asked what names she'd considered and in the Post Office Mrs Emmanuel was offering a large box of chocolates to the person who guessed it. She was charging ten pence a guess and intended using the money to buy the baby a present.

Although Amser now had more time to study, as the weeks

went by she found it difficult to concentrate and her body shape was making her feel uncomfortable. She became tired earlier each day and was worried she might not get the results she needed.

Amser was a bright girl but things had changed in such a short space of time. Not long ago failure wouldn't have entered her head and yet at that time she was worried a lack of money might have prevented her from fulfilling her dream. Now she had the money at her disposal but was weary and her mind was overburdened.

The pressure on Amser increased still further when she visited her choice of university known as 'Queens' in South Wales. She went with Rhonda and the girl's parents on the one and a half hour journey by train.

Looking around the massive building both girls were amazed to see so many other potential students. It hadn't occurred to them how big the university would be and when they looked at all the facilities it made them realise there would be a great deal of competition for places.

The task of getting selected seemed even more daunting when the minimum qualifications were emphasised for both Amser's teaching degree and for Rhonda to embark on law.

Amser was so concerned that back at school, without her knowledge, Rhonda went to see Mrs Reece. She said she was worried about her friend as all the pressure was taking its toll on her.

The teacher had already noticed a fall in the standard of Amser's work. Her recent mock examination results had been disappointing and she'd been having a problem concentrating in class. Mrs Reece thanked Rhonda for her concern and decided to talk to her colleague Mr Williams.

As a result the two teachers came up with a plan to help Amser. She was allowed to stay at home for some of the time and was given extra help by Mr Williams with her literature.

The days and weeks seemed to zoom by until the birth of her child was only days away. Then whilst sitting in class on the afternoon of 16th March her waters broke.

The pupils looked on as water flowed on the floor.

One of the boys sitting close by didn't understand what was happening and said to the teacher 'That's gross Miss' and moved away.

There were many voices of concern but the girls rushed to Amser's aid and formed a circle around her. There they waited for the ambulance to arrive and she was taken to Amber Sands General.

Rhonda was allowed to accompany Amser in the vehicle and her mum met them both at the hospital. Her mother and best friend waited outside the delivery room for over two hours but it enabled her dad who'd gone to work early to get to the hospital in time.

Amser was scared and in severe pain as her baby prepared to enter the world. The nursing staff were kind and reassuring but throughout the procedure Amser was remembering Richard. How she wished he was there beside her, holding her hand.

Mr and Mrs Edwards had never been so worried about their daughter. They waited patiently outside the room and when the news of a little girl was announced, tears flooded down their faces. Rhonda too was overwhelmed with joy and allowed to go in to see her friend with Amser's parents.

As they entered they could see the baby in her arms. Amser was crying and smiling at the same time. They all hugged and kissed each other and her dad for the first time in his daughter's life showed her love and affection. They all took turns holding the baby before a nurse suggested Amser should get some rest.

Five days later Amser and her little bundle were taken home and she told her parents the baby was to be called Bethan. Amser knew her mother and grandmother weren't very close but her granny meant everything to her and she knew the lady would have been proud. Mrs Edwards wasn't sure of Amser's motives but she too was touched by the decision.

News quickly spread around the town that mother and baby were home and there was a constant stream of visitors to the house to see Amser and baby Bethan. The girl was showered with gifts and she couldn't remember a time when so much attention had been paid towards her.

Somehow, Mr and Mrs Edwards managed to scrape enough money together to buy their daughter a second hand pram. There was a surprise when a lady called Phyllis Bryden who'd never spoken to the family before knocked on the front door. She was very nervous and spoke in a slow soft voice to Amser's mum without looking at her.

Without any introduction she said 'I've a cot I no longer have any use for. It's a bit old but it still looks OK. Would your daughter like it?'

On hearing this Amser came to the door. She knew who Mrs Bryden was. Her daughter was in the same class as her at school and the lady had recently given birth to a still-born baby.

This act of kindness put Amser's problems into perspective. Mrs Bryden knew Amser must have known about her tragedy as the girl reached out and took hold of her hands. Amser thanked Mrs Bryden and the lady raised her head and smiled.

She said 'That's settled then; you'll come and collect it, will you?'

Then without another word she turned around, walked away from the house and back down the road.

Another visitor was Mrs Emmanuel who'd collected £7.80 in her 'guess the name' competition. She arrived with two bags and gave the one in her left hand to Amser. It was a bright green colour and was bulging with a neatly wrapped present tied with a blue bow. The girl undid the soft parcel to find beautiful baby clothes and a small pink teddy.

'Thank you so much Mrs Emmanuel,' she said and planted a warm kiss on the lady's cheek.

She said 'This is Bethan's first cuddly toy.'

Mrs Emmanuel chuckled and said 'Nobody guessed the name Bethan then' and handed Amser the second bag.

It contained the chocolates she intended to be the prize.

'You might as well have them as well,' she added.

'I thought it might be Bethan. I know how much you loved your gran.'

Amser smiled and embraced the lady once more.

As soon as the baby was settled into a routine Amser took Bethan to school to see her teachers. Most of her friends had already visited her home but they all surrounded Amser and her baby when she entered the playground with her pram.

It was lunchtime and the girl made her way to the staff room. She knocked on the door and was invited to enter. On seeing Amser all the teachers got up and greeted her. They looked at baby Bethan who opened her eyes and smiled for them. Amser was very keen to see Mr Williams and thank him for all his help. She kissed him on his cheek and he went bright red.

Amser looked around the room. She couldn't see Mrs Reece. Then the door opened behind her - she didn't hear it because of all the chatter.

A voice said 'Hello Amser' and the room fell silent.

The girl turned around and moved towards the teacher and hugged her and kissed her. She wouldn't let the teacher go.

'Thank you, thank you so much, thank you for everything.'

Mrs Reece wasn't aware of the impact her words of encouragement and help had on the girl's life. She wasn't used to pupils showing affection towards her.

Then Amser released her grip. She took a step back and looked at Mrs Reece. The girl and the other teachers were astounded to see tears running down Mrs Reece's face. Amser picked up Bethan and invited Mrs Reece to hold her. The teacher's face gleamed as she looked down at Bethan in her arms before laying the baby back in her pram.

'I don't know what I've done to deserve such a fuss; promise me you'll complete your studies, pass your exams and go to university.'

'Yes, yes, I promise I will,' said Amser.

Again they hugged and there were more tears before she left the school. At home, as the family only lived in a small house, Amser had the baby in a cot in her room. There was now less space than before but somehow she managed to cope. The baby was very content and slept for long periods. She was also easy to feed and rarely cried.

Mrs Edwards helped look after Bethan in the evenings and

Mr Edwards did his best during the day whilst Amser revised her school work.

The exams came and went in a flash and when results day arrived Amser was home alone. She was ironing whilst Bethan was asleep when the expected letter was pushed through the letter box. She stared at it for a few seconds as it lay on the mat by the front door.

Amser believed she'd done well but at this moment doubts were flooding through her mind. She opened the envelope by slitting the top with a needle and took out the folded sheet of paper inside.

Holding her breath Amser opened it up to find she'd achieved grade A in Literature, English Language and Drama. She was overjoyed and kept reading the results over and over again.

Then there was a knock at the door. It was Rhonda. She'd also got fantastic results and the girls hugged one another. All the stress that had built up inside them evaporated and they were proud of themselves.

This wonderful news meant some major decisions needed to be made in Amser's life. Her place at university had to be accepted, accommodation had to be found in South Wales and of course there was Bethan. At least her granny's money would ensure she didn't have any financial worries and her friend Rhonda would be going to the same university so they could travel together.

One by one, things were arranged but Amser had become so attached to Bethan she couldn't imagine life without her. She pondered over the situation for hours at a time. Should she take the baby with her and get a childminder or would it be best to have her cared for at home.

Amser wasn't attracted to either option but decided to leave Bethan in surroundings familiar to her. Her parents had grown to love their granddaughter very much and Mrs Edwards knew a good local childminder. She was flexible and would have the baby whenever required so the necessary arrangements were made.

Chapter Nine

University heralded a new chapter in Amser's life. Having said her sad goodbyes to Bethan, she set off with Rhonda to Abeglan Railway Station. They'd managed to get accommodation together on the campus and were to be housed in a new purpose-built block of student flats.

The girls were allocated rooms next to one another on a corridor with a communal kitchen. They were very basic with just a bed, desk, chair and a wardrobe. There was also a separate area containing a toilet and a shower.

Rhonda disliked the arrangement. She was used to more home comforts and thought the accommodation was bland and on the small side. However, Amser fell in love with her room as soon as she opened the door. To her it was a little piece of heaven.

There was a dark blue carpet on the floor, the walls were painted in a light blue pastel colour and the window was draped with bright yellow curtains. There was even a long vertical mirror on the wall and Amser kept standing in front of it looking at herself.

When she looked out of her window she could see the river winding its way through the fields and loved to watch the sun shine on the water. It was a far cry from the old factory that greeted her when she opened her bedroom curtains in Walwyn Gate.

Here in South Wales there was nobody to shout at her. There weren't any chores to do and Amser was revelling in her independence. However, this was a tough time for the girl. She hated being separated from her daughter and often travelled home at weekends to see her.

Bethan was growing up and becoming more aware of everything around her. She now seemed more comfortable with her grandma, granddad and the childminder than she did with her. Amser was jealous and upset but she was able to re-establish the bond between mother and daughter during holiday periods when she spent every moment with Bethan.

Amser was enrolled on to a four year course and at first she and Rhonda became even closer friends. They looked out for one another and made sure there weren't too many distractions from each other's studies.

However, during the following year Rhonda became more attracted to the opposite sex. Sometimes she'd go out at night and not come home until the following morning. Amser could guess what she was doing and was worried about her.

One morning whilst Amser was eating her breakfast in the student kitchen Rhonda arrived home. Whilst pouring herself a cup of coffee she started talking about how tired she was and complaining about the lectures she had to endure during the day.

Amser sat there listening as her friend continued to moan about anything and everything that took her fancy. This was now a regular occurrence and she couldn't stand it any longer.

Putting down her tea cup she said 'Well you don't have to go out do you. If you stayed in and got your work done you wouldn't be worried about your studies. You're only interested in boys these days. What's happened to you?'

'Well I'm not a boring swat like you. When are you going to get a life Ams?' Rhonda replied.

Amser said 'If being tired and moaning all the time is getting a life I don't want any part of it. I know what you've been doing. I hope you're having safe sex.'

This comment ruffled Rhonda's feathers.

She said 'Well if that's not the pot calling the kettle black I don't know what is.'

'I had sex on one night with one boy. I've never slept around,' Amser replied.

'Yes and look where it's got you. I wouldn't want a baby on my hands,' said Rhonda.

The girls didn't often argue but it was inevitable they'd find new friends and have different ideas and values. Personality wise, Amser and Rhonda had always been poles apart but the girls knew there was a special bond between them.

After all the shouting and arguing the kitchen fell silent as they both pondered over what had been said. Rhonda knew her friend was looking out for her and decided to break the ice.

She said 'I'm sorry Ams. I shouldn't have said that about Bethan. I know you wouldn't be without her.'

Amser apologised as well saying 'I'm sorry too Rhon I shouldn't question your social life. What you get up to is none of my business.'

As usual after an argument there were hugs and kisses and they promised to make more time for one another in the future.

At the end of the second year there was a Student's Ball and tickets were £10. Amser didn't have to worry about money for her studies because of her granny's will. She was able to buy what food and clothes she liked but because of her upbringing her demands were modest.

Rhonda always had money and suggested they go to the Ball but Amser didn't know whether the trustees would allow her to buy a £10 Ball ticket. However, when Amser asked them they were pleased to oblige. In fact as she'd spent so little whilst away from home they suggested she have her hair set and buy herself some new clothes. They reasoned: if you're happy at university you're more likely to succeed.

So the girls went to the shops and Rhonda purchased a number of items in the space of twenty five minutes. However after three hours Amser hadn't found a single item of clothing she liked. Having tried on her eleventh dress she was deliberating in front of a mirror when her friend lost her patience.

'For god's sake,' said Rhonda.

'It suits you, it fits you, just buy it.'

'Mmm, I'm not sure it's my colour,' replied Amser.

'Look Ams there comes a point and you passed it some time ago.'

Amser could see the look of frustration on Rhonda's face. With some reluctance she made a purchase and then, as if to make a point, bought three more items in quick succession.

On the evening of the Ball the girls had a great time dancing to the student band known as The Galley Bashers. The music was loud and the sound was distorted but this was a celebration and nobody cared.

The young gentlemen were used to seeing Rhonda dressed in modern attractive clothes but as Amser had always made do with old attire she was almost unrecognisable.

Her light brown hair with beautiful curls flowed over her new long black dress. It clung to every inch of her body and Rhonda was jealous of the attention paid to her.

After that night many male students tried to date Amser but she always refused them. The girl still felt guilty being away from Bethan and, although it was in the distant past, Richard continued to stir in her mind.

Rhonda decided she must do something about this as Amser was missing out on so much fun. Her friend spent most of her spare time sitting in her room at university either reading poems or studying for her degree.

A few days after the Ball and three weeks before the students went home for their summer break, Rhonda made some arrangements without her friend's knowledge. On arriving back at the student lodgings she found Amser sitting at the kitchen table.

'I've got a date tomorrow night with Max the guy I met at the Ball,' she said.

Amser wasn't impressed. She remembered Max and didn't like him. He was very tall, spoke quickly and had a stutter. He seemed to want to make a joke out of everything and she thought he was rude and big headed.

Rhonda added 'I said I'd go if I could bring a friend.'

Amser immediately knew what her friend was up to.

'I don't think so. I'm not going to play gooseberry whilst you two are slobbering over one another. I've too much to do and I'm not in the slightest bit interested in a night out in Max's company,' she said.

Rhonda wasn't to be put off. She didn't need Amser to have a good time but was determined to expand her friend's personal horizons with the opposite sex.

'It wouldn't be with me and Max, I have asked him if he'll bring a friend,' she said.

Amser was furious and replied 'You think I need male company do you? Has it not occurred to you I might not want to go out with boys at the moment. Not everything is about sex.'

'Oh go on Ams, you never know you might enjoy yourself. I've told Max now and he's already asked one of his pals.'

'He'll have to un-ask his friend then because I'm not going,' replied Amser.

'I won't go then,' muttered Rhonda who was becoming a little agitated.

She was pacing around the kitchen, circling where Amser was sitting trying to think how she could persuade her friend to change her mind.

'Don't be silly, I'm sure you can handle both of them Rhon,' came the quick reply.

That comment made Rhonda so mad, she snapped.

'Look Amser, you're never going to see, err, what's his name, Richard again. He's gone, forget him,' she exclaimed.

Richard hadn't been mentioned for ages because Rhonda didn't think her friend would want her to. Now she'd uttered his name in anger and thought she might have gone too far. She valued their friendship and tried hard to recover the situation.

Putting her hands on Amser's shoulders she said 'I'm sorry, I shouldn't have mentioned Richard. Can you ever forgive me?'

Rhonda looked at Amser and waited for a response. She held her breath thinking her friend was going to say something that might terminate their relationship forever. After all the arguing there was now a silence as Amser considered what had been said. In truth it was just what she needed. Until now she hadn't been able to put Richard in the past tense and Rhonda's words helped her draw a line under the relationship at last.

Amser looked at her friend and smiled.

'It's OK,' she said.

'It is really. You're right I must move on. He's in the past. So where are we going for this date then?' she enquired.

Rhonda somewhat relieved hesitated a little and started to giggle.

Then very quickly she said 'We're having a picnic on Saturday afternoon.'

Amser couldn't quite believe her ears.

'Sorry, can you say that again, I thought you said a picnic.'

'I did, it might be fun don't you think.'

'Oh, come on Rhon, a picnic, you can't be serious. You're winding me up aren't you? I thought it might be the pictures, a drink or even a meal but a picnic, you're having a laugh aren't you.'

Once again Rhonda had got Amser into something she didn't want to do. She was one of those people who always seemed to be able to get her way. She was so persuasive and had answers for everything.

'No Ams,' she replied.

'It's all arranged, the weather is supposed to be dry and sunny and Max thought it would be fun.'

'I'm not surprised he probably thinks he's going to have a romp on the grass,' replied Amser.

Rhonda started giggling again. Looking at her friend, Amser could see she didn't think it was such a bad idea.

'You're outrageous, Rhon, you really are terrible,' she said.

However, the thought of a bit of fun in the park made Amser chuckle and for the first time in a long while the girls laughed together. Against her better judgement Amser agreed and once again Rhonda had got her way.

The girls were meant to meet the boys outside the Red Lion Public House which was a short walk from the local country park. Max said he and his pal would bring food and drink and when the girls approached from a distance they could see them holding large bags that looked full of goodies.

They both eyed Max's friend and Rhonda's first reaction was to say 'I can handle both of them if you still want me to.'

Amser however had changed her mind as she thought he was quite dishy. Standing almost six feet tall, he was slim with long wavy blond hair and as the girls got nearer he appealed to them even more.

Rhonda joked again 'You can have Max and I'll have his friend if you like.'

'No, you can have the mouthy stuttering giant, I'll have dream boy,' she replied.

Now only a few yards away, Amser couldn't wait to meet her blind date and by the look in the boy's eyes neither could he. Introductions were made and Amser shook hands with her new friend who was called David. They seemed to hit it off straight away and made polite conversation as they walked towards the park.

Max tried his best to disrupt the proceedings by telling jokes, pretending to trip over and singing. He also seemed interested in Amser and Rhonda was getting more agitated with every step. She began to wonder if making this date was a mistake.

It was a hot day and there wasn't a cloud in the sky. The sun was beating down and it was sapping the energy out of them. The party decided to settle in the shade, under a large oak tree next to the river where it was cooler. It was damp on the ground but Max had brought a large waterproof blanket which he laid out underneath the leafed branches.

It was a perfect setting for a picnic and the boys had bought sandwiches, beer, wine and strawberries. Whilst they were enjoying their lunch, boats of various shapes and sizes passed by them. There were holidaymakers and day-trippers on motor vessels whilst others chose to sail on the moderate breeze that hushed over the water.

Looking towards the right the party could see a road bridge. A constant stream of traffic passed over it but it was far enough away for the noise of the vehicles not to worry them.

There had been a great deal of rain in recent days and the river level was high. In these conditions good navigation was required to get under the bridge and time and time again boats approached the obstacle too fast. All too often they collided with the wooden supports on either side and sometimes bits of wood could be seen falling off the boats and into the water.

The boys and girls found this to be hilarious and were now enjoying one another's company. Then Max had an idea.

'We could hire a rowing boat for the afternoon,' he said.

The girls weren't sure as by now the lads had consumed a lot of drink. David was slurring his words and Max was stuttering more than ever. However, David thought it was a great suggestion and Max was almost intimidating as he pursued his desire to get the girls to agree.

Then he detected a slight interest being shown by Rhonda and put even more pressure on Amser to change her mind.

'Come on Amser, you can see Rhonda wants to go. You don't want to spoil things do you?'

Rhonda spoke up for her friend by saying 'I'm happy to stay here by the river.'

But she wasn't very convincing and David made it obvious he'd like to go on a boat. He didn't want Amser to stop them.

'Don't you like the river then?' he enquired.

'Yes I do, but I would prefer to stay here. We're in the shade and it's cool.'

'Well, we'll stay if you want us to but you can see we all want to go. It's really up to you,' said David.

They were all looking at Amser and waiting for her to speak. She felt under pressure and gave in.

'Alright, I'm not rowing though,' she said.

'Neither am I,' remarked Rhonda.

Having packed up their belongings they made their way down a narrow path to the river where the boats were moored. They were all shapes and sizes and painted in various bright colours.

An elderly bald man revealing a large bare chest and wearing grey shorts came out of his hut to confront the party. With the alcohol taking its toll, the boy's speech was becoming louder and the man didn't appreciate their request for a boat.

'I'm not sure you're in a fit state to take a boat out,' he said.

'Course we are,' retorted Max.

David added jokingly 'I'm an able seaman'.

The rest of the party fell about laughing but the boat man wasn't impressed.

'I don't think so. No you can't have a boat,' came the reply.

Rhonda, however, standing at the back, also with a drink or two inside her was determined not to be turned away. She undid the first and second buttons on her blouse and moved forward so the man could see her.

'Look,' she said, holding her hands on her hips and bulging out her chest.

'We're out having a bit of fun in this warm weather. Yes, we've had a couple of drinks but we work so hard during the week and want a bit of relaxation.'

Standing very close to the man, Rhonda looked straight at him and added in a slow soft voice 'We all have needs don't we.'

He was very unsettled by Rhonda's close proximity and couldn't take his eyes off her breasts.

'What do you all do during the week then?' he asked.

Rhonda had to think on her feet. She hadn't anticipated the question but an immediate answer was required.

Why it was the first thing that came into her head the girl will never know but she replied 'We're carers at the Walden Children's Hospice.'

Amser, Max and David looked on in amazement as the man broke down in tears.

He said 'My grandson died in the hospice last year.'

A feeling of guilt came over all of them. Rhonda in particular never expected such a response. However, she was still intent on getting the boat and put her arm around the man to comfort him.

'Of course you can have a boat. There won't be a charge,' he said.

To the party's surprise Rhonda replied 'Well that's very kind of you we'll donate the cost of the boat to the hospice funds.'

On hearing that comment the man put his hand in his pocket and found a five pound note.

'Put that in the funds as well, will you,' he said.

Rhonda was now feeling very uncomfortable. However,

although she tried as hard as she could to tell him it wasn't necessary, he was insistent and she had to take the money.

To make matters worse, by this time a family of four and another couple had arrived. They'd overheard the conversation and also wanted to donate to the hospice. The friends didn't know whether to laugh or cry but by the time they got into the boat they'd an extra £12 in their pockets.

David rowed the boat away with the boatman saying to his other customers 'What wonderful people they are.'

He'd forgotten about the alcohol and was waving both arms as they moved downstream. Amser, not wanting to go on the boat, was angry with Rhonda.

'How could you flaunt yourself like that?' she said.

'I wanted to go on a boat,' she replied.

'For goodness sake Rhon, we're hospice workers now, how could you?'

'It was the first thing that came into my head. I wasn't to know his grandson was in there, was I,' said Rhonda.

'What are we going to do with the money?' said Max.

'It's going to the hospice, together with the hire charge for the boat,' Amser insisted very loudly.

The others looked at her and didn't dare, try to change her mind.

The sun was still beating down, glinting over the tiny ripples on the water. It was very calm but a slight breeze continued to take the edge off the high temperature. The party were now enjoying themselves and even Amser had to admit hiring a boat had been a good idea.

As time went on the drink was taking its toll even more and David decided he would try and impress his blind date. The others all sitting together looked on as he took the oars out of the water and laid one of them inside the boat.

'What an earth are you doing?' asked Amser.

'I'm getting bored,' he replied as he stood up and stepped on to his seat.

The boat started to wobble from side to side and Rhonda

and Max laughed as water lapped inside. It was swirling around their feet but David wasn't to be put off. Placing two hands at the top of the other oar and dipping it into the water he started to punt.

The boat became unstable as more water entered the wooden structure. It was like a sailing vessel out of control. Rhonda and Max were still laughing as people on other boats voiced their concern and a man fishing saw his tackle broken.

He shouted out 'You moron,' in disgust.

David replied 'Fishing is cruel and a waste of time, you have to put them back anyway.'

The man was furious and Amser wasn't impressed with David's behaviour.

She was scared and shouted 'Sit down David, please sit down.'

The boy realising it was time to stop stepped off the seat but he slipped on the wet wooden base and whilst falling into the boat let go of the oar into the river.

'Oh dear, oh dear,' chuckled Rhonda 'I think I'm going to wet myself.'

Looking at the water in the boat, Max replied 'I think we've all wet ourselves already.'

This remark produced even more laughter although Amser stayed silent whilst she watched the oar floating further away from them.

'What are we going to do now?' she enquired.

David felt stupid but he wasn't going to show it.

'I lost the oar so I'll get it back,' he replied.

'And how are you going to do that?' the girl enquired.

Not another word was said. David got up again and stood on his seat. This time however, he used it as a launching pad and dived straight into the water. He didn't even take his shoes off. Amser screamed, as more water entered the boat. It was now up to their ankles but Rhonda and Max found this act of madness very funny as well and there were yet more hoots of laughter.

David was a good swimmer and the oar was recovered in seconds. Max managed to haul David back into the boat and

Amser looked at him in disgust. However, despite all her concerns she too couldn't contain herself and laughed at the sight of him dripping water from head to toe. He looked like a drowned rat.

By this time the party had enough on the river. It was late in the afternoon and Max rowed back to the boat hut. The man was waiting to greet them but voiced his concern when he saw all the water in his boat.

'Where has all that water come from?' he asked.

'Look at my poor boat.'

'It's OK,' replied Rhonda.

'We lost an oar and David dived in and got it.'

The man looked at David whose clothes were still saturated as he left the boat.

Before he could utter another word, Rhonda clasped the man's hand and said 'Thank you so much for your donation to the hospice, it was very kind of you.'

She added 'We've had a wonderful afternoon on the river.'

Looking at the smile on Rhonda's face he said 'Oh yes, you're welcome.'

Then the party made their way out of the park. Rhonda and Max made arrangements to see each other that evening but Amser didn't have any plans to go out with David again. She found him childish and foolish and when he asked to see her she told him she needed all her spare time to study. David was only being polite. He thought Amser was too serious for him and they parted with a handshake.

So nothing had changed Amser's view of men. She'd coped in the past without them and could manage without them in the future. Once more she immersed herself in her work.

Chapter Ten

Rhonda, although taking a law degree, continued to neglect her studies and had a string of boyfriends. She took risks with her time and did everything at the last minute. She was often late for both lessons and handing in assignments whilst Amser was organised, responsible and reliable.

Rhonda did manage to persuade Amser to go out from time to time although blind dates were off the menu. One Saturday evening they put on some decent clothes as they were booked into a posh local hotel for a meal.

It was called 'The Harlech' and the building was four stories high. In front of the hotel was a circular pond with a water fountain and the entrance was guarded by two large red lion statues.

Once the girls had made their way inside through a glass revolving door they could hear music. It was obvious there was a party going on and the sound got louder as they walked along the hotel corridor towards the restaurant.

Rhonda stopped in an instant by a function room door and Amser, who was behind, almost bumped into her. The door was open and they both looked inside. It was easy to see from the flowers on the tables and the banners draped all around that it was a wedding reception.

It was a large room and Rhonda said 'Look Ams there must be at least three hundred people in there.'

The girls stared for a long time at the people dancing, drinking and enjoying themselves.

Rhonda commented further 'I haven't been to a wedding for a long time.'

'Neither have I,' remarked Amser.

'I love weddings, I wish we knew the happy couple,' continued Rhonda.

Amser looked at her friend; she knew how her mind worked.

'Well we don't,' she replied.

'It says Jean and Robin here,' commented Rhonda, pointing to a board by the entrance door.

'No Rhon, we can't, no Rhon, really no,' said Amser.

Rhonda said 'Look Ams whilst we've been standing here people have been going in and out of the room. I bet they're not all guests. No one will know the difference as long as we keep away from the happy couple.'

Amser, as usual was more conservative than Rhonda but she did fancy a dance.

'I suppose we could go in for a while,' she reasoned.

'Of course we can,' replied Rhonda and before Amser could change her mind her friend took hold of her left arm and marched her inside.

As they walked, Rhonda was relaxed and comfortable. She was saying hello and smiling to guests whilst Amser kept looking straight in front of her and wished the floor would swallow her up.

Rhonda said 'I'm going to get some drinks.'

Amser couldn't believe how confident Rhonda was and sat down in a corner far away from the bar. Whilst waiting for her friend, a man came over and, after hovering around for a minute, he sat down beside her.

'Oh no this is all I need,' thought Amser.

The man was a little drunk and had a glass in his hand that looked like it contained whisky. He was swaying from side to side and backward and forward as he looked around the room. Amser was praying he wouldn't talk to her and looked away to avoid eye contact.

However, the man moved closer to her and enquired 'What side of the family are you on my dear?'

He looked very untidy. His shirt was hanging out of his trousers and the knot on his tie was loose and lop sided. When he spoke he moved his face very close to hers and his breath smelt of drink and cigarettes.

Amser felt uncomfortable as she tried to recall the names on the board outside. It was only for a few seconds but the man started nodding and it was un-nerving.

Then she remembered the bride's name and said 'I'm on Jean's side.'

'Mmm doesn't she look a picture,' he replied.

Amser's thoughts about him being drunk were confirmed.

He slurred his words and added 'She looks bootiful really bootiful.'

Then the girl almost laughed. The man had a Norfolk accent and his comment reminded her of a chicken advert on the television. Before she could answer the man said he was on the groom's side and was a work friend. Amser was relieved and agreed on the bride's appearance, although up until now she hadn't seen her.

With a sigh of relief Rhonda could be seen approaching with a tray of drinks whilst the man decided to get up and move on to bother someone else.

Amser looked at the glasses.

'Why have you got four drinks?' she enquired.

'Because they're free,' she replied.

'I got you a couple of lagers, OK.'

'I don't believe you,' said Amser. 'How could you ask for free drinks?'

'Well it would have looked suspicious if I'd insisted on paying,' she replied.

'Come on get those drinks down you, the buffet has started,' Rhonda added.

The girls were hungry; they intended to have a large meal and joined the queue. They could see the bride standing by a table with a young man who they assumed was the groom. The sight of the couple made Amser feel even more nervous.

They moved along the line keeping an eye on where the guests of honour were. The food looked delicious and the centrepiece was a beautiful white wedding cake standing on four tiers and decorated with red letter icing and a large red bow.

Having helped themselves to large plates of goodies they moved away from the table and Rhonda almost bumped into the bride. She looked at her uninvited guest but didn't speak and for the first time Rhonda felt uncomfortable. There was a certain thrill attached to gate crashing a party but the pressure was building inside both of them and they knew they'd have to leave soon.

Once they finished their food they danced for a while but then whilst Rhonda was in the restroom Amser's worst fear was realised. She was approached by the bride whilst seated at a table. She cringed as the lady stormed towards her.

'Who are you then?' she demanded to know in a loud voice.

This time Amser was able to remember the names of the principal guests.

Summoning up all her courage she replied 'I'm a work friend of Robin's.'

'No you're not,' shouted the woman.

'I'd know if you were. I know all Robin's friends. What are you doing here?'

A large crowd of guests had gathered around the table where Amser was sitting. The girl felt like a dying animal with vultures circling above her.

When Rhonda came out of the restroom she realised what was happening. Then the fire alarm went off and all the eyes focused on Amser were now looking for the nearest exit. People started moving as fast as they could and there was shouting and screaming.

In all the pandemonium Amser was able to escape through a door behind the stage. Rhonda watched her friend and followed her out of the hotel. Then both girls ran down the road until they were out of sight.

'That was horrible, I'll never do anything like it again,' said Amser.

'It was so lucky the fire alarm went off,' she added.

'It was a bit scary I suppose, it was a good job I had my keys in my pocket. I don't think I could have broken the glass without them,' replied Rhonda.

'Oh no, don't tell me it was you Rhon.'

Rhonda didn't feel any guilt at all and smiled.

'How could you, all those people, you've spoilt their evening,' said Amser.

'I had to rescue you somehow and anyway at least they'd all eaten,' replied Rhonda, chuckling.

'But the bride and groom, it was their big day,' said Amser.

Still giggling Rhonda replied 'Yes and they'll remember it for the rest of their lives. They should be thanking us.'

'I don't think I'll forget it either,' said Amser.

'Remind me not to go out with you in future.'

Rhonda continued to laugh and said 'If you don't go out with me you won't go out at all.'

Amser started to chuckle as well.

Then she said 'In all the pandemonium I hope the cake wasn't knocked over. That would be terrible.'

Rhonda looked at her friend with a cheeky grin and replied 'Oh yes that would be really terrible.'

The girls for a second or two had serious faces before bursting into more laughter. They'd had a great time and hadn't spent a penny. Arm in arm they strolled down the road away from the hotel.

Chapter Eleven

In the summer, after three years away from home, Amser reached her 21st birthday. Granny's house had been sold and the proceeds along with a large sum of money and some jewellery became hers. She was now very rich and her parents started asking questions about the inheritance.

Amser didn't want to discuss it and when pressured said 'I want to finish my studies before making any decisions.'

At the beginning of her last academic year Amser was given a work experience placement in Davis High School in Abergollen. The school catered for eleven hundred children and had a very good reputation for discipline.

The headmistress Mrs Megan Thomas was always dressed in clean, well-ironed clothes and her hair was groomed to perfection. She expected the same standards from her teachers and they didn't dare disobey her. Mrs Thomas believed if the teachers were well presented then the children could be asked to do the same. The parents liked this approach and there was a waiting list for places.

The school was a ten minute walk from the university campus and Amser was placed under the close scrutiny of Mr Hardy. This gentleman, a teacher of literature, was a massive man standing over six feet tall and weighing more than twenty stone.

Amser, sitting at the back of the class noticed the children making fun of him whenever his back was turned. She wasn't impressed by their behaviour but Mr Hardy was not a likeable man. Teaching was just a job to him and he didn't seem to have any interest in the children. He didn't like students either; they interfered with his routine and he regarded them as a nuisance.

Amser was bored as day after day she was only allowed to observe. However, in a funny kind of way this experience helped her. She wasn't learning many best practices but she learned what she wasn't going to do. Her own ideas about teaching were beginning to firm up in her mind.

At the end of a school day the headmistress came into the room. The children stood up but at that moment Mr Hardy was kneeling whilst retrieving some papers that had fallen from his desk. On seeing Mrs Thomas enter he tried to get to his feet. But in his haste the weight of his upper body caused him to slip and he landed back on the floor.

The children knew they mustn't laugh with Mrs Thomas present but there were grins on all their faces. Mr Hardy was in severe pain and in need of medical assistance. An ambulance was called and he was taken to hospital.

It was now mid-March and the Easter break was only three weeks away. Amser was tidying the room after the children had gone home when Mrs Thomas came to see her.

The headmistress was aware of Mr Hardy's practices and the lack of attention he would have paid to her development. She chatted to Amser about the accident in class and confirmed the teacher had sustained a broken ankle.

'That's awful,' said Amser.

'Yes,' replied the headmistress.

However she hadn't only come to tell Amser the bad news.

Looking straight at her, Mrs Thomas enquired 'Do you feel confident enough to take the class for these last few days?'

Amser came straight out of her comfort zone. It was one thing to sit at the back of the class but to stand at the front with thirty pairs of eyes watching your every move was completely different.

However, this was teaching, it was what Amser had been training for and it only took a second or two for her to make up her mind.

'Yes Mrs Thomas, I do. I would love the challenge.'

The headmistress liked Amser, who dressed well, spoke with a clear voice and gave the impression she was up to the task.

'Thank you Miss Edwards, I'll drop in and see how you are getting on tomorrow,' she replied.

When the headmistress left the room Amser took time to think about the days that lay ahead. Much as she relished this opportunity she also had anxiety. There were butterflies in her stomach as she contemplated the different classes of children that were to present themselves before her.

Mr Hardy had many faults but he did plan well for lessons. It was easy for Amser to find out what each class was doing and she'd already seen all of the children. Now was the time to put into practice all the things she'd learnt.

Continuing with the prescribed coursework, Amser used her personality and own style of teaching to get the best out of the children. They were encouraged to interact in a responsible way and she balanced criticism with praise.

The subject of literature that had been looked upon as boring by many pupils was now considered to be interesting and in a few days Amser was very popular. She spent time with the children and by taking an interest in each individual made them feel special.

The girl enjoyed her work and was saddened when the last day arrived. She'd become fond of many children and would have liked to continue teaching them. Now she knew how hard it would be for her to say goodbye at the end of each school year.

Her old teacher Mrs Reece came into her mind. Amser realised she too must have come to terms with this emotion. 'That's why she never got close to her pupils,' she thought.

Chapter Twelve

Whilst working at Davis High School Amser started to look for job vacancies close to her home town. However her applications kept being rejected and she decided to look further afield. Having already made up her mind she was leaving home it didn't matter where she worked as long as she and Bethan were happy.

The days and weeks disappeared as jobs continued to pass her by and Amser was getting concerned about her future. Then one morning amongst the post was a letter from Selwyn College, a secondary school in Rowan.

Rowan was a large town in North Wales. In some ways it was similar to Walwyn Gate as it also had a closed coal mine. However, any effect the demise of this industry had on the community wasn't visible. Lots of small businesses were thriving. There was a high level of employment and the streets bustled with people.

Amser opened the envelope and took out a large sheet of yellow paper. She feared yet another rejection and couldn't believe she'd been accepted for an interview. This job in particular was perfect for Amser as the school wanted someone to teach literature and drama. Reading the letter Amser could see she was one of three candidates and the interviews were to take place in four days' time.

The school was located over one hundred and fifty miles away. Amser didn't drive and the train journey was to take over six hours. It was therefore necessary for her to stay away for two nights. To make matters worse it was now late January; the weather was freezing and snow was lying on the ground.

Amser clothed herself with a thick woollen coat, her soft sheep-skin gloves and scarf. She also wore her long leather boots to keep her legs warm and help her walk on the icy ground.

As expected the journey was tiring. The train had to reduce its speed in various places because of the weather and was late arriving in Rowan. On exiting the station Amser could see a path had been cleared to the taxi rank.

She stood in a queue behind a man with a black briefcase and a woman with a large plastic holdall that she was clutching with both hands. Despite her warm gloves Amser's fingers were cold and she could feel the warmth in her boots receding as she waited in the street.

It was over five minutes before a taxi pulled up and the lady got into a passenger seat leaving her holdall on the pavement for the driver to deal with. As soon as the vehicle moved away another taxi came around the corner and pulled up beside Amser. It was the man's turn but he offered to share it with her.

The girl was very grateful as snow was now falling in large flakes. She didn't have an umbrella and it was settling on her hair and coat. The cab driver could see Amser was shivering and once she and the man got into his taxi he put the heater on full blast.

'Thank you so much,' said Amser.

'It's my pleasure,' replied the man with the briefcase.

'I couldn't leave you here in the dark on your own.'

Then as the taxi made its way down the road the driver enquired 'Are you getting warmer now miss?'

She replied 'Thank you I'm much warmer, yes thank you, both of you.'

The man and Amser were going in the same direction and her destination was to be reached first. She'd booked into a bed and breakfast house in a quiet road which was situated close to the school. It was run by Mr and Mrs Peach.

On her arrival, having made her contribution to the taxi fare, Amser was walking up the garden path when the door opened. Standing in front of her was a slim, tall, elderly woman dressed in black trousers and a thick green woollen jumper. She had rings on all her fingers, was wearing a necklace full of various coloured beads and the largest round earrings Amser had ever seen.

'Miss Edwards is it, come in, come in, you must be cold and hungry,' said Mrs Peach.

Before Amser could answer she was ushered inside and the lady called out to her husband to take Amser's bag to her room. Within a few seconds someone could be heard coming down the stairs. The sound of shoes on the bare wooden treads was very loud and they creaked with every movement.

Mr Peach, also quite elderly, was opposite to his wife in appearance. He was short and fat wearing a grey shirt with buttons bulging at the middle.

'So you're the school teacher,' he remarked and started laughing out loud.

The girl wasn't sure how to respond and Mrs Peach said 'Oh don't mind him Miss Edwards, he laughs at everything. He drives me bloody mad.'

Amser smiled and then removed her coat which the lady hung on a blue hook behind the front door.

'Everybody calls me Peachy,' she said as her husband took the girl's belongings upstairs.

Amser chuckled to herself 'I wonder if her husband is called Plumpy'.

As her bag was taken Mrs Peach said 'You come with me my dear.'

She invited Amser to follow her into the kitchen. As she entered she could see the room was for more than cooking. There was a large wooden table in the middle, an old Aga cooker and a mismatch of cupboards fixed to the walls. On one side of the room were two red rocking chairs and on the other side logs could be seen burning on an open fire.

'You sit yourself down there my dear,' said Mrs Peach, pointing to one of the rockers.

The lady removed some papers from the seat and gave it a firm whack with the palm of her hand to remove the surface dust. Then she cut Amser a slice of her newly baked fruit cake and gave it to her with a large mug of tea.

Having a further look around Amser could see there were piles of plates, dishes, cups and various other items occupying every inch of space. She'd never seen a room so untidy but she now felt cosy and warm and soon forgot about the cold outside.

'Can I call you Miss Amser,' said the lady.

'Amser will do,' she replied.

'Oh no, I can't do that, not a teacher Miss.'

The girl found it strange they'd both called her a teacher. They knew she was only there for an interview but it made her feel good inside and provided her with a bit of confidence.

Mrs Peach was kind but very nosy. She wanted to know all about Amser and why she was in Rowan. The girl wasn't about to tell the woman her life story as she was a stranger to her. However, there wasn't any harm in talking about the school and she liked to tell everybody about Bethan. It transpired Mr and Mrs Peach's son had been taught at Selwyn College a long time ago.

'In my opinion the school isn't as good as it once was,' said the lady.

'There's no discipline now and most of the kids around here seem to be unruly,' she added.

Although a little disappointed, Amser knew things had changed since she was a child. She wasn't going to be put off at least until she'd seen the school for herself.

At the time of her visit Amser was the only house guest and Mrs Peach made a fuss of her. The lady cooked Salt Marsh Lamb with leeks and cabbage which was followed by a rich creamy rice pudding. Amser couldn't remember such a nice home-cooked meal and when she'd finished eating she was full to the brim.

The meal had been perfect for a cold winter evening. Whilst sitting by the fire Mrs Peach told Amser about Rowan and convinced her she'd be happy if she got the job. Mr Peach continued to laugh every time he spoke. It un-nerved Amser a little and she chuckled to herself 'He would be a nightmare at a funeral.'

Later that evening Amser spent time in her room preparing for her interview at ten o'clock the following day. She hadn't forgotten there were two other candidates and thought about how she might impress the headmaster, Mr Stead-Simpson.

Her academic ability was very important but Amser was determined to show him how much she cared for the children and their education. Sitting in bed in her night gown Amser was beginning to feel sleepy. It had been a very long day and her head was starting to nod when there was a knock at the door.

'It's Peachy my dear,' said the lady as she entered.

She was armed with a thick blanket and a hot water bottle.

'We can't have you getting cold before your big day can we.'

Then she laid the blanket over the bed and placed the bottle within Amser's reach.

'Oh you're so kind Mrs Peach,' said the girl as the lady made her way out.

'It's Peachy, just Peachy, Miss Amser,' came the reply before closing the door behind her.

Although in a strange bed Amser rested well and was awoken from a deep sleep by her alarm at eight o'clock. Amser was a morning person and bounced out of bed but there wasn't any heating in the room. She shivered and rushed to get herself washed and dressed.

Downstairs she found a hot breakfast waiting for her. Amser was still rather full from the night before but somehow managed to consume bacon, sausage, egg and a round of toast. Mrs Peach had taken a liking to the girl and was determined to spoil her.

After spending a little more time looking at her notes Amser was ready. She felt refreshed and was looking forward to her interview. However, having made up her mind to be positive, enthusiastic and energetic, her thoughts were shattered a few minutes after arriving at the school.

She was asked to sit down in an area outside the headmaster's room and whilst waiting various teachers and children passed by. Some were polite and greeted Amser whilst others ignored her presence as if she wasn't there.

Her concern was raised when she heard two teachers talking. They were looking at a notice board close to where Amser was seated.

She was horrified to hear one of them say 'Shelley is being interviewed at the moment do you think she'll get the job?'

'She ought to, she's been helping out in class for a while now. She has the qualifications and her father is a governor,' said the other teacher.

Amser's heart sank. 'Had she come all this way for an interview when a decision had already been made?' she thought.

She was fed up, annoyed and felt disillusioned. Her interview was now only ten minutes away and somehow, she had to pick herself up and refocus on the task that lay ahead.

Amser had a serious word with herself. She wasn't the timid and shy little girl she used to be. She'd worked hard for this chance and was going to make the headmaster see she was the best candidate.

At that moment the door opened and a lady came out with Mr Stead-Simpson. They did seem quite at ease with one another and were laughing about something. As they parted with a handshake he told her she'd know by the end of the day if she was successful or not.

Then his attention turned to Amser and she was invited into the room. Already seated were two other assessors. The headmaster introduced a school governor called Mr David Jackman. He didn't smile and greeted Amser with a limp handshake. The other assessor was the deputy head teacher Miss Brenda Smith. She made Amser feel at ease by talking about the weather and asking her if she'd like to remove her coat.

The interview lasted an hour and fifteen minutes during which time Amser was asked questions about her application. The girl didn't let herself down. She answered the panel with confidence, without hesitation and with a passion for the job they couldn't fail to notice.

Once this process was complete Mr Stead-Simpson said 'Miss Edwards I'm pleased to tell you the interview is almost finished. We've only one more question for you.'

He paused for a moment and then said 'You've made a long journey to attend this interview. Can you tell us please what would be your reward if we offered you this job?'

Amser smiled, she didn't have to think about her response.

She replied 'If I'm given this job I'll put my heart and soul into it. I love children and long to teach them. It's very simple and yet it means so much. My reward is their education.'

The interview was over and Amser was shattered. Whatever the outcome she knew she couldn't have conducted herself any better. Mr Stead-Simpson then took her on a tour of the school before telling her she would have an answer by the end of the day.

After returning to the guesthouse Amser chatted to Mrs Peach about the interview. She shared her concern about Shelley and worried herself about the third candidate whom she hadn't seen.

At half past three the telephone rang. Mrs Peach picked up the receiver. She was as nervous as her lodger.

It was 'Selwyn College' and she handed the telephone to Amser.

The girl placed it close to her ear and waited to hear her fate. She held her breath as the headmaster began to speak and in a few seconds there was a smile on her face. Mrs Peach knew she'd been successful.

Amser said 'Thank you headmaster, yes, I would love the job.'

Mrs Peach was as pleased as punch. She didn't have any champagne or wine in the house but there was a drop of port left over from Christmas and they shared it with the remainder of the fruit cake.

The next day a taxi arrived early to take Amser back to Rowan Station. She hated saying goodbye to Mrs Peach. She was only the landlady but she'd been very kind and Amser kissed her on both cheeks.

Mrs Peach said 'If ever you want a bit of my fruit cake you know where to come. We've decided not to take in any more borders so we'll always have room for you.'

'Yes Peachy,' replied Amser and then with snow still heavy on the ground she made her way out of the house.

Mr Peach opened an upstairs window and called out 'Bye teacher' and then as usual laughed his head off.

Amser got into the taxi and waved as the vehicle made its way down the road away from the boarding house. It was only the start of her long journey back to South Wales. Now, however, she had her job and the time whizzed by as she re-lived her interview and thought about the school. Amser was excited and couldn't wait to start teaching but she still had to pass her exams.

Back at university Amser immersed herself even more in her work. Rhonda tried her best to get her friend to go out but it was an impossible task. Apart from Bethan the only thing on Amser's mind was teaching and she felt the job in Rowan was just perfect.

Chapter Thirteen

In June Amser was awarded a 2:1 degree so she could now plan for her future. Getting a job in Rowan had made it easier for her to disown her parents. This was a decision she'd made a long time ago and it was to cause her mum and dad great distress.

Amser was aware her daughter would lose her grandparents. Bethan loved them very much and was going to have to grow up without them. Sometime in the future she'd want an explanation and that's something Amser had to live with.

Mr and Mrs Edwards didn't have any idea what their daughter was planning. The weather on graduation day was hot and sunny and the family left early for the journey by bus and train. For the last time Bethan was looked after by the childminder in the town.

Amser's parents couldn't afford anything new but managed to purchase some suitable clothes from a secondhand shop. Her mum wore a navy blue dress and matching shoes. She even had her hair set. Her dad wore an old grey suit and put on a clean shirt and tie.

Amser didn't say anything but for once she was proud of them. Looking at her mum it reminded her how beautiful she was when she was a child. It saddened Amser to think how much her parents had changed and how her relationship with them had deteriorated.

As the family entered the university complex students could be seen everywhere in their graduation attire. Mr and Mrs Edwards and their daughter walked towards the ceremony hall and various people stopped and said hello to Amser. Students, both male and female, kissed and hugged the girl as they congratulated one another. Even some of the lecturers took time to praise Amser as they passed by.

Her parents couldn't believe how popular their daughter had become Then Amser saw Rhonda who was also graduating. Somehow, despite all Rhonda's irresponsibility, laziness and lack of commitment, she managed to get her degree. Amser had to work hard for everything she achieved.

Rhonda had arrived with her parents by car and although they liked Amser they hadn't got on with Mr and Mrs Edwards for many years. It all stemmed from the closure of the railway where both fathers had worked together and been good friends.

When Mr Edwards was made redundant Rhonda's dad was offered a job in Abeglan and the two men hadn't spoken to each other since then. They were both stubborn and glared at one another as their daughters chatted about their big day.

It was getting close to two o'clock and the start of the presentation. The two sets of parents made their way separately to seats in the ceremony hall and the girls went off to gather in their different award groups.

One by one the celebrated students were announced and invited onto the stage. The hall was packed and parents clapped and cheered as each child was honoured. After the presentation, cakes and sandwiches were offered in an enormous marquee close to the main hall where more people congratulated Amser. One of the university lecturers approached Mr and Mrs Edwards, having seen them standing next to her.

He said 'You must be very proud of your daughter. I'm sure she'll make a wonderful teacher.'

Amser's parents didn't know what to say, they didn't know anything about her time at university. In all honesty it had happened without them.

Realising Amser was talking to Rhonda a little distance away and out of ear shot Mrs Edwards quietly replied 'Yes she's a wonderful girl.'

It had been a special day and Amser had enjoyed all the fuss and attention paid to her. For a while she'd been able to put her leaving plans to the back of her mind. Now however, she was sitting on a train opposite her parents on the way back to Walwyn Gate. It was to be her home for one more night.

The noise of the carriage wheels seemed to get louder and louder as Amser considered how best to break the news she was leaving home. She sat there avoiding eye contact by pretending to be asleep. Amser wasn't a cruel girl but she knew whatever she said and however she said it, her parents were going to be very aggrieved.

Amser decided it would be best if Bethan was in bed first. She collected her daughter from the childminder and allowed her to sit next to her parents for her dinner. Amser also made an excuse about having a headache so her mum would bath Bethan one last time and tuck her up in her bed.

Amser then went upstairs to say goodnight to her daughter and to gather her thoughts again for what she had to do. In these quiet moments Amser looked around her room and considered what she'd be leaving behind.

She was a little distressed and a tear or two dripped from her eyes. Then however, she remembered the conversations she heard between her parents in the room below. She recalled the terrible things said about her and her granny and it gave her the strength to carry out her plan.

Amser walked down the stairs to where both her parents were sitting and watching the television.

Amser sat down beside her mum, took a deep breath and said 'I've something important to tell you.'

'You're not pregnant again are you girl?' her dad asked.

Amser ignored the question and her mum said 'We've had a wonderful day, whatever is it?'

'There's no easy way to say this: I'm going to teach in Rowan in the Autumn,' she replied.

Mr Edwards shouted at his daughter 'You're going off again, leaving us to look after Bethan. You have responsibilities here, you're not going anywhere.'

If ever Amser needed encouragement to go on then her dad's attitude had made things so much simpler.

'Don't worry; I'm taking Bethan with me. I've already sorted out accommodation,' she replied.

Amser hadn't done any such thing, in fact it was now her biggest concern.

The girl said 'I knew how you'd react so I've made arrangements to go first thing in the morning.'

Mrs Edwards was in tears.

'When will we see Bethan?' she asked.

'I guess you won't,' Amser replied.

'So that's all the thanks we get,' bellowed her dad.

'What about the money, it belongs to all of us,' he said.

Amser didn't want to say this but her father had made her angry.

She replied 'I heard you say you wouldn't have looked after granny if she was going to give her money to me. I also heard you both say I'd been a burden and you could have lived a better life without me.'

Mrs Edwards was distraught.

She said 'Oh my God, to think you have carried these thoughts in your head all this time; you must hate us very much.'

Mrs Edwards started sobbing.

Amser watched her mother's tears stream down her face. However, she wasn't going to comfort her this time.

'I don't hate you,' she replied.

'I don't know how I feel about you. I can live with the things you said about me. Looking back, I can see from the way you treated me that I wasn't wanted. However, what I can never forgive is the things you said about my grandma. I think she must have known and that's why you didn't get any money. I certainly don't think I should go against her wishes.'

Her parents were speechless as she added 'No you don't deserve any money. I'm going to make a fresh start for me and Bethan far away from here.'

Amser left the room and went upstairs to pack knowing she was only to spend a few more hours in Walwyn Gate. The only person who slept that night was Bethan and there were few words spoken in the morning. Amser brought her suitcase downstairs and went and got her little girl. Her mother watched as her daughter gathered her possessions in the hall.

At the stroke of nine o'clock a taxi pulled up outside and Amser opened the door to a bright sunny morning. The girl walked out with Bethan in her arms and the driver took her case. Her father had stayed inside but Amser looked back to see her mother standing on the door step. The girl turned again and walked towards the vehicle.

Her mum called out 'Amser, please Amser.'

The daughter turned again and walked back to her mother.

She said 'I'm sorry mum but I have to do this.'

Mrs Edwards said 'I'm sorry too, so sorry.'

Mrs Edwards gave her granddaughter one last kiss before Amser and Bethan got into the taxi. Then the vehicle drove off leaving Mrs Edwards crying and staring at her daughter and granddaughter through the vehicle's back window.

The taxi took Amser and Bethan to the railway station for the train journey to Rowan.

'Are we going on holiday?' enquired Bethan.

'It's kind of a holiday,' replied Amser.

Bethan then asked 'When are we coming home mummy?'

Amser said 'We're going to live in a new home.'

Bethan went on 'Are granny and granddad coming?'

'No they have to work here,' said Amser.

Bethan persisted 'When will I see them?'

Amser hadn't expected so many questions and she didn't want to lie to her child. However, if she told her the truth now she knew Bethan wouldn't be able to cope with it.

'I think they'll come and visit in the summer,' she replied.

There was one more thing Amser needed to do before saying goodbye to Walwyn Gate. She instructed the taxi driver to stop at her old school and asked the man if he would look after Bethan for five minutes. He was pleased to oblige as he knew Mr Edwards.

Amser entered the playground and made her way to Mrs Reece's classroom. She looked through the window and saw children hard at work in silence. Then Amser knocked on the door and entered. Mrs Reece looked up and beamed at her.

The girl apologised for the intrusion and said 'I'm sorry to disturb you but I'm going away today and may never come back. I've something of yours which I have to return to you.'

Mrs Reece had forgotten until Amser reached inside her bag and produced the poetry book she'd been lent.

'I'm to teach in Rowan having got my degree,' said Amser.

'I promised to return this book to you.'

Mrs Reece said 'I know you are Amser, did you think I wouldn't take the trouble to find out about you?'

She smiled and opened the inside page of the book and said 'I remember telling you never to deface books but I'm going to make an exception.'

She then picked up a pen and under the initial inscription she wrote 'To Amser with love from Angela Reece.'

Then she closed the cover and placed the book in Amser's hand.

Much to the amazement of her pupils the lady put her arms around Amser and hugged her. The embrace lasted several seconds and when they parted Amser turned around and looked at the children.

She said 'This lady changed my life, she can change yours too.'

Amser turned around once again and faced Mrs Reece.

'Thank you, thank you so much, I'll never forget you.'

Then she left the room and as she walked down the corridor for the last time all the memories of her childhood stirred in her mind. However, this was her chance to have a new life and embrace what her granny described as a wonderful future. She hoped it would bring both her and Bethan much happiness. With these positive thoughts in her mind she walked out of her school; she never looked back and reboarded the taxi.

After a few minutes the vehicle pulled up at the station entrance and mother and child made their way to the ticket office. The weather had taken a turn for the worse. The early sunshine had disappeared and the clouds had darkened. Small spots of rain began to gather on the pavement and Amser and Bethan hurried their way into the building.

Walking up behind Amser a voice said 'You didn't think you were going to get away without saying goodbye to me did you?'

Amser knew straightaway it was Rhonda and both she and Bethan turned around to greet her.

'I was going to write once we were settled,' said Amser.

Rhonda replied 'I know but I had to come. We've been through so much together and I'm going to miss you.'

'Dear Rhon, my best friend, my only real friend what would I have done without you these past years.'

Together they walked with Bethan up the wooden stairs and over the bridge to the platform beyond. They could see the train approaching from the distance and made their way down the steps. There was only time for a few words before the train rumbled into the station.

After the usual hugs both Amser and Bethan got on board and sat down by the window looking out over the platform. Two minutes later the train started to leave and the girls blew kisses and waved until they couldn't see each other anymore.

Chapter Fourteen

In a little over three hours Amser had re-lived her past. Bethan was soon to wake up and her mother read her stories until the train arrived at Rowan station. It was late afternoon and she didn't have any idea where to go. However, at least this time it was warm and there wasn't snow on the ground.

She was pondering what to do outside the station entrance when a taxi driver got out of his vehicle.

'Can I help you miss? Are you lost?' he enquired.

'A little, I need to find a decent hotel,' she replied.

'Would the town centre be OK?' he asked.

'That would be fine,' said Amser.

The taxi driver opened his door and mother and child got in. Within five minutes the vehicle was pulling up outside Hotel Rhonda.

Amser couldn't believe the name and smiled. 'It seems I can never get away from her,' she thought.

It was a tall, imposing, modern, building with steps leading up to two large glass doors. She thanked and paid the taxi driver before making her way inside with Bethan.

As soon as she entered a lady receptionist greeted them and after completing the necessary formalities she had them escorted to a comfortable room. It had a large double bed and a single bed for Bethan. It also had a small settee, a table with two chairs and a television.

Whilst Amser was emptying the case, Bethan went exploring and on opening the door to the en-suite she called out to her mother 'What's this?'

'What on earth was she talking about' thought Amser and she looked inside.

Bethan was pointing at the shower as she'd never seen one before.

'Oh it's for washing yourself. It's like taking a bath standing up.'

Bethan giggled thinking her mum was joking.

'Right,' said Amser. 'Get your clothes off and we'll take a shower together.'

They were both dirty after a day's travelling and undressed. Amser turned on the taps and her daughter was amazed to see water falling from above. It fascinated her and she wanted to get straight into the cubicle.

Her mother had to make sure it wasn't too hot and then they both entered. Shampoo and soap had been provided by the hotel and Amser washed herself and Bethan from head to foot. Bethan loved the warm water falling on her face and kept looking up at the spout.

When Amser came out of the shower area, having dried herself and her daughter, she finished unpacking whilst they both had towels wrapped around them. The day was becoming more and more like a great adventure for Bethan and despite the strange surroundings they were both able to enjoy a good night's sleep.

Bethan loved this place. It was warm and she had a nice cosy bed. The hotel also had a pool and it was the closest thing to a holiday the little girl had ever had. She was even able to take swimming lessons.

Bethan was happy and this was a great weight off Amser's mind. However a hotel wasn't an ideal environment for a child and she knew she must find somewhere more permanent to live as soon as possible.

Having so much money in the bank was a comfort and there were many properties for sale in the area. Amser didn't require anything big but she wanted the new home to be comfortable and to have a garden for Bethan.

Mother and daughter viewed three houses in quick succession. They were all far superior to anything Amser had lived in before but they each had their individual drawbacks. One was situated on a busy road and many lorries trundled up and down. The second property had a tiny back garden that was fully paved whilst the last one backed on to a railway.

Amser was getting fed up.

She'd just got back to the hotel with Bethan when there was a call from an estate agent.

'I think you'd like a property which has come onto the market in the last hour. It's in Princess Road,' he said.

'I would advise you to view it now as it will soon be sold,' he added.

'Did you say Princess Road?' Amser enquired.

'I certainly did, do you know where it is?' said the agent.

'I know somebody who lives at number five.'

'Well this is number seven; it's next door.'

Mr and Mrs Peach resided there and Amser was trying to picture the house that was for sale. When she stayed with them it was dark most of the time and all she could remember was a yellow painted gate.

The agent said 'It's a modern three bedroom detached house with a garden and a garage. I think you'll like it.'

Amser and Bethan decided to go out again and walked to the property which was almost a mile away. As soon as they saw the house they fell in love with it.

The white front door and windows had recently been repainted along with the garden gate. The front garden was smart; it had a small well-kept lawn with trimmed hedges on either side. Looking out into the back garden from the kitchen Bethan noticed a swing and a sand pit. She rushed outside with her mother following her.

They were yet to look in all the rooms but Princess Road was perfect; it was close to Selwyn College, the town amenities and the Peaches were next door.

Then whilst mother and daughter were standing in the back garden Mrs Peach heard Amser talking. She was hanging out her washing listening to her voice when she realised who it might be. She looked through a hole in the fence and was excited to see her.

Standing on a garden chair so she could be seen she called out 'Fruit cake for you Miss Amser.'

Mother and daughter were looking in the other direction and turned around.

Amser's face beamed as she said 'Oh Peachy I can't believe it. It's a small world isn't it?'

In all honesty Amser didn't know the woman very well but she was there when the girl got her job and she hadn't forgotten the affection shown towards her.

Mother and daughter went back inside the house and explored all the rooms. Everything was perfect and as soon as they finished they went next door. Mr Peach greeted them and planted a large kiss on Amser's cheek before bursting out laughing.

The girl just hugged him as she knew it was his way of saying hello. Then he bent down to talk to Bethan but his noisy presence un-nerved her a little. For once however Mr Peach tempered his approach.

He said softly 'Hello little lady' and kissed her on the forehead.

By this time Peachy had arrived from the kitchen. She greeted Amser with kisses on both cheeks. Then she turned her attention to the little girl.

'So you must be Bethan I remember your mother telling me about you.'

Bethan was clutching her teddy.

'So what's your teddy's name?' she enquired.

Bethan was shy and didn't speak so Peachy said 'If I can find you a piece of fruit cake do you think you could tell me the name.'

The little girl shook her head so Peachy said 'Is it Rover?'

Bethan giggled.

Peachy went on 'Is it Tweety Pie?'

Bethan giggled again.

Peachy said 'Your teddy can have some cake as well.'

Bethan nodded and they all went into the kitchen.

The room was as untidy as Amser remembered it but Mr Peach soon found places for them to sit by moving all sorts of objects including crockery, saucepans and biscuit tins.

By this time Peachy had cut five pieces of cake including one for teddy. She also made three cups of tea and poured a glass of fruit juice for Bethan.

'So are you going to tell me teddy's name then?' asked Peachy.

The little girl was getting to like her and replied 'It's Pinky.'

Peachy said 'If Pinky can't eat all her cake can you finish it for her.'

Bethan giggled again and nodded. She was fascinated by her enormous ear rings. They were as big as saucers and shone like gold.

On leaving Princess Road, Amser went to the estate agents and made a good offer for the property which was accepted the following day. The house was empty and so once all the usual searches had been completed she could look forward to moving in.

Amser spent time buying all her home necessities with the help of Bethan. Although only four years old, she was becoming as much of a friend to Amser as she was a daughter. Bethan seemed to have very good colour co-ordination sense. She amazed both her mother and the sales assistants in the local furnishing stores with her likes and dislikes of carpets, suites and curtains.

Bethan was so particular with the decoration of her own bedroom it made Amser cry. It wasn't that Amser minded her daughter's preferences. It was because she remembered her bedroom as a child and was happy Bethan could have such beautiful things.

The next task was to find a school for Bethan although a place wasn't required until the following year. Amser didn't have any idea what the standard of local infant education was like in Rowan.

She feared the better schools would have long waiting lists and wished she'd sorted things out in advance. However, she needn't have worried as one phone call to the local education authority resulted in a meeting at Williams Way Infant School. It was close to where Amser was going to live and she was to see the headmaster.

The teaching establishment did look a bit old-fashioned. It had arched windows at the front and imposing railings along the road each side of the entrance. A large board with white writing revealed the school's name which was also the name of the road.

On arrival the headmaster Mr Gareth Trott was standing at the school entrance. He was only five feet six inches tall but he was slim, had long blonde hair and was wearing a dark blue track suit.

'Come in, come in,' he said as he beckoned them.

'Miss Edwards isn't it and you're Bethan aren't you?' he went on.

Before either party could answer, the headmaster was talking about the weather, then the traffic on the road and then the lollipop lady as he led them to his room. He walked behind his desk and invited Amser and Bethan to take a seat.

However, as soon as they were comfortable Mr Trott was on his feet and moving around the room as he continued to talk about everything that took his fancy. Bethan and Amser were struggling to keep their eyes on him as he moved about the room at speed.

Then, he startled mother and daughter by perching himself on the end of his desk and saying 'So you want to send Bethan to my school?'

'Yes,' replied Amser.

'Good choice, good choice, not a better school around,' uttered Mr Trott.

'I'll see her in September next year then.'

Once again Mr Trott took to his feet and this time opened the door to his room for Amser and Bethan to leave. However, as they got up, the headmaster raced ahead of them.

As he sped away he called out 'I'm off to the gym now.'

'Only chance I get is when the kids aren't here, oh, are there any questions?'

Amser wasn't going to shout and Mr Trott was out of sight in a flash, having disappeared through some double doors at the end of the corridor. The meeting had lasted no more than three minutes and left Amser feeling a little confused. She'd met the most extraordinary person who seemed to be both eccentric and unpredictable.

'A headmaster's behaviour should be more professional' she thought. Yet there was something about Mr Trott that made her feel Bethan was going to the right place.

Finding a childminder might prove a little more difficult,

thought Amser. She was reluctant to think about leaving Bethan with anybody she didn't know or wasn't comfortable with. She searched the Yellow Pages and located a number of children's nurseries.

Silly as it sounds she was put off some of them by their names. Others she telephoned either didn't answer or didn't have any space available. Amser was able to place Bethan's name on waiting lists but with the new school term looming and the starting of her job, the situation was becoming critical.

In late August Amser moved into her house. All the furnishings arrived as planned. First the carpets came and two fitters worked hard to make sure they were all laid by lunchtime. In the afternoon, the remaining furnishings arrived and were assembled in the various rooms.

Amser had only seen as many new things in a furniture store and kept looking at all her purchases. The house felt warm and cosy and her favourite feature was the large windows. She hadn't realised how wide or deep they were. From her bedroom she could see the rolling hills of the countryside and in the far distance the sea.

Whilst Amser was looking around her house the doorbell rang. When she opened it a short plump woman was standing in front of her. She had grey curly hair and looked about fifty five years old.

The lady said 'I'm Iola, I live at number nine.'

'Come in, come in please, will you,' said Amser.

The lady entered and handed Amser a small package.

'It's a small welcome gift,' she said.

Amser put her hand inside and took out a love spoon.

'That's kind of you Iola, I'll hang it in the kitchen.'

Amser made her a cup of tea and whilst she was doing so Iola's eyes cast around the downstairs rooms. She'd seen the various vehicles arrive throughout the day and had come to see the deliveries for herself. Amser could see her taking notice of all the belongings when she entered the lounge with the refreshment.

'I've come here to make a fresh start and I have a teaching job at Selwyn College,' she remarked.

'Leaving problems behind, are you?' Iola enquired.

'A few,' said Amser.

'You have a daughter then,' remarked Iola seeing Bethan; sitting at a table colouring in a book.

'Yes, and I need a reliable childminder,' replied Amser.

'I don't suppose you know of anybody?'

'Well' replied Iola, still looking at all the new furniture.

'Good childminders are hard to find. I might know of somebody, if the price is right.'

'Who might that be?' said Amser.

'I might be prepared to look after Bethan myself,' replied Iola.

Amser wasn't sure about Iola, she'd only just met the lady and she seemed very nosy and a bit pushy.

Iola said 'I used to look after six children at a time but stopped doing it two years ago.'

'Why do you want to start childminding again?' Amser enquired.

'Because my husband has left me and I need the money,' replied Iola.

'I'm sorry,' said Amser.

'Don't be my dear, we spent over twenty years together but I never liked him. He spent all our money on drink and horses and has found himself a younger woman. Well she's welcome to him, I am glad he's gone. The only thing that's annoyed me is he's taken the cat.'

Amser didn't know what to say. She'd only met Iola a few minutes ago and knew nothing about her. However, she did think it would be convenient and agreed to think about it.

The more Amser and Iola talked the more they liked one another. As she left the house Iola invited Amser into her home the following day for a further chat. However, it was important Bethan was safe and secure and so Amser decided to ask Peachy if she knew anything about the woman.

Peachy had been looking forward to seeing Amser. She greeted both her and Bethan as if they'd been away for years. Walking down the hall towards the kitchen they could smell her delicious fruit cake.

Once again the little girl was attracted to Peachy's earrings. This time they hung like large spoons and were bright red. Then Mr Peach appeared from the sitting room and his presence un-nerved Bethan again. However, as soon as he opened his mouth he laughed causing Bethan to giggle.

Amser mentioned the visit of Iola and asked Peachy what she thought of her.

'I don't see a lot of her,' she replied.

'I know her husband left her but I think he was a bit of a pain.'

'I'm glad he took the cat, it was always messing in our garden,' remarked Mr Peach.

'She says she's a childminder,' said Amser.

'She used to be,' said Peachy.

'There was a time when we would see a number of children being taken to her. They used to pass by our window.'

'She isn't going to start that lark again is she?' Mr Peach enquired.

'No I don't think so, I get the impression it would only be Bethan,' said Amser.

'All I can say is, I think it would be alright,' remarked Peachy.

Amser went to see Iola the following morning as planned. Once inside her house Amser could see why she'd been invited. There was a children's playroom and outside there was a swing, a slide and a see-saw. It was obvious Iola had been telling the truth. When she showed Amser pictures of her three sons and two grandchildren, Amser started to feel at ease in her presence.

'Well what's it to be then, do you want me to look after your daughter, do you?' Iola enquired.

'I can provide references,' she went on.

Amser wasn't spoilt for choice and being next door was convenient.

'Yes please that would be great,' the girl answered and after a further discussion she agreed to pay a little extra on condition Iola would be as flexible as Amser required.

With all her school duties commencing in a matter of days, this arrangement took a great weight off Amser's mind. Now she could look forward to her new job with enthusiasm.

Chapter Fifteen

Amser went into Selwyn College the day prior to the start of term. She'd been allocated a classroom on the second floor overlooking the playing fields. The school had excellent facilities including woodwork and metalwork rooms, a brand new science laboratory and a gymnasium that was over eighty feet long.

For Amser however it was the library that held the most attraction. This large rectangular room was packed with books embracing every spectrum of the writing community. A shelf stretching right along one wall contained titles conceived by all of the best authors in the world. It was a treasure chest and the young teacher was keen to share its secrets with all her children.

Amser was excited and started preparing her room. She was determined to make an immediate impression on the children and worked for nine hours, only breaking for a cup of tea. By the time she'd finished, portraits of famous authors and sentences from their celebrated readings were everywhere to be seen.

Also there were posters relating to the enactment of well-known theatrical plays ranging from classical novels to modern day musicals. The room was packed with literary brilliance and reflected the teacher's passion for the subject that inspired her.

Having been up and down a step ladder and stretching her arms in different directions to fasten material to the walls, Amser's bones were aching. She went home very tired but didn't sleep that night. She lay on her bed feeling both nervous and excited watching the seconds tick by on her alarm clock.

The next day Amser arrived at school an hour before the children. She walked around the classroom a number of times and wiped her blackboard that had been cleaned the evening before. She adjusted some posters on the wall and even moved the position of her waste paper bin.

Amser started to imagine what her pupils might be like but

her main concern was Shelley Nevan the teaching assistant in situ who also applied for her job.

Shelley was a beautiful woman. In her mid-forties she was slim and had long blonde wavy hair. Her eyes were deep green and her skin was unblemished. She dressed in brightly coloured expensive clothes and drew the attention of everyone in her presence.

Shelley had moved to Rowan the previous January having taught English Literature in Bangor many years before. Amser hadn't considered any difficulties might arise with the lady until the headmaster telephoned her the previous week.

He told her Shelley had been biding her time in the knowledge that the vacancy would occur. Now with no suitable job opportunities existing locally she'd no option other than to continue with her classroom assistant duties albeit with another teacher.

It was now a few minutes before nine o'clock and putting Shelley to the back of her mind Amser concentrated on her children. She'd thought long and hard about how she should try and bond with them, earn their respect and help them realise their potential. Their future was in her hands and she was determined not to let them down. As she said in her interview 'Their education was to be her reward.'

Then a whistle was blown in the playground. In a moment or two her class would arrive and she could now hear the sound of shoe leather getting louder on the wooden stairs. Amser had already opened her door and unlike Mrs Reece she'd decided to remain seated behind her desk at the front of the classroom as the children entered.

They were noisy and a little unruly. They arrived armed with coats and bags and wanting to sit with their friends so there was a lot of pushing and shoving.

Amser called out 'Come on children find a seat you like and sit down so I can see you all.'

Two minutes later all the desks were occupied, and twenty eight pairs of eyes were looking at her. They were surprisingly quiet, all with their private thoughts about what Amser might be like. She knew she would be judged as she would judge them.

This was Amser's class although she would only see these faces for a short time each week. She had to teach many other children, with her time divided between literature and drama.

During the first few days Amser set out her stall. Children like rules and so boundaries were established but all her lessons were structured to encourage constructive criticism, imagination and creativity. It wasn't long before the pupils greeted them with enthusiasm and even some excitement.

Once Amser was settled into the school she wanted to speak to Shelley and clear the air. This wasn't easy as the classroom assistant always ignored her presence in the staff room and when passing in the playground or school corridor she resisted eye contact.

However on one afternoon when school work had finished Amser was walking past a classroom when she saw Shelley talking to a pupil inside. Something made her stop and take a closer look through the edge of a window from where she couldn't be seen.

Teachers were encouraged not to engage in one to one conversations with pupils in private areas. Amser was intrigued as this discussion was taking place in a classroom that was being redecorated and was out of use.

Voices were raised but she couldn't hear what was being said. However from Shelley's body language she could see the woman was very annoyed.

The pupil was a fourteen year old girl called Sophie. She had her back to the wall and was facing towards Amser. The teaching assistant was standing so close to the girl they were almost touching and then Amser saw Shelley take hold of Sophie's left arm. She was squeezing it so hard the girl was clearly in pain.

Sophie wasn't a very nice girl; she was often rude and arrogant. Her clothes were usually dirty, her hair was always untidy and her personal hygiene standards were a little lacking. However there was nothing that could justify such an act of aggression.

Shelley continued to clench Sophie's arm when as luck would have it Mr Stead-Simpson appeared in the corridor. Amser told him what had happened but by this time the confrontation in the classroom had ceased.

The headmaster was a well-spoken man in his late fifties who had been head of the school for many years. Amser had become used to his negative approach to almost every situation. He was always moaning about the extra responsibilities he now had and how the standards of pupil respect had deteriorated over the years.

When presented with an unpleasant situation Mr Stead-Simpson seemed unwilling to deal with it. To Amser's surprise he allowed both the pupil and assistant to walk out of the classroom without saying a word to either of them.

Shelley looked horrified by the headmaster's presence as she passed by and Sophie had already hurried off into the distance. Amser however was determined to pursue the matter and didn't waste any time.

'What were you doing to the girl?' she said.

Shelley turned around to make eye contact with Amser and Mr Stead-Simpson. She was looking very uncomfortable fiddling with the collar on her blue buttoned white blouse.

After pausing for a second or two she replied 'We were chatting, that's all.'

'It was more than that, I saw you,' Amser replied.

'You were gripping Sophie's arm and I could see she was in pain.'

Shelley tried to laugh off the incident.

She remarked 'I would never lay a hand on that dirty girl.'

Amser wouldn't let the matter rest and realising the seriousness of the situation Mr Stead-Simpson invited all three parties into his room. Sophie was already on her way out of the school when she was called back through an open window.

Whilst they were all seated by the headmaster's desk Shelley looked agitated and annoyed. Still fiddling with her blouse her face was deep red as she glared at Amser. Sophie was tearful and sheepish.

'Why were you in the room Mrs Nevan?' the headmaster enquired.

'It was something about nothing that happened outside the school, it's alright now or at least it will be,' Shelley said.

126

Sophie's head was bowed, she was clearly distressed.

'Is it all settled Sophie?' asked the headmaster.

The girl was hesitant but with Shelley's eyes peering at her she nodded.

Mr Stead-Simpson was prepared to let the matter drop but Amser had other ideas.

'I told you headmaster I saw them, Shelley Nevan was hurting her.'

Without further ado Amser got hold of the girl's hand and lifted up the sleeve of her jumper. It was much worse than she'd feared. Not only was there a large bruise but also finger nail indentations were visible as well.

'There look I told you: I saw it all, it was awful.'

Shelley sat in silence as she watched Mr Stead-Simpson walk over to Sophie. The girl stood up and he put his hands on her shoulders.

The girl was shaking as the headmaster enquired 'Tell me honestly Sophie, did Mrs Nevan hurt you, did she do this to you?'

Sophie now an emotional wreck, her face wet with tears, nodded.

On hearing this Shelley knew there was no way back. She'd done something dreadful and had been found out. Getting to her feet she went to strike Amser with her umbrella but the blow was stopped by Mr Stead-Simpson's arm.

'Nosy cow, why couldn't you mind your own bleeding business,' ranted the lady waving her arms about.

'But why would you want to hurt the girl?' Amser asked with the headmaster between them.

'Just look at her, would you want the girl anywhere near your son; I've tried to warn her off but she won't listen,' she replied.

Mr Stead-Simpson had heard enough.

He said 'Mrs Nevan collect your things and get off the premises you're suspended. Your position at the school will be reviewed with a view to the termination of your contract. I'll be speaking to both the police and Sophie's parents to see if they'll be criminal proceedings.'

Shelley stormed out of the classroom but looking back she shouted out 'You've got my job Edwards and now you've got me out of the school. Make sure that filthy girl keeps away from my son.'

By this time Sophie was huddled in a corner on the floor. She was in need of some comfort. On a normal day Amser would have been home by now but she knew Iola would be pleased to look after Bethan.

She said 'Headmaster would you leave Sophie with me please. I'll make sure she gets home safely.'

Mr Stead-Simpson hadn't had a teacher attack a pupil before. It had shocked him and he was grateful for her assistance. Despite Sophie's terrible ordeal, Amser found it hard to show much sympathy towards her. The girl was one of a very small number who disrupted her classes and her appearance appalled her.

'Right girl let's get out of here,' she said.

Sophie got to her feet and Amser escorted her home which was close to where the teacher lived. Not a word was said between them until the last second when she opened her front door.

The girl turned around and nodded before saying 'Thank you Miss Edwards, truly thank you.'

From that day on Sophie didn't show any more interest in her school work. However she was always washed and better dressed and whilst in Amser's classroom improved her behaviour.

With all Amser's teaching responsibilities, over the coming days and years, Iola was a godsend. Not only was she a reliable childminder but she also had good local contacts and was able to find a nursery place for Bethan three mornings a week.

The little girl loved mixing with other children where she was read stories and played all sorts of games. Bethan had always been a good talker but this environment improved her confidence.

It was also a comfort having Mr and Mrs Peach living next door. Amser and Peachy did their shopping together on a Saturday morning. They walked to the local supermarket which was only a mile away.

The brick exterior of the shop was painted a bright yellow colour but curiously it was called 'The Red House'. It was a long single storey building with a glass covered walkway that extended right along one side. The entrance and exit were both situated together at one end and sometimes people had to push past one another to get in and out. It seemed to be busy all the time.

Amser always took two large cloth bags with her and Peachy pulled an old rickety basket on wheels. This contraption squeaked as it moved around its axle and sounded very noisy in the shop on the stone tiled floor.

With so many people around, shopping was not a pleasurable experience. When they finished they enjoyed tea and scones from the small café at the side of the store which they saw as their reward for completing the weekly endurance test.

Whilst they were out Mr Peach amused Bethan. She got used to his strange mannerism and he looked forward to her visits. The man became very fond of Bethan. Sometimes Mr Peach would sit Bethan on his lap, tell her stories and draw animals with a pencil. She thought he was very clever.

His drawing of horses excited her as they looked alive and ready to walk out of his sketchbook. Mr Peach encouraged Bethan to use a pencil but she was unable to grasp what he tried to teach her. It seemed drawing wasn't to be her forte.

However, Mr Peach did think there was something special about her fingers. She seemed very particular about the way she touched things. It was as if she treasured their every movement and unlike anything he'd seen from a child before.

On one of her visits he was a little more serious and said to Bethan 'My darling little girl, you may never be a sketch artist or a painter but you have love in your fingers.'

Bethan giggled. She didn't know what he meant. Mr Peach didn't know either but there was something that moved him.

Apart from drawing Mr Peach was interested in flying kites. Before he retired he was a carpenter and used to carve wood into beautiful designs for glass cabinets, chair legs and banisters. He worked from home and had a workshop at the bottom of his garden.

Now he had time on his hands and spent ages on his hobby. It was because of the necessity to delicately use his fingers during his working life that he noticed Bethan's.

Mr Peach made kites from all sorts of material in many different colours. When the weather was dry he would take Bethan to a large grassed area close to Princess Road where all sorts of recreational activities were undertaken.

It was a gathering place for kite flyers on Saturdays and they all knew one another. Sometimes there would be twenty kites flying at once and there was a local rivalry to see who could fly the highest and fastest. Bethan loved watching the spectacle in the sky and sometimes Mr Peach let her hold the strings.

Chapter Sixteen

The following September soon arrived and it was to mark the beginning of a new and exciting chapter in both Amser's and Bethan's lives. Bethan was a bright girl and had been ready to start school for a long time. With the help of her mother and Iola she was able to count and read at a level well beyond her age.

On her first day she was up earlier than usual and Amser dressed her in the red and white uniform of 'Williams Way' school. How proud her mother was to see her little princess standing in front of her with her yellow lunch box in her hand.

Amser's term didn't start until the following morning so she was able to walk her daughter to school. Iola stood at her door as they came out. She'd become part of Bethan's life and cried when she saw the little girl.

Amser knew how much the lady had done for both of them and enquired 'Iola, would you like to walk Bethan to school with me?'

Iola, thought about the question. Of course she wanted to say yes but she knew despite all her caring and love for Bethan, she wasn't the child's mother.

She replied 'No Amser this is your moment, taking your daughter to school for the first time is something you never forget. I've had my children and I have my memories. Don't mind my tears; I'm a silly woman.'

Mr and Mrs Peach were also outside their house watching as the little girl and her mother passed by. Bethan waved to them and Peachy responded by blowing the girl a kiss whilst the old man just laughed.

It was only a short distance to the school so Amser and Bethan walked down the road and around the corner into Williams Way. As they approached the gates Bethan saw children she knew from nursery and waved at them.

After two minutes a bell sounded. Amser bent down and adjusted Bethan's clothing. She wiped a food smudge away from her chin with a handkerchief she had wetted from her lips. Then Amser straightened the ribbon in her hair and by this time most of the children had gone into the school.

'Go now Bethan, you'll be late,' she said.

Then she kissed her on the forehead and the little girl walked towards the entrance. Amser watched her for every last second until she disappeared inside before turning around and making her way home.

It seemed so daft but, although she was going to see her daughter in a few hours, at this moment she felt alone and the odd tear slid down her cheek.

Once again Amser thought about her childhood.

She said to herself 'Whatever happens in the future I'll make sure my daughter is loved and cared for. I'll never let her down.'

Amser hadn't told Iola much about her life in Walwyn Gate but the childminder knew she'd be sad. She'd been waiting in her front garden and watched as Amser came down the road.

Iola called out 'The kettles on,' as Amser opened her garden gate.

Bethan's mum, still feeling rather glum, didn't need any persuading and went straight around to next door. Tea had already been made and Iola brought out some homemade biscuits on a large pink tray. Amser took one and then Iola handed her a note from Bethan which Iola had helped write.

Amser was a little surprised and opened it.

It read 'I thought you would be sad today so I made you some biscuits Mummy, love Bethan.'

'We made them last Friday,' said Iola.

'I said you would be thinking of her today so what shall we do to cheer you up.'

Bethan said 'Let's make mummy some biscuits.'

There were more tears of course but Iola was a jolly person and they soon started to laugh as they discussed Bethan's upbringing and all the fun times they had enjoyed with her. Amser became contented again and in no time at all Bethan needed picking up from school.

As soon as Bethan saw her mum she ran across the playground; she'd so much to tell her.

Amser said 'Have you got a nice teacher?'

Bethan replied 'Yes she's called Mrs Hinkin. We were all given sweets because we stayed silent for a whole minute.'

The teacher was a kind and gentle person with a pretty face and wavy blonde hair. She'd worked at the school for over 30 years and taught the first infant class. After one day Bethan had fallen in love with her.

The girl was so excited about everything. She was talking so fast about the things she'd done and her new friends that Amser couldn't keep up.

'Bethan, slow down will you,' she said.

Ignoring her mother's request she started talking about the headmaster.

She laughed and said 'I saw Mr Trott slip over in the playground.'

Amser was a little concerned.

She said 'You shouldn't laugh at someone else's misfortune. He may have hurt himself.'

To Amser's horror, Bethan said 'He did mummy, he fell over a boy's satchel and there was blood pouring from his arm. He had to go to hospital for some stitches.'

The little girl had a huge grin on her face and giggled again. Amser couldn't help herself. She remembered how Mr Trott whizzed all over the place when she and Bethan visited him the previous year.

She said to Bethan 'You're a naughty girl,' and then started to laugh as well.

'Oh well the main thing is Bethan's happy' she thought.

Chapter Seventeen

The next day Amser was to start her second year at Selwyn College. Having had twelve months to settle in she'd established a good reputation. The children loved and respected her because she played games with them during breaks, stayed behind after school to run clubs and was always involved in the school plays.

Bethan and Amser thrived with every passing day. It was a wonderful time in both of their lives.

Each year at Williams Way Infants School, with the encouragement and expertise of Mr Trott and his teachers, the children took part in a Christmas play. The event was famous in the community and the school hall was always packed to see the show.

When Bethan was six years old there was extra excitement ahead of the annual performance as in this particular year the play was to be very different. The children had been practising hard after school and had been making scenery and props for some weeks. They'd been told to keep everything a secret and Bethan wouldn't tell her mother anything about it.

On the evening of the play, when all the parents had taken their seats, the curtain opened to reveal a room in the home of a very poor family with a little boy. As the story unfolded it became clear the child thought there was no such person as Father Christmas. Both his mum and dad tried hard to convince him but as he never got the presents he asked for he didn't believe them.

Lots of things happened in the play involving all of the children but the story centred on this one little boy. He was so sad and disillusioned that his parents made up their minds he was going to Lapland to see Father Christmas for himself.

It was very hard as they only just had enough money to live and buy the food they needed. However, by working extra-long hours and making more sacrifices they managed to save enough cash for the boy and his dad to make the trip. Everything was arranged and they set off for the airport.

The audience was amazed to see the children's colourful scenery. It had been painted to make the stage look like an airport terminal building and then changed in a few seconds into an aeroplane.

It was an amazing story but the climax was when the boy arrived at Santa's home. Now seen on a reindeer sleigh he was asked to put his hands over his eyes for the last few minutes of the journey. The audience waited as the lights in the hall were turned off and the curtain was lowered so they too could experience the same surprise as the little boy.

Then the sound of a sleigh on snow could be heard on the school's sound system and whilst this was going on all of the children except this one little boy had gathered on the stage out of sight. Moments passed as the sound of the sleigh continued and then the children began to sing:-

Would you like to know about Father Christmas
And where he keeps his sleigh
Well he lives in a house with a big red door
Where his reindeer play all day
And every day he's making toys
To give the millions of girls and boys
And while he is working all day long
You can often here him singing his song.

Whilst the curtain was down the children had worked hard to transform the stage setting again. Then with the pupils singing, the lighting on the stage was turned on and the curtain was raised.

The parents in the audience looked on as the little boy opened his eyes in amazement. On the stage sitting outside a small house with a bright red door, Father Christmas could be seen with a hammer in his hand making a dolls house. All around him were piles of new looking toys and a little further away were four reindeers made out of cardboard, old pieces of carpet and twigs for antlers.

The children could now be seen standing together in a choir-like formation except for two boys who were with a teacher high up on a specially-erected platform. Then Father Christmas started to sing:-

Little boys and little girls
Rely on me each year
To make them smile
For just a while
When Christmas time is here
And when the snow falls
And the robin sings
I know I'll soon be on my way
Sailing through that holy night
With my reindeer and my sleigh.

As this was happening pieces of white cotton wool were dropped from above and it looked like snow was falling. Finally the children joined Father Christmas to sing the whole song again. It was magical for everybody and of course the boy now believed in Santa.

Mr Trott had come up with some wonderful ideas for his school's Christmas plays. This time he had surpassed all expectations and there was a warm glow in the hearts of all the parents as they left the hall.

The following night was Christmas Eve and Bethan was in her nightie sitting on her mum's lap beside her bed.

'Is there really a Father Christmas?' asked Bethan.

Amser replied 'Of course there is. You know what his song said: when the snow falls and the robin sings he'll soon be on his way.'

'Yes mummy but that was only make-believe.'

Amser opened the curtains and to Bethan's surprise snow was falling. She could see the roofs and gardens had turned white as she looked out into the darkness.

Cuddling up close to her mother, Bethan said 'Will he come tonight?'

'Well he's always come before but you must go to sleep now. He doesn't visit children who are awake,' said Amser.

Bethan got into bed and Amser tucked her in. She kissed her daughter on the cheek and turned out her light. Later, when the girl was asleep, Amser crept back in with a large white pillow case. It was full of presents and she placed it at the end of the bed.

Christmas Day arrived and Bethan was awake before it was light outside. As Amser lay in her bed she could hear her daughter rustling paper and opening her presents.

Amser had bought her a number of gifts and there were presents from Rhonda, Iola, Mr and Mrs Peach and some of her school friends. However, the biggest surprise was downstairs waiting in the lounge. Bethan had asked Father Christmas for a bicycle and she felt disappointed it wasn't in her bedroom.

The little girl ran into her mother's room and said 'He didn't bring me a bike,' she said.

'That's what I wanted more than anything,' she moaned.

Amser was a little disappointed in her daughter.

She wanted her to have lovely things but 'had she taught her to be selfish and take things for granted,' she wondered.

For a moment she was very stern with Bethan.

'Do you realise how lucky you are my girl. Have you got any idea how better off you are than most children?'

Bethan of course had little knowledge of hardship. She'd been protected by her mother and couldn't understand how different things were for other children.

The girl wasn't used to being told off and was surprised by the severe tone in her mother's voice. 'It was unlike her,' she thought.

Amser did however make Bethan feel guilty.

'I'm sorry mum, you're right, I'm lucky aren't I,' she said.

Amser had calmed down and realised she may have over-reacted.

She comforted her daughter and said 'Father Christmas can't bring you every present you would like. How would he carry them all in his sleigh?'

Bethan giggled and said 'He would need a very big sleigh mummy.'

Bethan got herself dressed and walked downstairs. On walking into the lounge she saw her new bike standing against the coffee table. The handlebars and frame were dressed with blue Christmas wrapping paper but she could see her special present had been painted bright red. It had a shiny bell and lights at both the front and the back. She thought it was perfect.

'So Father Christmas did remember then,' she said.

'It seems he did,' replied Amser who had followed her into the room.

'I don't think he could get it up the stairs though,' she went on.

Bethan was keen to ride her new toy but almost six inches of snow had fallen overnight. It would have been impossible for her to move the wheels around outside.

Bethan pleaded with her mum to let her try and as it was Christmas Day she was allowed to practise on the carpet. At first Bethan wobbled and used the walls in the hall to steady herself. Up and down she went and it wasn't long before she could get from one end of the hall to the other without stopping.

'Look mummy, watch me mummy I can do it.'

Amser looked on as her daughter completed the short distance. It was a very small milestone but to Bethan it was everything; she was very happy.

After breakfast mother and daughter wrapped themselves up in their winter clothes and struggled through the snow to get to church. Bethan loved walking in her pink wellington boots and pelted her mother with snow balls along the way. She was laughing more and more as her mum got wetter and wetter. Amser was laughing as well and walked into the church dripping from head to toe.

A turkey had been left in the oven and when they returned, whilst Bethan was playing with her toys, lunch was prepared. Iola and Mr and Mrs Peach came in to share the day and they all tired themselves out playing games with Bethan.

By seven o'clock Bethan had fallen fast asleep on the lounge carpet. Amser picked up the little girl in her favourite yellow blanket and carried her up the stairs to her bedroom. Amser loved these moments when her beautiful Bethan was in her arms. She was dependant on her and they were moments she was to treasure for ever.

Chapter Eighteen

Whilst Amser devoted as much attention to her daughter as she could, she had many responsibilities at her school. The success of her teaching methods had impressed the headmaster and she was promoted to head of drama, a position she'd always aspired to.

Amser was also a member of the Parent Teachers Association and attended monthly meetings. One evening the following autumn there was a discussion about a forthcoming visit to the theatre.

As the children were now enthusing about literature Amser arranged for year nine to see a production of the classical novel entitled *Little Women*. However an examination of the finances for the trip revealed two children hadn't paid for their tickets.

Amser was very annoyed and said 'I don't know how many times I've reminded the kids. Enough is enough, they're not going.'

One of the parents in the group called Mrs Grande listened as the teacher continued to moan about the offending children. This lady was very timid; she stayed silent throughout the meetings and voiced her opinions with the nod or shake of her head. It was difficult to comprehend why she was on the PTA.

Mrs Grande didn't like Amser because she was always confident and blunt in her assessment of every situation. Unlike when she was a child Amser expressed her opinions loudly and Mrs Grande felt intimidated by her.

On this occasion, for some reason the parent felt a little braver. Mrs Grande's husband had died some years ago and she'd brought up a child with very little support. She didn't have any spare money for the nicer things in life and hadn't been able to allow her daughter Holly to put her name down to see the play.

Summoning up all her courage she remarked 'It's alright for you Miss Edwards, you can always put your hand in your purse and find a fiver can't you. It's not like that for everybody around here.'

These words stirred the emotion in Mrs Grande's head; she burst into tears and ran out of the room. Amser and the other members of the PTA were stunned. There wasn't any appetite to continue with the meeting and the shortfall in finance was left unresolved.

Amser left the school and as she made her way home she pondered over what had happened. She'd been chastised by a parent and made to feel very small.

However, as the moments ticked by Amser began to balance the argument. She started to realise she'd forgotten how hard life could be and felt ashamed of herself.

'What must Mrs Grande think, she must have such a low opinion of me,' she thought.

Amser had been dealt a severe blow and her confidence had been knocked sideways but in a strange way the parent had done her a huge favour. It wasn't long before she stopped feeling sorry for herself and thought about putting things right. She'd been embarrassed but realised what Mrs Grande or other people thought of her was of no consequence. It was the children who mattered.

Amser loved her job but after tossing and turning all night she was both tired and anxious. She'd been unable to get Mrs Grande out of her mind and was keen to get to school as soon as possible.

She shouted at Bethan for not getting up, for not eating enough breakfast and for not getting ready for school in time. The little girl knew something was wrong as whatever she did wasn't good enough.

'What's the matter mummy?' she said.

Amser replied 'Just hurry up Bethan will you, you'll be late.'

Amser was stressed and knew by the time she entered the school gates the previous evening's PTA meeting would have been discussed amongst her fellow teachers.

After leaving Bethan with Iola she ran to Selwyn College in her work shoes carrying her handbag and brief case. She looked a little uncomfortable in her haste but was a woman on a mission.

On entering the premises she rushed to the staff room and as she imagined a large number of teachers had gathered inside.

Several conversations were taking place but when Amser opened the door the room fell silent. She decided now wasn't the time to talk to anyone and after picking up a pile of exercise books she went to see the headmaster.

On knocking on the head's door, she noticed it was ajar. It opened and she could see inside. Mr Stead-Simpson was lying back in his chair with his feet stretched out on his desk reading the Times newspaper and eating a banana.

'Not a very good example to the children' she thought.

He was startled to see Amser and put his feet to the ground.

'I suppose you've come to tell me about last night,' he remarked.

'Mmm, I'm sure you've already been told,' she replied.

'From what I've heard you were reminding your colleagues a trip to the theatre has to be paid for, that doesn't seem unreasonable to me.'

'I've thought about this long and hard since the meeting yesterday evening. There are two things I would like to discuss with you headmaster,' said Amser.

'And what might they be?' he replied.

'I want to pay for the two remaining children so they can go on the trip but I don't want their parents to know I've done it.'

'I'm not sure I should let you do that,' he said.

'Why would you want to? All the other children have paid, haven't they?'

'Headmaster, I've been here a while now. I've never asked you for anything and you know how I feel about the children. Whatever the rights and wrongs of what happened, it will help ease my conscience. If I give you the money, will you please see the PTA receives it, perhaps through a budget under spend or something of the like?'

'You said there were two things on your mind.'

'Yes,' replied Amser.

'But the second is far more complicated.'

The headmaster looked puzzled.

'Can I ask, in your assessment, how many pupils in the school come from poorer families?'

'It depends what you mean by poor. Is it going hungry, not being clothed properly or not being able to have a new toy?'

'I guess I mean all those things but how many don't have anything to look forward to, have no self-esteem or aspirations because of their parental situation.'

Mr Stead-Simpson joked 'Well most of them could do with something in their sorry lives' and started to moan about discipline and respect again.

Amser looked at him with her hands on her hips.

She ignored his attempt to amuse her and said in a loud voice 'Headmaster, I want to do something about it.'

Mr Stead-Simpson couldn't believe his ears.

'So you want to do something about it. How are you going to do that?' he enquired.

'Many of the parents don't care about themselves or their children. A lot of the kids are out of control. I've watched the standards in this school deteriorate as the years have gone by. At times I've thought it can't get any worse but it always does.'

Not to be deterred Amser said 'I want to set all the children in year nine a challenge. I want to give them an opportunity to do something for the community and for themselves. For those who work hardest there would be two rewards.'

The headmaster said 'Rewards, did you say rewards?'

She replied 'Yes I did. The children would be sent on a special holiday because it's something many of them never have. However I also want them to know the feeling of joy that comes from doing something for other people; that would be their second reward.'

The headmaster started to fidget with his hands and laughed out loud.

'Surely you can't be serious? The kids in year nine; some of them are morons.'

Amser, still not to be deterred, continued to ignore the man's degrading comments.

She added 'I've chosen year nine because the children are old enough to make a difference in the town and yet they're still a year away from their O Level studies.'

Mr Stead-Simpson at last realised Amser was serious and started to take notice of her. He was impressed with her resilience and stubbornness. Despite all his negative comments about the children and their parents she never wavered in her delivery.

Amser had only been thinking about her idea for a few hours but spoke with clarity in her voice, sounded confident and determined. The headmaster sensed the emotion in the teacher's every word as her eyes sought the commitment she required.

'Even if I agreed it was possible, who's going to pay for it all?' he enquired.

Amser hesitated for the first time and then responded, nodding her head positively.

'That's the tricky bit but I have an idea.'

The headmaster's ears were alert; he couldn't wait to be told how the money was to be found for what he still considered to be a very dubious venture. He was now sitting back in his chair with his arms folded, looking at his teacher.

'May I ask what that might be?' he said.

Amser deliberated. All of this time she'd been standing in the headmaster's room but at this moment she decided to sit down in front of him.

Then she coughed before saying 'I intend to gain the support of local business people.'

Mr Stead-Simpson thought Amser had taken leave of her senses.

'Oh Amser, come on; how are you going to do that?' he asked.

'I intend to get them to judge for themselves whether the children have made a difference in the community. Then they'll only be spending their money if they consider it is worth it,' she said.

Amser went on 'Look, just like you I know the kids around here are not viewed as model pupils. If we can get them to take up the challenge and make a positive contribution locally then small donations from businesses will be money well spent. Look at all the recognition they will get for it and the school.'

Mr Stead-Simpson had listened to his teacher. She was young, enthusiastic and cared about the children. However, he was far from convinced by her arguments and didn't believe the kids would want to get involved. Even if they did, he didn't think donations would be forthcoming.

However, there was nothing to lose. Either his long held opinions on pupil behaviour would be cemented further or else he would get the surprise of his life.

Having considered all the pros and cons he said 'OK Amser, I can't say I believe you will be successful but I can see how serious you are. You have my support. I hope it works. I really do.'

Amser smiled and said 'Thank you headmaster and, oh, there is one more thing.'

Mr Stead-Simpson raised his eyebrows, lifted his chin and beckoned a further comment.

'Can I have the use of school facilities out of hours for meetings please?'

'Yes, yes just keep me informed,' he replied.

Amser left the headmaster's room and breathed a sigh of relief. The meeting had gone well, in fact much better than she'd expected. Despite all the sarcasm and adverse comments she got everything she wanted. This however, was the easy bit. She still had to find her benefactors and there was the small matter of persuading the children to take part.

Chapter Nineteen

Over the next two weeks Amser spent her spare time assembling the names of possible donors. The businesses she chose were both large and small and reflected day to day life in the community. She pondered over the list at home, adding names and deleting them over and over again.

Amser didn't relish asking for money and the more she thought about it the more doubts crossed her mind. She began to wonder if she'd ever get the project off the ground.

However, with the words of Mrs Grande still ringing in her ears Amser wasn't to be deterred. She was determined to find the good in the children and prove their worth to the residents of Rowan.

This was an almighty challenge and now not only was her reputation at stake, but so was her judgement. She'd put herself on trial in the eyes of the headmaster and could already feel the burden of responsibility weighing on her shoulders.

Sitting at home Amser's thoughts drifted in one direction and then another. She wanted a perfect solution, something that would make her feel confident and at ease with her objective. However, as much as she tried, she was unable to come up with an imaginative plan.

Amser decided to telephone the names on her list and ask for short meetings but she wasn't prepared for the amount of resistance she encountered. Most of the local business people wanted to know why she needed to meet them and as soon as money was mentioned excuses were made not to see her.

'I'm too busy,' said the local newsagent proprietor.

'I don't give donations,' commented the toy shop owner, rather bluntly.

One by one Amser crossed names off and when she'd finished only the butcher Jack Hinds had invited her to see him. This meeting also proved fruitless but on leaving the shop a man in his forties, with jet black hair, wearing a dark blue suit, walked across the road towards her. Amser could see him in the corner of her eye.

'Miss Edwards, is it?' he enquired.

Amser replied 'Yes can I help you?'

'Please excuse my approach, my name is Mr Hinds.'

Amser looked puzzled and waited for him to speak further.

'You telephoned me last week about a donation, I'm the antique dealer,' he said.

'I believe I was a little blunt with you.'

Now recalling the conversation Amser replied 'A little I think. How do you know who I am; have you been following me?' she enquired.

'Mmm well yes and no, the butcher is my brother. He told me you were going to see him and I'd been waiting for you to leave his premises. Our shops are opposite each other.'

'I noticed there were two people named Hinds on my list but I didn't link the butcher and the antique dealer together,' said Amser.

'Why should you, they hardly go hand in hand and how he touches all that meat I'll never know,' said the man.

Still standing in the street he said 'Miss Edwards would you like to come into my shop for a cup of tea. I am so intrigued about what you are doing.'

As they walked across the road Mr Hinds said 'By the way my name is Gerald, would you mind if I call you Amser?'

Her first thoughts about him were positive. He was well mannered and looked quite dishy so she didn't have any objection.

On entry Amser could see the shop was very cluttered and untidy.

'How on earth do customers manage to move around freely and browse the goods for sale,' she thought.

Mr Hinds apologised as she moved a large blue painted vase so she could squeeze between it and some medieval body armour. Amser hadn't been in an antique shop before and was fascinated by the variety of items on sale.

Her eyes moved around the room gazing at the interesting

objects but in particular she liked three stuffed animals she had spotted in glass cases. They were sitting on top of an old book-shelf that had become loose over the passage of time. The cases had slid forward looking like they might fall off. Amser was enchanted by the animals. There was a badger, a fox and a red squirrel.

Studying them closely Amser remarked 'They're wonderful.'

'They were possessions of Lord and Lady Falkener at Kimberley Hall in Chester in the late eighteen hundreds,' said Mr Hinds.

Amser asked all sorts of questions about the antiques and although Mr Hinds was pleased to satisfy her curiosity it made him realise he'd far too much stock.

'How in the world do you get rid of it all? I don't think I could remember everything I had for sale if this was my shop,' she remarked whilst blowing dust off an old coal scuttle.

For the first time in ages Mr Hinds was having a good look at his antiques. Some items had been in his shop for years without anybody showing the slightest interest in buying them. He didn't have an inventory and some goods obscured from view he'd forgotten he'd bought.

The teacher and the antique dealer were getting on well as they browsed around and it was a while before the conversation returned to Amser's project. Mr Hinds liked the teacher. She was chatty, bright and bubbly and he wanted to help her.

On reaching the back of the shop Amser moved a bed pan from a wooden chair and was able to sit down.

She could see Mr Hinds was embarrassed and said 'I don't mind moving a bed pan Gerald as long as there's nothing in it.'

He replied 'No I don't think so, I emptied it last week.'

There were grins from both of them and then Mr Hinds made some tea before moving a sewing machine and sitting down next to Amser.

'Now tell me all about your idea. I want to know what you're doing and why you're doing it,' said Gerald.

Amser could sense he was interested and there was an eager-ness for information. She hadn't discussed her past with anyone in Rowan but it was important for him to understand her feelings and why she was determined to make this challenge work.

She compared her childhood with her life in West Wales and spoke about Bethan and the enormous joy she got from teaching. Then Amser paused and Gerald realised there was another reason.

'What are you not telling me, there's something more isn't there, what is it that's motivating you?' he asked.

He could see the anxiety building up inside her as she looked at him and prepared to answer.

It was hard for the girl but after deliberating a little more she told him about Mrs Grande. She explained how a few words had affected her emotionally and refocused her mind.

'It got me thinking about the children. Oh I always am but this was different,' said Amser.

She paused again before saying 'I want to give some of the children the kind of opportunity I never had.'

With sadness in her eyes and almost apologetically Amser added 'I wish it could be for all the children in the school but at least it's a start.'

The antique dealer was intrigued and interrupted her.

'What opportunity Amser, what are you talking about?' he enquired.

The glumness on the teacher's face disappeared. There was an excitement in her voice as she started to enthuse about her idea.

'I want to send them on a special holiday. I do mean something very special but nothing is for nothing so they would have to earn it. The children would be given a chance to express themselves and make a difference in their local community. I believe it will unlock the joy of giving that lies dormant in their hearts.'

Mr Hinds thought about what Amser had said. The local reputation of the children had been tarnished over a number of years. Many were rude and arrogant and he could understand why Amser's first reaction from business had been negative.

Amser could see from Mr Hind's eyes he didn't think her idea had much chance of success. She understood why there were so many reservations but became impatient as he pondered over what she'd said. She was fidgeting with her handbag and playing with her fingers. Her idea was fixed in her mind and she wouldn't be put off.

Focusing her eyes on Mr Hinds she said 'Look, nothing is going to stop me doing this. If business won't help me, I'll find the cash myself.'

She got up and made her way to the door, knocking over a lampstand with a large red and white striped shade.

Mr Hinds called out 'Amser my dear, please don't be hasty.'

'Don't you 'dear' me,' she snapped back.

'I'm not a silly girl, the children will have this chance if it's the last thing I ever do for them.'

Mr Hinds, although surprised by her reaction, was now in no doubt how serious she was.

He re-phrased his words and said 'All right Miss Edwards, but you have to understand, if you ask a business for a donation they'll want to be sure they'll get something for it.'

Amser had already opened the door and was on her way out of the shop. She stopped herself in her tracks and came back inside.

Standing with her hands on her hips she listened as Mr Hinds said 'I'm Chairman of the Chamber of Commerce, come to our next meeting on Thursday at twelve o'clock. Tell everybody there what you've told me and you'd better think of something to convince them it's in their interests to support you. Oh and one last thing, don't be stroppy with them like you've been with me.'

Amser smiled and giggled at Mr Hinds and said 'No, Gerald err I mean yes Gerald I will.'

Amser bounced out of the shop almost knocking over another antique. This time it was a porcelain figurine of a ballet dancer on a shelf. It looked fragile and wobbled on its base but she was able to catch it before it fell to the ground.

The young woman, somewhat relieved, turned around smiling and said 'Thank you.'

Gerald shook his head and said 'Remember Thursday at twelve o'clock; don't be late.'

Chapter Twenty

On returning to school Amser went to see her headmaster again. Trying to excite this man about anything was a huge challenge and meetings with him were demotivating. When she told him about the lack of donor interest he didn't empathise or provide any words of reassurance.

Moving his body from side to side in his swivel chair he looked pleased with himself and remarked 'I'm not surprised. I don't like to say I told you so but I did.'

However, Mr Stead-Simpson was taken aback when she informed him of her invitation to address the local Chamber Of Commerce.

He laughed out loud and said 'Well, Miss Edwards, you're a devil for punishment; they'll eat you alive.'

Amser was already feeling nervous about the forthcoming meeting. She had some concern ever since leaving Mr Hinds's shop. However, she wasn't going to let this rather irritating man see her anxiety. As he continued to try and un-nerve her, Amser stood her ground and let him say whatever he liked.

When he'd finished she said 'I hear what you say headmaster, I'll be going into the lion's den at 12 o'clock on Thursday. I don't know how long it'll last.'

Standing there with her hands on her hips, she added 'Can I have the time off please?'

'You will be wasting your time, those commerce people will pull you to pieces but I suppose you'll have to find out for yourself,' he replied.

'Thank you headmaster,' said Amser as she broke into a smile.

On leaving the room she breathed a sigh of relief. It had been a struggle but she'd got what she wanted. However, before the Chamber of Commerce meeting Amser was as worried as at any time in her life. There was a brick wall in front of her and somehow she had to climb over it.

She had to sell her idea and make people believe their money wouldn't be wasted. 'But how?' she thought.

She considered the challenge from all angles before coming up with an idea she thought might work. The Red Dragon Public House was situated in the middle of Rowan. It was a large grade two listed building with a high pitched roof.

On the top was a weather vane displaying a bronze corgi dog. The front of the building boasted a large black painted clock that was always ten minutes fast. The clock had been set like that for as long as anybody could remember but none of the town's folk knew why.

Some years before, the then new publican put the clock to the right time. However, he received so many complaints he had to change it back again. The locals set their watches by this clock and it was known as 'Rowan time'.

The pub was always busy. It hosted all kinds of social activities including the monthly Chamber of Commerce meeting. By the time Amser arrived there were already a large number of people seated at a long narrow oak table in a private room. The door was ajar and she could see them chatting in small groups.

However, as soon as she entered, the room fell silent and her heart was in her mouth. Amser was well presented in a light blue two-piece suit and was carrying a black briefcase under her right arm.

Mr Hinds had forewarned the members of Amser's expected attendance but there were few smiles and only one or two nods from the male-dominated gathering. It wasn't one of the friendliest welcomes she'd ever encountered but undeterred she made her way to an empty seat between the antique dealer and his brother.

Mr Hinds realised Amser must be feeling a little uncomfortable and as soon as everybody had arrived he took the opportunity to introduce her to The Chamber. However, his colleagues, many of whom she'd contacted, hardly uttered a word between them. They didn't like their meetings disrupted and had already judged the teacher's presence to be a waste of time.

Mr Hinds decided it would be best if Amser was allowed to make her donation pitch straightaway and with the reluctant approval of the members Amser took to her feet. She moved to the end of the table where she'd be seen by everybody.

She took a moment to compose herself. She straightened her collar, fiddled with her watch strap and re-positioned her brief-case on the table in front of her.

Then looking at all the frowning faces she took a deep breath and started to speak 'Good afternoon ladies and gentlemen. Thank you for allowing me to talk to you today. I'm here to offer you an opportunity to get involved in a major community scheme which in my opinion you cannot afford to ignore.'

Amser's opening remarks had been rather brave and presumptuous but despite the dismissive looks on people's faces at the outset she now had their attention.

She went on 'Look, we all live here together. We rely on each other, our mothers and fathers, our council, our police force, our fire brigade, our local business, our schools and of course our children.'

The audience looked on as Amser got more and more confident with her delivery.

She added 'I'm well aware of the fallen values that seem to have been accepted in the town not only by our children but by people in general. I want to do something about it.'

There was silence around the table as Amser explained she would like to offer the fourteen year old children in her school a deal.

'I want to offer up to thirty of them a holiday in return for hard work,' she said.

This prompted the first response from the table.

'You'll never get the kids around here to do anything for anybody,' remarked a red faced man sitting with an elbow on the table and his hand pressed against the side of his face.

He was the fishmonger known as Ginger Tom and the smell from his grubby clothes filled the room.

Then a lady called Milly Mott from the wool shop with white, curly hair and a high pitched voice commented 'I've had my car scratched and a window broken in the last year, they've no respect.'

Other members of The Chamber also voiced their concerns and at one point several people were speaking at once until Mr Hinds brought the meeting to order.

Amser having got this far wasn't to be deterred. She opened her briefcase and took out a pile of papers. Then whilst the Chamber members were still muttering she walked around the room and handed a sheet to everybody present.

Amser found it difficult to retain the interest of the members and speaking loudly she said 'Can I ask you please to look at the questionnaire I've given you.'

For a few seconds the room was quiet as the members looked at their hand-out. Some of them studied it whilst others just browsed over it. There were more mutterings and so Amser decided it was time to intervene.

The teacher drew their attention by shutting her briefcase with the swift movement of her hand causing a loud thud.

She said 'OK ladies and gentlemen I can see there will be lots of questions so please let me explain how the project will work. To start with the children need to be told about the venture. I'll be making it crystal clear how lucky they are to have been selected and any reward will be well earned. I'll be telling them any abuse of the challenge won't be tolerated and they shouldn't enter if they don't think they can stay the course.'

Then, knowing it would cause a negative reaction, Amser said 'All the kids interested will be given the opportunity to use their initiative and imagination.'

'Initiative and imagination, the kids around here,' laughed Mr Bevan a local newsagent.

He had thick lips and spoke with a lisp 'I think you'd better go back to where you came from. Err West Wales is it Miss Edwards?' he remarked.

Amser ignored this rude comment and every other criticism thrown at her as best she could. However the members had worn her down. She'd talked with passion and enthusiasm about the children and her community.

She'd been determined to stay professional but became animated and there were tears in her eyes as she did everything in her power to woo her potential donors. However with one or two exceptions even the most sceptical people in the room couldn't fail to see her determination to make this venture work.

Somehow she managed to stay strong and said 'Yes, initiative and imagination. We forget our children do have talents, but we're not always good at bringing it out of them.'

'So it's our fault is it?' Mr Bevan interrupted again.

'It's all of our's,' said Amser.

With her arms stretched out on the table in front of her and making eye contact with everyone in the room one by one she added 'We're letting our children down and they're our town's future. Look at the questionnaire again please, will you. You'll see once a child has chosen a project and carried it out, its success will have to be verified by someone in authority and not a parent or guardian.'

'What kind of project?' enquired a lady with blonde hair tied in a bun, wearing a peach coloured blouse. She was the toy shop owner called Mrs Peeps.

'It doesn't matter, its success will be judged on what's achieved,' replied Amser.

'Over how long then?' asked another person.

Again the response was the same although Amser did say 'All the ventures would need to be completed by the following April and the holiday would take place over the first two weeks of the school summer term.'

A man at the end of the table, sitting quite away from Amser, started grinning. He thought he'd discovered a basic flaw in the notion. His name was Bill Johns a solicitor from Messrs Smith and Johns. He'd the reddest hair she'd ever seen that was short and parted in the middle. He wore a black suit with a white shirt and red bow tie.

In a posh voice he said 'Can you tell us please who's going to judge the questionnaires?'

Amser had been waiting for this question. She knew if her venture was going to have any credibility then her answer was going to have to satisfy her audience.

Looking straight at him she smiled and said 'Well you are of course. That's if you want to be involved along with other interested people around this table.'

There were no more questions. Amser had made her pitch and sat down. She'd said everything she wanted to and at least had made the attendees listen. Mr Hinds thanked her for coming and suggested she leave the room for a few minutes so her proposal could be considered.

Amser was mentally fatigued and pleased it was all over. She made her way to the lounge bar area where she waited whilst enjoying a cup of hot black coffee.

Meanwhile, the Chamber members talked about the venture and about Amser. Almost everybody was impressed with the teacher but there were mixed feelings about the children and what they could achieve. Some of the Chamber members were adamant they wouldn't get involved but there was some interest kindled by Mr Hinds.

Amser was called back into the room and this time amongst the glum faces there were some smiles. She sat down once again as Mr Hinds got to his feet.

He said with some sadness in his voice 'As you know Miss Edwards the members have taken their time to review your proposal and it's fair to say there's still a lot of adversity around the table.'

Then his facial expression changed.

He couldn't contain his joy as he added 'But we have thirteen members who are prepared to support you. They will provide up to £2500 each on the basis they can refuse as many questionnaires as they like.'

Amser was overwhelmed and without hesitation confirmed she was prepared to accept this condition. Then Mr Hinds read out the list of donors. Amongst those to be involved was of course himself together with his brother the butcher, Mr Blake, the proprietor of the Red Dragon, Mr Tudor the owner of 'Moving Parts' a car showroom business, Mrs Freed who ran a large clothing store, Mr Johns the solicitor and Brian Steele a local insurance broker.

Amser went around the room and shook the hands of her donors.

Then before leaving she said 'Ladies and gentlemen I'd like to thank all of you for listening to me this afternoon. It may not be apparent at this moment but today is a big day in the life of some of our children and in our community. Those of you who have been kind enough to commit to this venture will help make a difference which will be there for all to see. I promise I won't let you down and neither will our children.'

All the Chamber members clapped and Amser left the room. It was back to school now and a further visit to the headmaster beckoned.

It was half past two and Mr Stead-Simpson was discussing the school budget with his administrator when Amser looked into his room. She decided not to disturb him and was walking down the corridor when the headmaster came out. He'd spotted his teacher peering through the window and was anxious to know what had happened.

'How did you get on Miss Edwards?' he enquired.

'Did you get any support from the Star Chamber?' he said jokingly.

To his surprise she replied 'Everything I wanted,' as she walked towards him.

Then she read out the names of her donors. The headmaster had known some of these people for years. He was aware they had similar concerns to him about the children and he found it difficult to believe they wanted to be involved.

He stood there looking at his teacher as she added 'We need an after-school meeting for year nine and their parents. We have reached the stage where the children can be involved.'

Mr Stead-Simpson was amazed. If he hadn't realised it before he knew now that in Amser he had a very special teacher.

Chapter Twenty One

The next day letters went home with the children and the meeting took place the following Monday evening at seven o'clock in the main hall. It was often difficult to get parents to come into the school and Amser made sure there was enough information in the letter to encourage families to attend. It was the mention of a free holiday that did the trick and by the time the meeting started the hall was packed.

The headmaster took to his feet and welcomed everyone. For once there wasn't any negativity or sarcasm in his voice and there was a buzz around the hall as the kids talked amongst themselves. A holiday was something some of the children only dreamt of.

Then Mr Stead-Simpson took time to talk about Amser before introducing her to the invited parents and guardians. Amser had been waiting for this moment since the day she started the project. She was excited and leapt to her feet in an instant. The teacher explained to the audience how the project would work and stressed it was open to all children in year nine.

However when she'd finished her presentation and invited questions it soon became clear there was a lot of suspicion.

'What's the catch?' asked one lady.

'Who are these donors?' enquired another.

'There must be something to pay, we can't afford anything,' said another.

'It will be same as usual if you've got money its fine but if you haven't, well hard luck,' shouted a voice from the back of the hall.

Amser stood there as one person after another voiced their opinion. She was a little shell-shocked.

When the hall fell silent she said 'OK I've listened to you and I understand your concerns. I make this commitment now: the holiday is going to be free. I'm not interested in who's got money and who hasn't; this is a challenge for all of the children in year nine. They have to earn their holiday, that's all. There are up to thirty places and it's up to the children to make a difference in our wonderful community and impress the judges. It will be a very special holiday I can assure you.'

The parents had been sent a copy of the questionnaire; they were told when the competition was to begin and when it would end.

Amser said 'You'll have noticed there's a number at the top of the form that is repeated at the bottom on a tear-off slip. Also there's a place for the child's name on the slip.'

She added 'When the questionnaires are returned I'll go and see what the children have done. I'll speak to the people involved to make sure the forms have been completed accurately. Then I'll keep the slips at the bottom and hand the questionnaires to the judges. They will therefore make their decisions without knowing who the children are or their backgrounds.'

There was still a lot of mistrust in the audience. Many of the parents thought it was a bit of a cheek asking children to help in the community.

'That's what we pay our taxes for,' one man remarked.

Also, although it was clear the pupils wanted a holiday, it wasn't clear whether they would want to earn it.

When all the parents and children had left the school Amser felt a little disappointed. It had been much easier convincing her headmaster and her donors. At this moment it was difficult for her to see how the project would be a success.

However, the word holiday is very powerful in a child's mind, especially in the heads of children who never have them. Away from Amser and in their homes, they were starting to think about the competition. Unknown to Amser they were talking to their parents and to their friends.

One by one the children were coming up with ideas as to how they could help their community. The more children wanted to get involved, the more it prompted other children to want to take part as well.

As the weeks went by a change was taking place in Rowan. Old people were having their shopping carried, gardens were being attended to, fences were being repaired, a community hall was repainted, litter was being removed from the streets and unwanted graffiti was cleaned from walls. The children involved were now improving the reputation of their school so fast it was impossible to ignore it.

As April approached questionnaires started to be received by Amser and as promised she followed up each one to make sure they'd been completed honestly.

In any community you're always going to find children who will try and deceive you. Amser had to refuse one application because weekly washing said to have been carried out by a girl for an old aged pensioner was found to be a lie. The senior male citizen said he'd never seen the girl.

A boy was also refused because he lied about weeding gardens. Amser was very upset and disappointed because adult signatures had been forged. Other applications had to be dismissed when she found out children had been paid for what they did.

There were tears amongst the offending children and Amser's refusals led to parents making complaints. However she referred them to the rules of the project and refused to make an exception for anybody.

There was, however, one boy called Martyn who Amser did feel sorry for. He was a bit of a loner and was looked after by his grandmother Gladys Jewell as his parents had split up and disowned him. She could tell by the way he dressed that money was tight and life was hard for him.

Martyn wasn't the brightest button in the box and his classmates often taunted him. He was desperate to go on the holiday and started delivering vegetables to old people. He took them carrots, parsnips and potatoes. They thought it was wonderful.

He said he got them from a kind market stall holder at the end of the day but he'd been digging them up from allotments. After making four visits to the people's homes, the following week he was caught red-handed with a spade in his hand and a large bag of produce.

Two tall men with large body frames looked down upon him. One was wearing an old green overcoat, wellington boots and a dirty brimmed hat. The other man was in a black mud-stained duffle coat with the hood up, covering most of his head. They scared him half to death.

One of the men took a tight hold of his right arm and wrenched him to his feet. Then they both demanded to know what he was doing. The boy was shaking with fear as the men waited for an answer.

In the absence of a reply the man in the hat shouted 'Stealing, that's what you've been doing boy. Don't you realise it's wrong to take something that's not yours.'

'I've been giving it to people in the town,' he replied.

'People, what people,' they both demanded to know.

'Old people,' said Martyn.

The man in the duffle coat thought for a moment. He seemed to recall something about a school encouraging community work. He remembered reading about kids doing things to help others who were finding it difficult to help themselves.

'Hold on a minute, do you go to Selwyn College boy?' the man enquired.

'Yes sir,' he replied.

On telling his friend, the man in the hat, said 'I don't care what bloody school he goes to, stealing is stealing; we need to call the police.'

Martyn pleaded with both of them not to do this and after a heated discussion it was agreed they would go to Selwyn College. On hearing the news Mr Stead-Simpson was very annoyed and called Amser to his office where the party had assembled.

The dream of a holiday was now over for Martyn but realising how severe this punishment was the men decided not to take any further action.

On the whole the community plan had been an outstanding success as there had been so many genuine acts of kindness and generosity. The valid papers were handed to the judges who had gathered in the school hall one evening to make their choices.

These donors were of course already aware of the positive impact the competition had in Rowan. They were feeling rather pleased with themselves having decided to get involved because of the publicity that would follow.

They considered forty one papers and were so impressed with the standard they passed twenty eight. Amser was very pleased to see Mrs Grande's daughter Holly had been selected. She'd been making cakes and serving them with tea and coffee in a local old people's home every week since the competition began.

So the selections had been made and all the successful children and their parents were invited back into the school. Unlike at the first meeting there was only excitement in the hall. The children were anxious to know where their holiday would be but before the announcement was made the donors had to be introduced.

They all received great applause as one by one they stepped onto the stage and gathered around the headmaster. Then the Mayor of Rowan was welcomed and he paid great tribute to the children for their tremendous efforts. There was more applause.

When the clapping had stopped the headmaster stood up and the hall fell silent.

He said 'Many parents here know me well, they're aware of my opinions on various matters that don't always match theirs. However, today is a cause for celebration. I don't often single out a teacher for praise but I must make an exception as we have a lady here who is an example to us all.'

He chuckled and added 'Goodness knows she is stubborn and she can be irritating as well.'

Then he smiled at his audience before saying 'This wonderful lady has not only restored my faith in our children but she's also installed in them both pride and responsibility.'

He chuckled again and added 'I don't suppose she's done the school any harm either.'

'Ladies, gentlemen and children can I once again introduce Miss Amser Edwards.'

Every parent and child stood up and clapped until their hands were burning. Amser had always told herself nothing would stop her making this project work. However, she'd never contemplated a night like this with so many people expressing their gratitude.

Amser wasn't looking for praise; the success of the venture was all about the children. She was embarrassed and waited for the audience to quieten and sit down.

She smiled and said 'Hello everybody, it was nice of you all to come and I do thank you for the wonderful welcome. However it's the children, your children, who deserve all the applause.'

There was more clapping and when she could be heard again Amser turned to her pupils and said 'I knew you could do it kids, how proud I am of you all. I think I promised you something didn't I?'

'Yes, yes,' shouted the children.

'I think I mentioned a holiday didn't I?'

The children were getting more excited.

They were joking with one another. 'I bet its two weeks in Tenby,' said one boy.

'No,' said another 'we won't go that far, more like two weeks in Llandudno.'

Amser had teased the children for long enough.

'OK,' she said.

With that remark Amser nodded to one of her colleagues off stage. In a few seconds the schools sound system started to play 'When You Wish Upon Star' then the curtain opened behind Amser to reveal a large picture of the Magic Castle in Disney World.

For a moment the whole audience went quiet as if they couldn't believe their eyes. Then they all burst into applause and cheered and cheered. The children were jumping up and down whilst the parents looked on; some of them couldn't speak, some were in tears whilst others were grinning and laughing.

It took several minutes for everybody to calm down and then all the children were invited onto the stage to have their photo taken with the donors, the mayor and of course Amser.

On their way out of the hall parents were thanking Amser.

'Don't thank me, I told you it's the children we should all thank.' she replied.

Gerald Hinds appeared in front of her.

He remarked 'Well my dear Amser it looks like you've done it.'

He had a big grin on his face and Amser knew she needn't scold him this time for calling her dear. She put her arms around him and hugged him.

'Thank you so much Gerald, if it wasn't for you.'

Gerald interrupted her and said 'Stop right there Amser. I've heard what you've been saying to everybody. It's the children; they've done it for themselves. It's nothing to do with me. In fact Amser they've done it for all of us. I suspect Rowan will never be the same again.'

Then Mrs Grande passed where Amser was standing. She looked at her for a second before hurrying by without saying a word.

News of what the children had achieved spread far and wide. Local newspaper coverage led to a radio interview for Amser. It even attracted an article in the national press. Seldom had a school received so much attention and more and more enquiries were received from parents who wanted to send their children to Selwyn College.

With all the euphoria time seemed to pass in the blink of an eye for Amser. The holiday was now only two weeks away when she saw Mrs Grande in the playground.

Amser called out to her 'Mrs Grande can you spare me a moment?'

The lady looking a little nervous started walking towards her and they met half way.

Before Mrs Grande had a chance to speak the teacher said 'I'm so sorry for what I said in that PTA meeting. It was a long time ago now but it's been worrying me ever since.'

Mrs Grande replied 'Oh no please don't apologise. I've misjudged you. It was so rude of me not to thank you for my daughter's holiday.'

She added 'I need to thank you for more than that. I'm so proud of my Holly. She now wants to help everybody all of the time.'

Amser couldn't a get a word in edge ways.

Mrs Grande continued 'I can't explain it, but I was angry. It seemed you could do anything you wanted whilst I couldn't do anything at all. I know that isn't true now. I'm so pleased for my daughter, going somewhere I could never afford to take her. Please let me thank you now, I'm sure you will all have a wonderful time.'

Amser smiled and replied 'I'm not going on the holiday Mrs Grande,' as she reached into her handbag.

'I have spent so little time with my daughter lately and I couldn't go to Disney World without her. I decided to let someone else have my place.'

'That's very good of you,' replied Mrs Grande as she watched Amser pull out two tickets.

One had Holly's name on it and the other displayed the name of Mrs Grande.

'No,' said the lady.

'No, no, I can't accept that. I don't deserve it. I cannot possibly take it.'

Amser replied 'Mrs Grande, it's Kitty isn't it?'

'Yes,' she answered.

'Kitty, look I don't think you've any idea what you've done.'

'I don't want to go into detail but life hasn't always been so kind to me and I'd forgotten. Those words you said to me "you can always find a fiver" will ring in my ears forever and look what has come out of it.'

'I know you have a passport because your daughter has told me. I had to check, sorry. Holly also told me about the help you give to the old people's home.'

'Thank you Miss Edwards but it's impossible. I can't get time off work,' Kitty uttered.

Amser looked at her and smiled.

Mrs Grande realised this problem had been overcome as well.

'You think of everything, don't you,' she remarked.

'Holly told me you work for 'Drapes & Drapes' as a curtain maker. I went and told them about the holiday and that Holly was going. I didn't have to say anymore.'

'Your boss, Mrs Pimkin, said that you're always helping them out by doing extra work and it's a shame you can't go as well.'

Mrs Grande replied 'I do what I can.'

Amser was warming to Kitty and was pleased to say 'Mrs Pimkin wanted me to tell you, you've two weeks extra paid holiday this year but you have to take it in two weeks' time.'

'I don't know what to say,' replied Mrs Grande.

'Then don't say anything Kitty, give me a hug and let's be friends.'

This meeting took a great weight off their shoulders and the two ladies embraced as if old acquaintances had been re-united.

The day of the holiday arrived and all the children and parents were assembled over half an hour before the coach was due to arrive. They waited outside the school gates and as the minutes ticked by the children were getting more and more excited.

Selwyn College wasn't situated on a fast road but it was often busy with traffic and even these fourteen year old children had to be told to keep on the pavement. Ten minutes later than planned a bright shiny red coach arrived to take the party to Manchester Airport.

The pupils formed a line to board the vehicle with the accompanying teachers following behind. Both the local and the national press were there to cover the departure and photos were taken as every child hugged Amser by the coach door.

When everyone was settled the vehicle drove away. Most of the children were leaving their parents for the first time and there were many tears as they waved their goodbyes. Amser's project was to leave a lasting legacy at the school. There was now a queue of businesses wanting to be involved and the headmaster was keen to see the scheme working each year.

Enquiries were also received from schools in other parts of the country. They wanted to create similar initiatives for their children and sought as much information as possible. The school's teaching vacancies also attracted masses of applicants and when older children applied for jobs after leaving school they were proud to say they'd attended Selwyn College.

Chapter Twenty Two

Amser didn't know what she'd have done without Iola over these past months. Such was the importance of the school project she'd been neglecting her daughter and felt guilty.

Bethan however, was a very contented child. She'd grown to love Iola and Amser knew she'd been well looked after when she wasn't at home.

There was also Mr and Mrs Peach next door. They made such a fuss of Bethan whenever they could and Mr Peach was like the granddad she never had. He took her to the park, they flew his kites and at home he played all sorts of games with her.

Above everything else she was most contented sitting on his knee watching him drawing horses and listening to him laughing. Mr Peach adored the little girl and would have done anything for her.

It was now September once again and autumn had come early. Leaves were already falling from the trees and they were looking tired and ready to sleep.

Bethan was now seven years old and had moved up into the junior part of her school. It was contained in a separate building next to the infants and had its own playground and entrance.

It was there a major change took place in the little girl's life. As a child Amser always wanted to play a musical instrument but her family circumstances prevented her from doing so. Now Bethan had such an opportunity available to her.

Williams Way School had an outstanding reputation for its music teaching. The music room was situated at the end of a long corridor away from the main school building. The walls of this walkway were covered with framed photos of classical composers. They were large and imposing, each with a small oblong plaque at the bottom stating the composer's name. The school was proud of its photo collection which had been featured in the renowned *Classical Times*.

Bethan could have learned to play any instrument she liked. In her first lesson along with other children she was asked to sit on the floor with her legs crossed and listen to three classical recordings. The music chosen was by Rachmaninov, Beethoven and Gershwin and the teacher, Mrs Pugh, believed this was the best way for children to choose an instrument they would enjoy playing.

Mrs Pugh was a softly spoken lady who always wore knitted jumpers and pleated skirts. She had grey curly hair and wore glasses for reading with white frames which were attached to a chain around her neck.

Whilst they listened to the music Mrs Pugh sat in front of them moving her hands about as if she was conducting the orchestra. She would often hold a long piece of chalk and use it like a baton.

Bethan, like most of the children, thought the lesson was boring. She wasn't used to listening to classical recordings and started fidgeting. However, after the music had come to an end the sound of the piano was still playing in her mind. She'd always liked the sound of this instrument and this option seemed to be the obvious choice.

Three other children in the class also chose the piano but others selected the violin, cello, clarinet, flute and the trumpet. Over a number of years the school had assembled a large selection of instruments and after persuading two children to change from their original choice everyone had what they wanted.

In the school there were two dedicated music lessons each week for every class. However, because there was such a desire amongst the pupils to learn to play an instrument, large after-school music clubs were held in the main hall every day.

Wednesday was for year four, the beginner's class. It was always a noisy affair as the children got used to their instruments. Much of the day's music lessons were taken up with theory but the after-school club was where the pupils were encouraged to learn to play.

Mrs Pugh grouped the children according to their instrument preferences and time was taken with each sector to develop any individual talent. The school was very fortunate because three of the teachers had a wealth of musical expertise amongst them and were able to help the children.

The progress was astounding over the months that followed. From the din that could be heard bellowing from the hall at the start of the school year, came the first signs of an orchestra by the end of the following summer term.

From her first lesson it was clear music was to play a large part in Bethan's life. She was keen to learn everything there was to know about her chosen instrument and Amser bought a piano so she could practise at home.

Mrs Pugh was impressed by Bethan's progress in her first two years and wondered if she'd like to consider playing the harp. The teacher noticed how the girl caressed the keys of the piano with such ease and gentleness and deliberated over this possibility for a long time.

The school didn't possess such an instrument and Mrs Pugh realised disrupting her pupil's progress with the piano might be a dreadful mistake. Nevertheless, in her opinion the harp was the mother of all instruments, a treasure in the world of music.

Mrs Pugh invited both Bethan and Amser to a meeting one afternoon after school. They didn't have any idea what it was about and were intrigued. Amser left her own school early to attend and met Bethan outside Mrs Pugh's room. On hearing them talking, Mrs Pugh opened her door and invited them in.

'Come in please it's good of you to come, thank you so much,' she said.

Amser detected Bethan's teacher was a little anxious.

'Whatever the meeting is about, it is troubling her,' she thought.

Mother and daughter were invited to sit down in front of her desk. Amser could see the woman was organised. Children's exercise books were arranged in neat piles and pens and pencils were lined up next to one another to the right of where she was sitting.

In front of them a pot of tea, a small jug of milk, some sugar lumps and three china cups and saucers had been laid out on a pretty round tray.

As Mrs Pugh poured the tea she said 'I've been thinking quite a lot about Bethan these last few weeks; in fact your daughter has been on my mind most of the time.'

Then she paused and smiled before adding 'Oh there's nothing wrong, far from it. I can tell you Miss Edwards your dear Bethan is a pleasure to teach.'

'What is it then Mrs Pugh, why do you want to talk to us?' she asked.

The teacher replied 'This isn't an easy thing to say but I'm worried we may be wasting Bethan's exceptional talent.'

She added 'In all the years I've been teaching only once before has a child excited me so much with her fingers. The piano is a fine instrument and with her natural ability I'm sure Bethan could become an excellent pianist.'

'Yes I suppose I'd come to the same conclusion watching her play but why do you think it would be a waste?'

Bethan added 'I love playing the piano mummy I don't want to stop.'

Mrs Pugh was finding it hard to explain her thoughts and beginning to doubt her own judgement.

Amser could see her daughter was becoming upset and said to Mrs Pugh 'What are you trying to say to us?'

At last the woman answered 'I think Bethan should learn to play the harp.'

Amser was dumfounded. This instrument was alien to her and her daughter. They'd never seen one or heard one being played in person and Bethan started to cry.

'Why now Mrs Pugh and what's so important about the harp?' Amser demanded to know.

Amser was irritated, moving her feet backwards and forwards, and she reached out the palm of her right hand as she was talking.

She said 'My daughter loves the piano. Why should she change now after two years?'

The teacher replied 'Yes I know I'm asking a lot but she has exceptional talent. In my opinion she should be given the opportunity to play what I consider to be the most beautiful instrument in the world.'

The girl was still sobbing and Mrs Pugh didn't want to cause her distress. She opened her desk drawer and produced a packet of chocolate biscuits. On offering one to Bethan, it was rejected but, when her mum took one, she changed her mind and her tears dried up.

Mrs Pugh grasped the moment and said 'Learning to play the harp is not as difficult as you might think. The strings on this instrument are the same as the white keys on the piano and it would be easy for you to pick up the basics.'

Amser was unsure and Bethan kept saying 'I want to learn the piano mummy I don't know anything about the harp.'

Mrs Pugh reached into her drawer again and took out a cassette. Mother and daughter could see it contained music by harpist Elinor Bennett.

'Let me play this for you,' said the teacher and when the music started she stayed silent.

After a couple of minutes Mrs Pugh said 'Can you hear how beautiful the instrument is Bethan. A sound all of its own, don't you think,' as she turned up the volume.

Mother and daughter, although initially dismissive of any other instrument, did listen to the music. They enjoyed it very much but Bethan still wanted to play the piano and there were more tears.

The teacher understood the girl's anxiety and said 'I've been deliberating over this decision for ages and wonder if I might impose on you a little more.'

'What now?' Amser thought.

Mother and daughter listened as she said 'I'd like you both to go and see Mrs Jones. She's an old friend and a retired music teacher who specialises in the harp.'

She reasoned 'If Bethan saw and heard the instrument in a quiet room it would help her decide.'

'I think you'd both feel more comfortable about it.' she said.

Mrs Pugh wasn't a forceful woman but Amser could tell she'd

given the matter a great deal of thought. She was enthusiastic about Bethan's ability and so Amser took her to see Mrs Jones.

Arriving outside the teacher's house Amser could have been forgiven for taking her daughter home straightaway. The garden was guarded by a black iron gate. It had grass two feet high either side of a broken concrete path leading to the front door. All the window frames were crumbling and at the very least could do with a good clean along with the glass.

Bethan remarked 'Mummy it looks like a witch's house.'

However, in view of Mrs Pugh's recommendation Amser persevered and replied 'Shush Bethan she might hear you.'

The girl giggled as the gate creaked when her mum opened it. On reaching the door Amser lifted an imposing, black, iron knocker and banged it twice to announce their arrival.

They waited a few moments before the door opened. In front of them stood Mrs Jones, a tall thin woman over sixty years old. She had masses of untidy, grey, wavy hair and a deep jagged scar on her right cheek. She was wearing an old green cardigan with holes in the sleeves and bright red slippers.

'Miss Edwards and Bethan, is it?' she enquired.

Before either party could reply she added 'Of course it is, come in, come in.'

Mrs Jones moved to the side of the entrance to allow them both to pass and they walked inside. The lady spoke in a loud voice and was abrupt in her manner. They didn't like the look of her and couldn't believe how untidy her house was.

There were piles of books, boxes and sheet music lying all over the hall and even on the bottom stair runs. In the distance more piles of papers could be seen in the kitchen along with dirty plates, cups and saucers. The whole area they were in smelt dirty and musty.

Then they reached the parlour and Mrs Jones opened the door. Amser and Bethan feared the worst. They expected to be greeted with more clutter but to their amazement this room was sparkling clean and tidy.

Blue velvet curtains draped the windows. There was a light

blue carpet on the floor and porcelain ornaments decorated her mantelpiece.

However, Bethan's eyes became fixed on the middle of the room. There, standing beside a red stool, stood a shiny, black pedal harp. It was beautiful and imposed itself on the surroundings.

Bethan had never been so close to such an instrument. It was larger than she expected and she couldn't take her eyes off it. The doubts she had about learning to play the harp were already beginning to disappear. She was excited and couldn't wait to touch the strings.

Mrs Jones said 'Bethan sit down on the stool.'

It was a little low down for her and the teacher found Bethan a green velvet cushion to prop herself up with.

'Look at it,' the teacher said.

'Feel it Bethan, run your fingers over the strings and pluck them gently. Close your eyes and imagine you're playing in front of an audience. It's alive and will respond to your every touch. When you can play it you'll be fulfilled but it takes dedication, time, patience and a great will to succeed.'

'Let me sit there for a minute will you,' asked the teacher and Bethan stood up.

Mrs Pugh moved away the cushion and made herself comfortable by adjusting the stool position and her body posture. Then without saying another word she started playing Llwyn Onn (Ash Grove) as both Bethan and her mother watched and listened.

They were enchanted by the soft sound of the strings. They'd listened to Mrs Pugh's cassette but it didn't prepare them for this magical experience. The room became energised as she played. The sound was inspiring and uplifting. It created a feeling inside both of them which was impossible to put into words. Now they understood why Mrs Pugh wanted them to see her friend.

Mrs Jones stopped playing and looked at her guests. She was well aware of the effect this instrument could have on people.

She said 'Miss Edwards, Bethan I can see you like my harp.'

They were spellbound and didn't know what to say and so with a smile on her face Mrs Jones said 'I live alone but I'm not alone if that makes sense. I come into this room every evening and play to myself.'

She added 'It's over fifty years ago now but a teacher like your Mrs Pugh suggested I start learning to play this instrument. I seem to recall it was a hard choice at the time as I too had been learning the piano. I was only ever going to become a teacher but if Mrs Pugh is right then who knows what the future might hold for you Bethan.'

Then she looked at the girl sternly.

Leaning forward and with a serious face she said 'I would like to explore the talent your teacher says you have but I don't waste my time. I only give lessons to those who want to learn. The harp is not a toy for a day, it's a companion for life. Do you understand what I'm saying?'

The teacher was a little intimidating but Bethan's mind was made up. She'd been motivated by the woman's enthusiasm for her prized possession and enchanted by its sound. The girl couldn't wait to get started.

'Yes Mrs Jones,' she replied.

'I will, I will. I'll listen to everything you say and do whatever you want me to do. I love the instrument so much, please, when can I begin?'

Amser, too, was impressed by the beautiful harp. However, she wasn't keen on Mrs Jones, although it was easy to see how committed she was to her instrument. Mrs Pugh had recommended her and she did seem genuine but this woman's appearance and living standards appalled her.

Whilst she was thinking, Bethan was pleading with her to say yes.

She said 'Please mum I want to do this. I won't let you or Mrs Jones down I promise.'

With Mrs Jones sitting there and listening it would have been very difficult for Amser to say no and with the nod of her head and a smile she indicted her approval. Bethan raced over to her mother and kissed her.

'Thank you, thank you,' she said.

Lessons of course had to be paid for but Amser knew she'd be able to afford them. Arrangements were made for Bethan to be taught one evening each week and she was also to enjoy a double lesson on Saturday mornings.

Bethan still played the piano at school. She was part of the orchestra and performed in evening concerts. However, this instrument no longer enthralled her. The harp was now where her heart was. She was always early for lessons and her progress astounded Mrs Jones. Never had she taught a pupil with such enthusiasm and such devotion to her music.

First she learned how to play two and three line pieces until she developed her sight reading. The theory examinations were boring but Bethan stuck to the task and passed grade after grade. Mrs Jones seemed to get the best out of Bethan and she got so much pleasure out of teaching her. The harp took over the girl's life. She now knew she wanted to be a professional harpist.

The arranged music lessons meant Bethan was no longer able to see Mr Peach on a Saturday morning. She did call in and see him and Mrs Peach whenever she could but her regular visits had given him a new lease of life and he missed them.

He enjoyed the things they'd done together and longed for her to knock on the door. She used to make him biscuits, talk about her school work, her friends and of course the harp. Now music took up most of Bethan's time but the old man was comforted by what he once said to her about her fingers.

Chapter Twenty Three

Amser became prouder of Bethan with each passing year. Her daughter was now thirteen and settled into a senior school called Hartswood High. It was about a ten minute walk from where she lived. Amser's only connection with her past was the occasional correspondence from Rhonda. It didn't seem possible it was nine years since she and Bethan left Walwyn Gate.

One day a letter lay waiting on Amser's return home from school. She knew from the writing it was from her friend and was surprised as they'd swapped letters the previous week.

Amser sensed something was wrong and opened the envelope with a knife she took from the kitchen.

Taking out a folded piece of paper she saw it started with the words 'My dear Amser.'

Rhonda always commenced her prose with 'Hi Ams'.

'Whatever could it be?' she thought and with some anxiety sat down on her bed.

The letter went on 'I'm so sorry but I have to tell you, your dad has passed away today.'

Amser looked at the date on the letter. It was the day before yesterday.

Rhonda wrote 'He suffered a massive heart attack having just got home from work. One minute he was sitting in his chair reading his newspaper and the next he was doubled up in pain. Your mum telephoned for an ambulance but although the vehicle arrived within ten minutes your dad died before getting to the hospital.'

The letter went on 'Dearest Ams I know you and your dad weren't close but this news must come as a terrible shock. I wish I was there to comfort you.'

Amser stared at the letter, she didn't cry, or feel any sadness at all. Rhonda meant well, she always did, but time hadn't healed the differences between her and her parents. Although, she never wished her father dead she was determined not to get upset about it.

In the years that passed since leaving Walwyn Gate she had erased all her childhood memories as best she could. Not one photo could be seen on display of her mum or dad anywhere in her home. She never mentioned her parents to her daughter.

In the letter, Rhonda invited Amser to telephone her for details of the funeral but even though she knew how upset her mum must be she had no intention of going back.

'It would be sheer hypocrisy to return to Walwyn Gate now,' she thought.

Nevertheless, the sad news had shaken her and then Bethan arrived home from school. The girl could see something was wrong. Amser wasn't as strong as she thought and when she saw her daughter she burst into tears. Bethan, now much older, was far more inquisitive than when she first came to Rowan.

'What's the matter mum?' she said.

'Nothing,' said Amser.

'Mum, you're upset. I can see you're upset, you're crying, what is it?' Bethan enquired.

Amser had a special relationship with Bethan now. They told one another almost everything and, despite Bethan's age, at times they were more like sisters than mother and daughter.

Amser gave Bethan the letter and she sat down and read it. Then moving closer to her mother she cried in her arms. This event prompted Bethan to start asking questions she'd never asked before.

She remembered being told as a little girl her grandma and granddad would come and visit. When they didn't come she was informed they didn't want to travel to Rowan. She accepted the situation at the time but now Bethan wanted more information.

However, despite their closeness, Amser didn't want to talk to her daughter. She didn't want her to know how she'd been treated as a child. Amser had made sure her daughter was loved and cared for and never experienced the sadness and heartache she'd encountered in the past. She was determined to protect her.

Bethan became upset and started shouting 'Why won't you

talk to me about it? My granddad's dead and I didn't even know him. I can't see my grandma either.'

It was unlike Bethan to behave in this way. The death of her granddad had disturbed her more than her mother and she felt let down. Amser wouldn't answer her daughter and Bethan became more and more upset.

'It's not fair mum, he was my granddad and your mum is my grandma.'

Amser stayed silent but Bethan was determined to get a response.

'What about my dad then?' she said.

'Who's my dad?' she went on.

'Where is he? Why can't I see him? I've never even seen a photo.'

Amser knew one day her daughter would want some questions answered and had always intended to sit her down and talk to her when the time was right. However, she knew in her heart the time would never be right. Now when their lives were full of good things, the death of her father had brought matters to a head.

Her past now had to be relived but she didn't know what to say or how to say it. She was scared of the truth and, although she had her reasons, she was frightened of Bethan's reactions.

Amser looked uncomfortable. Sitting with tears flowing down her cheeks she put her hands on her daughter's shoulders and tried to calm her down. But Bethan moved her mother's arms away and stood up. She wasn't in any mood to be controlled and became even more aggressive.

'I need to know about my dad, you have to tell me mum, I've a right to know,' she insisted.

Amser also now standing had never seen her daughter so angry. Looking straight into her eyes from only a few inches away Bethan was intimidating her.

Amser still hadn't spoken but was trying to think what she should do. Bethan, seeing her mother was so distressed, calmed herself down and started to behave a little better.

She said softly 'Mum you have to tell me, you know you do.'

Amser bent down and took a tissue from a box lying on a small table beside them. She dried her eyes and wiped her face. Then they both sat down once more this time facing each other.

Looking at her daughter with a feeling of guilt showing in her face she replied 'Yes I know I must, God knows I've wanted to for long enough.'

She added 'Do you think it's been easy for me keeping secrets from you?'

Bethan snapped back at her mother 'But it's not only about you, it's about my dad as well.'

This comment prompted an immediate response 'I don't know where your father is and he doesn't know you exist. I wish he did Bethan.'

Amser never intended to say this without explanation but her daughter had been relentless in her search for the truth. The words just came out and there was intent in her voice as if she was trying to upset her.

Bethan's mood changed again. She stood up and walked to the other side of the room. She became very animated. First her hands were on her hips and then round the back of her head.

'I can't believe it,' she mumbled to herself as she prowled around.

Amser, still seated, watched in horror as the girl continued to fret about her mother's admission.

Then Bethan shouted 'Why can't I be like other children?'

Her voice was so loud it was frightening Amser. Bethan walked over to her mum again and stood right in front of her.

She looked down at her and said 'You slept around then did you? Is that why your parents disowned you?'

Amser was distraught and for the first time in her daughter's life she lost her temper. It was an instant reaction but in a moment of madness she got to her feet and slapped Bethan's face. It wasn't a hard slap but Amser knew that, however much she'd been provoked, she'd gone too far.

As a child, when times were hard and she suffered from neglect, the one thing her parents never did was to lay a finger on her.

Amser was mortified and fearful she had tarnished the wonderful relationship she'd always enjoyed with Bethan.

'How was it possible to destroy so much in such a short space of time,' she thought.

Bethan looked at her mother and Amser could see the disappointment in her daughter's eyes. The girl didn't say another word; she stormed out of the room, slammed the door and ran upstairs. Her mother collapsed on the sofa with her head in her hands.

In a few seconds Amser heard her daughter's bedroom door being slammed closed. Such was the force of Bethan's action the whole house shook and a long mirror on the landing fell from the wall and crashed on the carpet.

Amser was desperate to talk to Bethan but needed to give her time on her own. The shock of the news about her granddad and information about her father had been overwhelming and difficult for a child to cope with. Her reactions were understandable and it was her mother who somehow had to put things right.

These moments alone gave Amser time to think and a few minutes later she made her way upstairs. On seeing the mirror face down she feared the glass must be broken. Amser wasn't superstitious. She didn't avoid walking under ladders but as a child she'd learnt not to open an umbrella indoors or put shoes on the table. She'd also been told a broken mirror was a sign of bad luck. These things had never made any sense but the sight of this object decorating the carpet troubled her and she chose to ignore its presence.

Amser knocked on her daughter's bedroom door and said 'Bethan my darling would you mind if I come in please?'

Bethan didn't answer and so Amser added 'Please Bethan can I talk to you?'

Still there was no answer and nothing could be heard from inside the room. Bethan was lying on her bed gathering her thoughts but her mother was getting a little worried; she wanted to be sure her daughter was OK.

There wasn't a lock on the door but Amser wasn't going to make things worse by invading her private space.

She pleaded with her daughter 'Bethan, we need to talk, please let me in.'

'It's too late for that,' she replied.

It was a relief for Amser to hear her daughter's voice but the reply was short and blunt.

Amser pleaded again 'Bethan please let me in. I need you to understand.'

'Not everything is about you mum. Your needs, your wants how about me?' the girl shouted.

'I know Bethan, I do, please let me in; I promise I'll tell you everything.'

There was silence again and Amser waited for a response as she stared at the bedroom door. Moments passed that seemed like hours to a woman who was now frantic. She was on edge and had to talk to her daughter.

She called out 'Bethan I'm still here and I'm going to sit down outside your room until you let me in. I'll sit here all night if necessary.'

Then she slumped to the floor and lent against the adjacent wall with her legs stretched out in front of her. A few seconds later the door opened. It creaked as the gap widened until Bethan could be seen looking very glum-faced.

Amser got to her feet in anticipation of her daughter's next move and was relieved when she said 'I suppose you'd better come in.'

The girl sat on her bed with her arms folded.

She looked up at her mother standing in front of her and said 'All right mum, tell me then, tell me will you.'

Amser sensed so much sorrow in her daughter's voice. She'd lost the girl's respect and was unsure whether whatever she said would be believed at this time. She'd been desperate to talk to Bethan but, having been granted her wish, was worried she may not be able to put things right.

Amser felt sick; neither she nor her daughter had eaten for hours. Her stomach was churning from a lack of food and her anxiety.

Plucking up courage she said 'Bethan, my darling Bethan I'm very sorry please can you find it in your heart to forgive me. I've never hit you before and you must know I love you very much. I know it's my fault but I've kept so many things cooped up in my head for so long. I have always dreaded a day like this but I never thought I would ever strike you. Please don't let this come between us. It's no excuse but I'm pleading for your forgiveness.'

The girl's tears had soaked her tee shirt and there was still redness in her eyes. It's times like this you find out how strong a bond is between mother and daughter. Bethan had been disturbed by her mother's action but she loved her deeply. She hadn't forgotten her mum had always supported her. She'd everything she wanted and couldn't have been loved any more.

Bethan rose to her feet and replied 'Oh mum I don't want us to quarrel and I know you wouldn't want to hurt me but you have to tell me now, there can't be anymore secrets.'

Mother and daughter hugged as if they hadn't seen each other for years. Tears of joy were shared as they kissed each other's faces before sitting down on the bed together.

Amser said 'Yes I promise I'll tell you all I know but both our stomachs are rumbling; I think we need some food.'

When they came out of Bethan's room the sight of the fallen mirror drew their attention. Amser in particular was distressed by it and cringed as her daughter picked it up from the carpet. Surprisingly after such a heavy drop the glass was fully intact.

Amser beamed 'Maybe this was a sign things were going to get better,' she thought and all of a sudden her confidence returned.

Bethan wanted pizza and an order was placed by telephone. Twenty five minutes later there was a knock on the front door from a tall slim man who'd arrived on a motorbike. He was wearing a helmet and didn't say a word. He extended his hand for payment and then provided two large boxes and a receipt. The man was off as quick as lightening before Amser even had a chance to say thank you.

After finishing the meal the time had come for Amser to reveal all. Mother and daughter once again sat down on the couch where they'd argued earlier.

They faced each other and Amser said 'OK this is it, the truth I promised you. You want to know about your dad. I can honestly say I don't know where he is but I can tell you his name is Richard.'

Amser smiled and held the tips of Bethan's fingers.

She paused before adding 'I made love with him once and for what it's worth I haven't made love with another man either before or after that time. I only ever saw him on that one occasion.'

Amser didn't go into the reason why but she said 'My parents didn't know about Richard but they had things for me to do when I had planned to meet him again. You can imagine how upset I was. I had no way of knowing I was pregnant and by the time I did it was too late. He lived far away, I didn't have his address and he didn't have mine.'

Bethan took time to absorb all the information.

Amser went on 'Look Bethan it sounds so dirty now but you have to believe me when I tell you that, apart from giving birth to you, the moments me and your dad had together were the most special moments in my life. You could say you are a love child because I fell in love with him the first moment I saw him and I believe he did with me too.'

She sighed and added 'I knew him for a very brief time and yet every second will live with me forever. We never intended to have sex but a time arrived when somehow it seemed the only thing to do, the right thing to do and now I have you, my darling, darling Bethan.'

Amser went on 'Afterwards, came all the guilt and worry but after finding out I was having a child, never once did I ever think about giving you up. You were always wanted and I never considered life without you.'

Bethan enquired 'Why did you say that?'

'Say what?' asked Amser.

'Say you never considered giving me up and I was always wanted; it seems such a strange thing to say.'

Amser had promised there would be no more secrets. She was referring to her own parents' regrets but didn't want to tell her daughter.

'Oh I don't know,' she replied.

'It was such a hard time but from the moment I knew I was pregnant I wanted you and I needed you.'

Holding Bethan's hands she added 'Yes, I'm sorry you've had to live without a father but I've had to live without him too. I don't even have a photo.'

Bethan was now feeling sorry for her mum and in a far more receptive mood. There were more kisses and cuddles as Amser was consoled.

Bethan's mind was now working overtime 'Is that why we moved away?' she enquired.

Amser said 'I suppose it was partly, but there were many reasons. Overall I just didn't get on with my mum and dad and I had a job to go to in Rowan. It was best for all of us.'

There were no more questions. Bethan accepted the situation and thanked her mother.

'Wait there,' said Amser.

Bethan watched as her mother went into her bedroom. Then she listened to the sound of something being dragged on the carpet. Amser came out clutching an old brown shoe box with white ribbon around it, tied in a bow. The box had been under her bed since the day they moved into the house. It had a thick layer of dust on it and Amser blew the substance off into the air.

After removing the lid Bethan could see all sorts of papers of various shapes and sizes. There was also a wooden whistle, a metal badge with a picture of a panda on it and Amser's book of poems. The girl could see they were her mother's treasured possessions.

Amser moved various items around until she found what she was looking for. She removed two photos from the bottom of the box; one was of her as a child and the other was of her mum and dad at her graduation. Amser looked at the photos for a second before handing them to her daughter.

The girl held them side by side and Amser waited for her

response. She was aware Bethan should have been shown the photo of her grandparents a long time ago.

'How will she react?' thought Amser.

Then Bethan turned towards her mum and the girl's face beamed.

'My grandma looks like you,' she said.

With relief Amser replied 'Yes, I think she does.'

Bethan adored the photos.

She said 'Would you mind very much if I kept them, I promise I'll look after them.'

'Of course you may,' she replied and from that day on the photos were displayed on a small chest of drawers which sat beside Bethan's bed.

The day of the funeral passed and Amser had sent a pretty bouquet of flowers. She also sent a letter to her mum, together with a photo of her and Bethan at Bethan's request.

It was a turning point in their lives as the death of Amser's dad had led to Bethan learning about the past.

Amser smiled as she thought to herself 'Well at last my dad has done something for me'.

It made her chuckle but then she burst into tears as she thought about her childhood again and all the heartache she'd left behind.

How she wished things had been different. However, they say time is a great healer and as the weeks and months went by Amser thought less and less about her dad and once again she succeeded in putting her mother to the back of her mind. During that time her relationship with Bethan became even stronger.

Chapter Twenty Four

One day out of the blue Amser had another communication from Rhonda. This time it was a telephone call. She asked if she could come and visit her.

She said 'I'm fed up with writing, don't you think it's about time we got together for a good old natter.'

'I would love you to come,' said Amser.

The one person she missed from her past was her best friend and arrangements were made for Rhonda's visit to North Wales. On a bright Monday afternoon in August she arrived at Rowan Station.

Amser had been counting down the days and was waiting for her as she stepped off the train. The girls hadn't been together since the day Amser left Walwyn Gate and they were both excited.

As soon as they saw each other they kissed and hugged and talked about how their looks had changed.

'You don't look a day older,' Amser said.

Rhonda replied 'Well you look much older Ams, I hardly recognised you.'

The girls were laughing and giggling like they always did and they took the short journey by taxi to Amser's home.

Amser welcomed Rhonda into her house and introduced Bethan.

Rhonda said 'I can't believe it, how you've grown up.'

Bethan was now five feet three inches tall and very slim. She had long flowing golden hair.

'I guess I have but I don't remember you,' she replied.

'Never mind,' said Rhonda.

Sitting down beside Bethan she said 'Tell me all about yourself. I want to know everything you two girls have been up to.'

Bethan liked her mum's friend and told her all about the harp, her school and all the things she did with Amser. Rhonda realised there was a special bond between mother and daughter.

It didn't take long for Rhonda to feel at home and the two

girlfriends got on so well together it was as if they'd never been apart.

Amser said 'I'm very happy here in Rowan. Bethan is settled, I've good people around me and I love my job.'

'No man in your life then?' enquired Rhonda.

'I don't need one and anyway all my time is taken up with my work and looking after Bethan.'

Then Amser enquired 'How about you Rhon, you haven't told me anything at all. What have you been up to? I suppose there's at least one man on the scene?'

Rhonda was very cagey. She seemed reluctant to talk about herself but was very keen to talk about Amser's mother. Rhonda lived in the same house she was brought up in. Over the years she'd often bumped into Mrs Edwards and had been going to see her since Amser's dad's death to make sure she was alright.

'She is finding life very hard without your dad. I don't know how she copes,' she said.

Amser said 'Yes it must be hard on your own after being with someone for a long time,' but she didn't want to talk about her mother.

'Come on Rhon tell me about you, I haven't seen you for ages. What have you been doing? How's your sex life? Are you happy at work?'

Rhonda wasn't her usual jolly self.

She said 'Oh you don't want to know about me. Tell me more about life in North Wales.'

Amser could sense something was wrong. Sitting on the couch together she faced her friend and placed her hands on Rhonda's shoulders.

Looking straight into her eyes she said 'Rhon what is it? What's the matter?'

Rhonda hesitated and cast her eyes away from Amser before saying 'I didn't come here to tell you my troubles, don't let's spoil things. I'm so pleased to see you.'

But Amser wouldn't let it drop.

'Rhonda, tell me, I beg you, what's the matter?'

192

Tears started falling from her friends eyes.

'I've so many problems,' she said.

'Life has been so difficult these past months.'

'Just tell me, will you, you and me don't have secrets do we?' she replied.

Rhonda, still not looking at Amser, said 'I've lost my job and I'm heavily in debt. I don't know which way to turn.'

Rhonda was not a girl that cried without reason. Amser hadn't seen her friend looking so solemn before and wanted to know more.

'How much are you in debt?' Amser enquired.

'Quite a lot,' she replied.

'Just tell me Rhon, how much in debt, tell me will you?' Amser insisted.

'£14,000,' said Rhonda as she continued to sob.

'Goodness gracious, how on earth did you manage that?' said Amser.

She tried hard not to get annoyed but her voice pitch was becoming higher as she continued to interrogate her friend.

'It's so easy,' said Rhonda.

'I love beautiful clothes and my credit cards have been so tempting to use. Now I don't have a job and I can't afford to make the repayments.'

Amser looked at Rhonda who was facing her once more. She wasn't well dressed for someone who'd been spending lots of money on clothes.

She'd arrived in Rowan in tatty old jeans and a blouse that had been washed so many times the blue colouring was almost out of it. Even more surprising were her shoes. Rhonda had always adored them but all she had with her was a pair of ordinary sandals.

'There has to be another motive but what could it be,' Amser thought.

The one thing that stood out from her friend's visit was her determination to talk about her mother. Rhonda had been mentioning her at every opportunity and Amser recalled how she tried to get her to go to her dad's funeral.

Then the penny dropped. Amser realised her friend didn't want the money for herself, she wanted it for her mum.

'What an earth was she going to say now,' she thought.

Having come all the way to Rowan, it seemed Rhonda was desperate to get some money and she knew her friend had plenty of it. It saddened Amser to think her mum was in such need and she pondered over what she should do.

She realised it must have taken her friend a great deal of courage to approach her with a begging bowl. The last thing she was going to do was let Rhonda see she could tell she was being deceived. Amser didn't like being lied to but was aware if Rhonda had told her the truth she would have refused to help.

Whilst this conversation was going on Bethan sat listening. She was trying to find out a little more about her family from the scraps of information on offer. Amser had become irritated by Rhonda's intrusion into her life.

Once again she was reminded of the past she wanted to forget. However, ever since the funeral she'd been worried about her mum. She'd been having trouble sleeping and in truth her friend had brought matters to a head.

Amser had always felt guilty about keeping all of her granny's money. She knew her mum had been led on by her dad and wasn't so much to blame for the past as he was. She was timid and shy whilst he had been loud, aggressive and persuasive.

She could never forgive what had happened but decided to help her on the pretext of her friend's lie.

She said 'Rhonda we've known one another for many years and you're my only real friend. I want to help you.'

'No, I won't let you. I've got myself into this mess and I'll get myself out of it. I shouldn't have told you,' she replied.

Then so typical of Rhonda she made a joke out of it all by saying 'If I need to eat I'll gate crash a wedding.'

Just for a moment the mood of the conversation changed as the girls fell about laughing. Bethan looked on in amazement, wondering to herself what was so funny.

Amser said to her 'I will tell you later I promise. You won't believe it though.'

'Come on Rhonda, let me give you the money, you know I can afford it.'

'That's the trouble,' she replied.

'I know, you know, I know. It must give you the impression this is why I came.'

Still trying to hide her thoughts Amser said 'I don't think that, you're my friend and I'm pleased you're here. I'm going to help you and that's the end of the matter. Then you can start again.'

Rhonda wasn't stupid; she knew her friend had worked things out. Perhaps it was best she had as it made Rhonda feel better.

'I don't know what to say,' she replied.

'Say yes then,' said Amser.

Without waiting for a response she reached into her handbag and took out her cheque book. Then having acquired a pen from an adjacent table, and resting on a small round tray, she made out a payment for £20,000.

'I said I only needed £14,000,' said Rhonda.

'I know but as things have been so difficult for you, I would like to give you a head start for the future,' she replied.

Rhonda's eyes filled with joy and she thanked her friend with a huge bear hug. Then whilst their arms were entangled they over-balanced and fell on the carpet with Rhonda landing on top of Amser. The girls burst into hysterics as they rolled around on the floor. Bethan couldn't believe her eyes but was pleased to see her mum having fun and began to laugh as well.

Laying side by side and looking up at the ceiling; with the money issue settled, Amser said 'Listen Rhon let's go out and have some fun tonight. We haven't done that for ages.'

'That's a great idea,' Rhonda replied.

However, a further thought crossed Rhonda's mind.

'Oh Ams I can't, I haven't brought anything to wear.'

'Don't worry Rhon I'm sure I can find something,' said Amser.

Arrangements were quickly made for Iola to sit with Bethan, a taxi was booked and the girls got themselves ready. Rhonda borrowed a deep red, close-fitting top which was even more pronounced as she'd put on a bit of weight since the girls' university days.

Amser remarked 'Goodness Rhon you look so tarty.'

However, her friend saw this as a compliment rather than a cause for concern and just giggled. Then Rhonda somehow managed to get into a pair of Amser's grey flared trousers after a lot of pulling. They didn't flatter her middle at all and the outfit was completed with Rhonda's sandals which would have looked more at home on a seaside promenade rather than in a decent restaurant.

Amser put on her dark blue silky dress she often wore on special occasions. It was held up with two thin straps and was frilled at the bottom. Rhonda looked at her and noticed it fitted her like a glove. Every inch of the material complimented her figure and she looked stunning.

It wasn't often Rhonda was lost for words and, being envious, all she would say was 'I suppose you'll do'.

The girls were excited and having indulged in liquids, creams and sprays there was the smell of perfume and makeup everywhere. They'd only just finished beautifying themselves when the taxi arrived and they were on their way into town.

Rhonda didn't need any persuading to enjoy herself and some immediate flirting with the driver reminded Amser how mischievous she could be. She hoped that being older would have calmed her friend's sexual appetite. However, it only took Rhonda two minutes to come up with a master plan for the evening.

'Let's pretend we're sisters tonight,' she suggested.

'Well, we've always been pretty close, that's OK with me,' replied Amser.

'Yes, but being just sisters would be boring. Let's make out we are more than sisters.'

'You mean like lesbians, Rhon?'

'Let's say incestuous lesbians,' she replied whilst giggling.

'It will be such a laugh don't you think?'

Amser felt uncomfortable and closed the small window in the taxi behind the driver so he couldn't overhear the conversation.

'Mmm I'm not sure. I've never pretended to be anybody else before. I don't think I could do it,' she said.

Rhonda tried to convince her friend she hadn't done it either but Amser didn't believe her.

'Oh come on, don't be such a boring old fart,' she grumbled.

Rhonda was set on the idea and pleaded for her friend's approval. Amser knew there wasn't any point in arguing about it. In the past she'd never been able to change Rhonda's mind. She agreed with some reluctance, not having any notion how the evening might turn out.

The journey to Rowan only took six minutes and the taxi pulled up outside Amser's favourite Italian restaurant. It was called Realaroma and was situated on one side of the market square. In this area people could wander freely without worrying about traffic.

Seats had been positioned so that passers-by could stop for a while and gaze at the attractive flower beds which had been cut into beautiful manicured lawns. The dazzling array of colours always reflected the seasons of the year and in spring a line of pink cherry blossom trees guarded the main path across the square.

One side had a cobbled surface that was centuries old and each Friday stallholders displayed their wares. Rowan was always a busy place but people came from miles around to make their special purchases from this historic area.

In the evenings the square wore a different hat. It was then a much quieter place and lit by lamps in square iron casings that swung from metal posts in the breeze. Although of a fairly modern construction, they looked like gas lamps and the area had a Victorian feel about it.

Shops of various sizes looked onto the square selling all the town's needs. Realaroma stood out from the other establishments. Pastel pink curtains draped the windows either side of the entrance and, looking inside, candles could be seen alight on each table.

The name Realaroma was written in large red letters in an arch above the entrance. On each side of the door, hanging baskets could be seen filled with all kinds of pretty plants.

Amser hadn't booked a table as it was a mid-week evening and she didn't anticipate any problems getting in. However, on peeking through the entrance glass door, Amser was amazed to see the restaurant was busy. There wasn't one empty table and she suggested to Rhonda they should try elsewhere.

However Rhonda liked the look of the place and wasn't to be put off.

'We're here now Ams, I'm sure we'll be alright,' she remarked.

Then without another word she entered the restaurant with an air of confidence. Amser followed her friend as she always did and wasn't surprised to hear a waiter explain the restaurant was full for the evening.

Rhonda, now with an evening of fun fixed in her mind, amazed Amser.

She said 'Look I'm here with my sister because it's her 32nd birthday. I haven't seen her for nine years and I go home tomorrow.'

Rhonda focused her eyes on the waiter and waited for him to speak. Nothing was said for a few seconds as Rhonda continued to glare at the man.

Then Amser was shocked to see her friend break down in tears and hear her say 'Please Mr Waiter, you can find a little table for us can't you?'

Amser was very embarrassed. She noticed other customers sitting close by had heard the conversation. They were muttering over their food to one another.

A lady in a long white dress and curly black hair remarked 'Who do they think they are?'

Then looking at Rhonda's clothes she added 'She would be better off in the chip shop across the square.'

Amser wanted to leave but Rhonda had also heard the lady.

Moving over to where she was sitting and looking down upon her Rhonda said 'Keep your comments to yourself unless you want me to shove your napkin down your throat.'

'How rude, how very rude,' the lady whispered to her friend who was sitting opposite her.

These acts of aggression and emotion were too much for the

waiter to bear. He was concerned by Rhonda's behaviour, but after consulting a colleague, the girls were shown to the far side of the restaurant.

In a few seconds a small teak-coloured table was brought out of a store room. It was covered with a green striped cloth and two place mats were laid out side by side. Still waiting, the girls watched as two yellow chairs were brought out from the kitchen and they were invited to sit down.

Amser had witnessed her friend's acting skills before but couldn't believe what had happened. She scanned around the restaurant and was relieved not to see anybody she knew. Rhonda's tears dried up and Amser reminded her she was now thirty one years old and not thirty two.

She looked at Rhonda with a serious face but it made her friend giggle and then they both burst into laughter. Because of Rhonda's outrageous behaviour Amser had forgotten Rhonda's saucy plan but this was about to change when she called over the waiter to order some drinks. It was the same man who greeted them on entry and he looked a little nervous.

'Two bottles of lager please, one for me and one for my beautiful sexy sister,' commanded Rhonda, putting her arm around her friend as she spoke.

On hearing this comment the waiter looked at Amser, and then Rhonda remarked 'Mmm, couldn't you just eat her?'

The waiter didn't say a word. He nodded and the girls weren't sure if it was to confirm he was getting the drinks or if he agreed with Rhonda's remark.

Amser was bursting at the seams as she witnessed the waiter almost run from the table. They both watched as he tripped over a crease in the carpet and the girls giggled again.

'Do you think we'll get our drinks?' said Rhonda.

Amser replied 'If you carry on like this Rhon he will probably want us on video.'

More laughter followed and within a couple of minutes the poor man returned with two bottles of lager. He removed the metal caps and placed them on the table together with two glasses.

'Are you ready to order now ladies?' the waiter asked.

The girls hadn't even looked at the menu but Amser, who was feeling more and more uncomfortable with both the waiter and Rhonda asked for a recommendation.

The waiter mumbled 'A chicken pasta dish in a red wine sauce.'

Before Rhonda could speak Amser replied 'Thank you we'll both have that.'

The waiter somewhat relieved left the table in haste again.

Whilst they were waiting more drinks were served and Rhonda, decided to spice up the evening a little more. She moved her seat much closer to Amser and started to run her fingers through Amser's hair whenever the waiter was looking their way.

When he walked towards them with their meals she put her hand under the table pretending to feel Amser's legs. By now Amser was a little more relaxed. She didn't often drink alcohol and having consumed three bottles of beer she was ready to join in the fun.

As the waiter arrived she jumped a little as if she'd been touched by Rhonda and said 'Can't you wait until we get home?'

This time it was Rhonda's turn to stop herself from laughing and it was made worse when the waiter offered to move them to a quieter table which had become free.

'No thanks, my friend is enjoying it right here and mmm so am I,' Amser replied.

The girls calmed down a little and took time to enjoy their food. They were having such a laugh and the evening passed quickly.

At eleven thirty they left Realaroma but not before Rhonda made one last attempt to arouse the waiter. The restaurant had a policy of adding ten per cent to each bill but the girl decided to offer the waiter something a little different.

'How would you like more than a ten per cent tip tonight?' she said, putting her arm around Amser as she spoke.

The waiter was standing alone with the girls in a quiet area by the cloakroom.

Rhonda said 'I'm going to show Amser what she means to me tonight.'

Then she reached over her friend's shoulder and moved her hand towards her breast as she smiled at the waiter.

Amser froze and the waiter physically trembled as Rhonda added 'I don't know what I'm going to do without my older sister.'

The waiter was a very short gentleman, in his forties with black balding hair.

Looking at him straight in the eye Rhonda went on 'Mmm little man, I'm sure you could be a big man tonight,' as she ran her index finger across his cheek.

'Why don't you come home with me and Ams and keep us warm?'

That was enough for Amser. She searched through her purse to pay for the meal and the tip. The waiter didn't say a word and on leaving the money on the counter, Amser almost pushed her friend out of the restaurant door.

'What on earth did you think you were doing Rhon, you acted like a slut. The waiter almost had a heart attack and by the way, I'm not older than you.'

Rhonda had a little more to drink than her friend and was finding everything funny. She was talking loudly, singing and laughing as Amser was getting more and more wound up.

The girls started to make their way to the taxi rank in the next street. As they stumbled and swayed a door on a parked car was opened and Amser was knocked to the ground. This was the last straw for Amser but Rhonda laughed until she realised her friend might be hurt. The man got out of his car and started looking at his door and by this time Amser had got to her feet.

'Excuse me, you knocked me to the ground,' she said.

'It was your fault, the pavement is at least ten feet wide, why did you need to walk so close to my car?' he replied.

Seeing the state of the girls he went on 'Oh I see you're drunk aren't you. You should be ashamed of yourselves.'

Amser now recovered from the shock and with drink inside her, was in no mood to be chastised. Rhonda too didn't like the man's attitude. Then as they continued with the argument Amser felt quite ill. The cold chill of the night air after being in a warm restaurant had caused her to feel a little lightheaded. She could feel her stomach churning and in the next moment was sick all over the man's coat and trousers.

'Oh dear,' remarked Rhonda.

'Oh dear oh dear, I think we'd better go home,' she added.

Amser, still feeling woozy, couldn't believe what she'd done. However, the words I'm sorry seemed inadequate as she looked at her body fluid dripping off the man's shoes.

Both girls hurried away, leaving the man standing by his car covered in sick. Amser had somehow avoided staining herself and her clothes seemed none the worse for the fall.

When Amser and Rhonda reached the taxi rank there were two vehicles waiting and a driver opened the back door of his cab. The girls climbed inside and began the short journey back home. For a moment they were quiet as they reflected on all that had happened but the silence was too much for Rhonda to bear.

She said 'Well Ams at least you weren't sick over the waiter. Thank God he was only four feet ten inches tall, otherwise you might have spewed over his face.'

Amser said 'He was taller than that, much taller.'

Rhonda replied 'He's the only waiter I've come across who had to reach up rather than down to put plates on the table.'

There was more laughter.

'Oh Rhon it was awful, I was so embarrassed,' said Amser.

She replied 'Don't worry Ams, I'm sure the man is used to knocking over people with his car door and letting them be sick all over him.'

The two friends became tired of the conversation as the taxi got closer to Amser's home. They were both ready for bed and a good night's sleep.

The following morning both girls had large hangovers. Their faces looked drawn and their hair was uncombed as they tried to negotiate the various areas of the kitchen. Rhonda's head was spinning as she made herself some toast and Amser was unable to face any food at all. She sat down at the kitchen table with her hands on the surface and her head lowered between her arms.

Bethan entered the kitchen as bright as a new summer's day. She quickly assessed the situation.

'A good night last night was it? Did you manage to get a drink anywhere?' she enquired with glee.

There wasn't any laughter, just a sense of satisfaction on Bethan's face that her mother could make a fool of herself once in a while. It became obvious that the slightest sound provided some discomfort and Bethan was intent on making as much noise as possible. Cutlery was rattled, her chair was dragged across the kitchen floor and she was told over and over again to turn the sound on the radio down.

Amser lifted her head to say 'Really Bethan do you have to make so much noise?'

The girl replied 'It's not my fault if you get yourself plastered, I'm doing what I always do.'

'Well go and do it somewhere else will you,' she replied.

After breakfast Rhonda packed her clothes. She'd just re-appeared in the kitchen when there was the noise of a taxi pulling up outside. Amser, still feeling a little rough, hugged and kissed her friend.

Rhonda's visit had been very short but as usual her company had proved to be challenging, exciting, embarrassing and exhausting. The girls were a tonic for one another and they agreed not to leave it too long before they saw each other again.

Rhonda also embraced Bethan and planted a kiss on both her cheeks. Her breath smelled of stale garlic and the girl was glad when they parted. Then Rhonda boarded her taxi which was to take her to the railway station. Amser waved her friend off and, as sad as she was to see her go, she breathed a sigh of relief.

All of a sudden life returned to normal and Amser was left to ponder over the real reason for her friend's visit. She didn't like being lied to but, despite the deceit, was comforted in the knowledge that her good deed was going to make life more comfortable for her mother.

Chapter Twenty Five

Amser went back inside. She was still feeling the ill-effects of the previous evening and collapsed on the couch. After a few moments with her eyes closed she was disturbed by small spots of water dripping on her face.

She sat up and called out to her daughter 'I think we've got a leak Bethan, come and see.'

Bethan ran down the stairs and they both looked up at the ceiling.

'Look there,' said Amser pointing to the spot.

'Wherever is it coming from?' she asked.

'I think it must be upstairs,' Bethan replied with mischief in her voice.

Amser had already realised the source of the problem must be above and snapped back at her daughter.

'I'm not stupid girl.'

Then she went upstairs and established the shower in the bathroom was above the leak in the lounge. The water controller was turned off so Amser knew the problem wouldn't get much worse unless the shower was used.

Amser now had to set about finding a plumber. The Yellow Pages was full of listings of tradesmen. Some only had names and others had colourful advertisements. All sorts of guarantees of work, reliability and quality of materials were offered but it was impossible to make a good choice without a certain amount of luck.

Amser thought about getting a pin to make a selection at random. She even considered asking Bethan to choose a letter from the alphabet to narrow down the search. However, whilst reading all the advertisements she happened to spill some coffee on one of the pages. The liquid settled mostly over a plumber called Russell Emmanuel and Amser liked the name.

'I can't believe you're choosing a plumber on the basis of a coffee spillage mum,' remarked Bethan.

'Neither can I but I have to pick one of them,' she replied.

Amser started dialling and got straight through to an answerphone.

'You're through to Russell Emmanuel the best plumber in Rowan, leave a message, name and contact number,' said a recorded voice.

Amser thought the plumber's message was both boastful and a little abrupt. She would have put the telephone down but there was something about the voice. She couldn't quite put her finger on it but she was intrigued and decided to proceed.

'I've a leak in my lounge ceiling which I think is coming from the shower above it, can you come and have a look please?' she asked.

Amser left her telephone number, last name and address details and awaited a response.

The voice continued to interest Amser. She listened to the recording over and over again. It was strange but she was sure she recognised it.

The plumber didn't telephone back and the voice puzzled her even more until there was a knock at the door that evening after dusk. On opening it both Amser and the plumber were startled to see each other.

It was dark in the street the previous evening and Amser was a little worse for wear but she recognised the man who knocked her off her feet with his car door. The gentleman also recognised the lady who had been sick all down his suit.

'OK lady, I'm on my way. I'm sure you can find another plumber.'

The man turned around and walked back towards his van as Amser, still in a state of some surprise, stood speechless. Then, after recalling her thoughts, she decided to call out to him.

'If you help me I promise I won't be sick on you.'

Looking back at Amser, he saw the serious look on her face change. She smiled and even chuckled as he considered the opportunity.

He replied by saying 'Well, I can't bring my van up your drive so I'm not going to knock you over again.'

'My thoughts exactly,' said Amser.

'I'd better take a look at the problem then,' replied the plumber and he walked towards the house.

Amser showed Mr Emmanuel the lounge ceiling and Bethan entered the room behind them.

'Did I hear you say you were sick over this man, mum?'

'Be quiet girl,' she replied.

Bethan wouldn't be silenced. She thought about the situation and it didn't take her long to realise what had happened the previous night.

'It was when you were out with Rhonda, was it?' she enquired.

Before Amser could reply, Bethan was quick to add 'If I disgraced myself, I would be told in no uncertain terms I would be letting you down, and yet you were drunk on the street and spewing up on passers-by.'

'It was an accident. Anyway, it was his fault. If he hadn't knocked me over with his car door it wouldn't have happened,' she remarked.

Mr Emmanuel countered by saying 'Well, if you'd been sober you wouldn't have swayed towards my car in the first place.'

'I wasn't that drunk,' remarked Amser.

Bethan said 'Well you had a hell of a hangover this morning.'

Mr Emmanuel started to laugh and Amser, with a stern school teacher look on her face wasn't amused. He wouldn't stop and Bethan began to laugh as well.

'I don't think it's funny,' said Amser.

This serious remark prompted Mr Emmanuel and Bethan to laugh even more and the lady became very irritated.

'For goodness sake I had a night out and had one drink too many. How often do I go out?' said Amser.

Bethan still trying to contain her laughter replied 'Well if that's how you behave you'd better not go out too often.'

Mr Emmanuel was still laughing but the conversation was getting more and more lighthearted by the minute.

'Look, it seems things have blown out of all proportion. I will sort out your plumbing problem for nothing if we can start again,' he said.

Amser wasn't sure how to respond. She didn't want any favours from anyone, especially a stranger.

'Also he'd said 'start again'. What did that mean?' she thought.

She didn't know what Mr Emmanuel's motives were and felt a little uncomfortable. However, despite all that had happened he did seem rather nice.

She liked him and responded by saying 'That's good of you but I'll only agree if you let me cook you dinner afterwards.'

Bethan listened in amazement. She hadn't heard her mother be so forward with anybody before, let alone a male stranger whom she'd only met in the dark.

Mr Emmanuel agreed and confirmed his name was Russell. Without further ado the plumber went upstairs and looked in the shower room. It wasn't easily noticed but there was a hairline crack in the tray causing water to escape and drip through the ceiling.

He noticed a wooden scrubbing brush hanging on the wall and on enquiring further established it was dropped into the tray from time to time. Russell explained how the hard rimmed wooden surface could cause so much damage and said it needed to be replaced.

'What the brush,' Amser said.

The lady was being a bit playful.

The plumber smiled at her and answered 'No the tray of course,' thinking to himself 'What a stupid woman you are.'

Amser and Russell were now being very polite to one another and Bethan was amazed to hear the small talk developing between them.

'I'll order a replacement tray and come and fit it on Wednesday, if that's OK.'

'That's fine, I will cook you dinner then as agreed,' replied Amser.

'Lovely job,' said Russell.

The following Wednesday Russell's van pulled up outside Amser's house. A front window was open and she heard the sound of the engine. On opening the door Amser was very concerned to see the vehicle in such a bad state. Apart from being filthy, the wheel trims were missing and there was a large oblong-looking dent on the driver's door.

Amser was aware appearances can be deceiving but this wasn't the start she was looking for. Russell stepped out in his dark green overalls and noticed her eying up his prized possession.

He remarked 'Don't worry, it's me who's going to do the work not my van.'

Then he opened up the double doors at the back and took out a shower tray that was still in its shop wrapping. Having exchanged the usual pleasantries, Russell went upstairs and repaired the shower.

It was late in the day and Amser had already started cooking dinner. When he came down he found her in the kitchen with her hands in a mixing bowl hard at work.

'Is it alright if I change my clothes, I can't have dinner looking like this?'

'You can use my bedroom and the bathroom upstairs; dinner will be in about twenty minutes,' replied Amser.

Before dinner was served Russell entered the kitchen again. This time he was dressed in grey pleated trousers and a smart thin blue striped shirt. He was over six feet tall, had long dark brown hair and Amser thought he was very handsome. Then however she noticed he was carrying chocolates and flowers and became very annoyed.

Amser said 'The deal was a dinner for some plumbing work. Nothing else was mentioned and so I'm still in your debt.'

'I don't see it like that Miss Edwards. After all it only took me an hour or so to fix your shower, I expect you've been preparing the meal for ages.'

Amser had but she replied 'Don't flatter yourself Mr Emmanuel I haven't taken that long, you're only the plumber.'

As soon as she said it Amser regretted her comment.

She thought 'What an earth am I doing, it's not often I've a good looking man in my house.'

She could see from Russell's facial expression he was gobsmacked. Regardless of the work he did he had been invited to dinner and thought it only right to bring a gift for the lady.

To make amends Amser quickly apologised.

She said 'I'm sorry, I'm not used to being spoilt, it's very good of you,' and planted a warm kiss on his left cheek.

The mood lightened and Russell was asked to take a seat in the dining room with Bethan so that Amser could dish up unhindered. Sitting opposite each other, Bethan had a good look at Russell. He was a natural smiler and made her feel at ease with his constant grinning. Whilst they waited they chatted a little more about the chance meeting after Amser left Realaroma.

Bethan said 'My mum has never been in such a state before as far as I know.'

'Yes I can see now it was out of character but I suspect that getting to know your mother will be a real challenge,' he said.

Then Amser came into the room wearing oven gloves and carrying three hot plates. They all enjoyed a good helping of roast chicken served with vegetables and gravy.

Russell said 'It all came out of a packet did it?'

This time however Amser felt much more relaxed and said 'OK it might have taken me a few minutes to get it ready, these microwaves are wonderful you know' and giggled.

Russell said 'Thank you so much. I don't have time to cook for myself, this is a real treat for me.'

Bethan was as quiet as a mouse listening to the grown-up chatter.

Throughout, Russell was calling the lady Miss Edwards until the girl said 'Mummy can Russell call you Amser?'

It was very strange but it hadn't occurred to either Amser or Russell until they were enlightened.

Amser saw Russell often after that day as their personalities seemed to gel and they enjoyed each other's company. They visited the theatre, went for picnics in the forest and long walks by the sea. She was even persuaded to attend a rugby match although she hated sport. Russell, under some protest, was taken to an art gallery. Such was the developing bond between them it didn't matter where they went as long as they were together.

During their courtship Russell also took an interest in Bethan. He was keen to earn brownie points from Amser but it wasn't difficult as he liked the girl. She was bright, bubbly and grown-up for her age. She'd an opinion on everything and was interesting to talk to.

Russell looked forward to seeing her almost as much as seeing Amser. As soon as he arrived at the house Bethan would run down the stairs to greet him with a hug and start talking about her day at school or her beloved harp.

Often this would happen whilst Amser was getting ready to go out and when she appeared Bethan would say 'Oh mum can't you stay in tonight?'

Amser would smile and say 'We won't be late my sweet, make sure you go to bed by 10pm.'

For the first time in her life there was a male presence and the girl started to look up to him as a father figure. Bethan was disappointed on the days he didn't come around and even a little jealous when he took her mother out and left her behind.

Amser was pleased her daughter was getting this attention and was as comfortable in her life as she'd ever been. However, with all her needs taken care of, she hadn't once stopped to think about Russell. She didn't realise he'd become so attracted to her and was unaware he wanted to make his place in both their lives a more permanent fixture.

Despite all the time they'd spent together, Amser and Russell had no more than kissed and cuddled but one evening whilst sitting in the local Indian restaurant Russell became very serious. It was unlike him and it worried Amser.

'Whatever is the matter? What's wrong?' she enquired.

Russell fixed his eyes on hers as he reached inside his jacket pocket and produced a small red cubed box. Amser, realising what was coming, didn't move a muscle. Russell placed the box on the table between them un-opened and took hold of Amser's hands.

'Dear Amser, you provide me with so much warmth even when I'm not with you; I love you with all my heart,' he said.

Then slipping his fingers away from Amser's hands, he opened the box to reveal a small bright sapphire ring clustered in diamonds.

Still looking at Amser and holding her hands again he mentioned the words she was frightened to hear 'Will you marry me my darling?'

Amser was mortified; they'd never talked about marriage not even in jest. She hadn't considered it and although she was very fond of Russell she wasn't sure she wanted this commitment or even to live with him.

Amser felt uncomfortable; in a moment she had to answer but she'd only just become aware of Russell's feelings and was desperate not to hurt him. Still holding hands, but clutching a little more firmly, Amser had made her decision.

'Russell, we have become such good friends, you know I'm very fond of you, I can't imagine life without you but marriage is such a big step. I'm not ready to take it,' she said.

She added 'Thank you so much for asking. It's so kind of you.'

Russell's mood changed. There was redness in his face and he was upset.

Pulling his hands away he said 'It's so kind of you! That's what you say when someone carries a heavy bag for you, gives you a gift or makes you a cup of tea.'

He went on 'Amser, I've been so patient. I have looked after you and Bethan for a long time. Bethan has told me about her dad and I've never asked you for sex. I always thought you would tell me when you were ready. I've never asked you for anything.'

'I thought you liked things the way they were,' she replied.

Russell said 'Yes I do, of course I do but in any relationship there's usually a little more. It seems we've reached a crossroads.'

Amser was trembling and replied 'Oh no please don't do this; can't we go on like we've always done?'

Russell said 'It's too late now. I need you so much but we both know you will never be ready. I can't live in someone's shadow forever.'

There was no reply. The relationship had come to an end and Amser cried looking at his sorrowful face. In a few moments she'd lost the dearest person in her life other than her daughter but she couldn't commit herself to marriage. Russell was crying too but he was right: there would always be Richard between them.

They left the restaurant and Amser was taken home by Russell for the last time. Not a word was said on the short journey and Amser's mind turned to what she was going to tell Bethan the following morning.

She got out of the car and walked up to her front door. Russell was hoping she would turn around and rush back into his arms but Amser didn't look back. As she inserted her key in the lock Russell drove away and a feeling of sadness and emptiness filled every vein in her body.

Once inside Amser was mortified to find Bethan waiting for her in the lounge. The girl was full of smiles and couldn't contain her excitement.

'Did he propose then?' she asked.

Amser was shocked as she added 'Did you say yes?'

Amser knew her daughter and Russell had become close but she hadn't imagined Bethan would have been forewarned about his proposal. How she wished she'd been.

She went into the kitchen to make a cup of tea but Bethan followed her. She was determined to find out what had happened.

'He did ask you didn't he?' Bethan enquired.

'Yes, yes he asked me.' she replied.

'You accepted then, did you?' the girl enquired further.

Amser couldn't bring herself to speak. She couldn't look at her daughter and there was a solemn look on her face. Bethan became angry and in the few minutes her mum had been home Bethan's world had been torn apart. Her face was covered in tears.

'How could you mum, he's such a generous loving man, don't you like him?'

'Of course I like him. I like him a lot, but I don't love him and he says he won't wait.'

'So it's his fault is it?' the girl exclaimed.

'No of course it isn't. It isn't anybody's fault but I can't commit my life to him.'

'If I was older I would have married him, I love him,' remarked Bethan.

She added 'There's not a queue of people waiting to wed you mum.'

That was a dreadful remark for her daughter to make but Amser knew she was right.

She replied 'Yes I know.'

Bethan was a mature girl for her age. Despite her own anxiety she could tell from her mum's mannerisms that turning down Russell had been a difficult decision. She looked sad and there were tears in her eyes.

Amser needed comfort and Bethan hadn't forgotten the row she and her mother had a few years before when her granddad died. She was determined not to let that happen again.

She put her arms around her mother and said 'I'm sorry mum, I shouldn't have said that. You have the right to marry who you like.'

'If only he would have waited, who knows what might have happened?' Amser replied as she cuddled Bethan even closer.

After that night Amser didn't speak to Russell again. His dirty old van was seen on the street from time to time but if their paths crossed they acknowledged one another with no more than a nod of the head.

Bethan however, always went out of her way to talk to Russell if her mother wasn't present. He'd always liked the girl and continued to take an interest in her school activities. Secretly, Bethan hoped her mother would miss going out with Russell and one day there might be reconciliation.

Chapter Twenty Six

As time went by, and with practice, Bethan became more and more proficient on the harp. She didn't miss a single lesson with Mrs Jones and at school Mrs Pugh delighted in her progression in every musical sense. She was now fifteen and had already excelled in exams beyond her years. Her command of the harp was now at such a high level Mrs Jones felt she was ready to enter a prestigious regional music competition.

However, when Amser spoke to the teacher alone, she said 'I'm not sure, I don't like the idea of my daughter performing on such a renowned stage. It's one thing to perform in a school hall in front of parents but it's quite another to play in front of strangers. I would be worried she might be overcome by the occasion.'

Mrs Jones replied 'Miss Edwards I ask you to consider what we've been working for. In all my years as a music teacher I've never known a pupil as talented as your Bethan. She has a gift from God, please don't let her waste it.'

Amser replied 'I'm concerned what failure might do to her self-esteem, you know as well as I do there will be an array of musical brilliance on display.'

Mrs Jones wasn't to be deterred and, overstepping the mark, said 'Don't you think we should ask your daughter what she wants? She's all grown up now and this is such a wonderful opportunity for her.'

She added 'I'm telling you she's special, very special indeed.'

So desperate was Mrs Jones for Bethan to take part she even offered to transport her harp to the venue for her to play.

Amser agreed subject to her daughter's approval. She knew if Mrs Jones was prepared to move her treasured harp out of her house she must be serious. To her knowledge it had sat in the teacher's parlour for over forty years.

When Bethan was told about the competition she got very excited, especially as it was to take place in St John's Abbey in Rowan. Her application was submitted by Mrs Jones but there wasn't any guarantee the girl would be selected despite her impressive credentials.

The ages of the contestants usually ranged from seventeen to nineteen. However, such was the teacher's reputation an acceptance letter was received ten days later. It came with four complimentary tickets and both Mrs Jones and Amser were given one each.

Bethan took the remaining two to school. At the end of the day she went to see Mrs Pugh. This lady had agonised over whether getting Bethan to play the harp had been the right decision for a long time. She knew about the concert from a telephone call from Mrs Jones and was delighted for Bethan.

As soon as Mrs Pugh saw the girl she said 'I've heard you're in the regional competition, congratulations.'

'That's what I've come to tell you, isn't it wonderful,' she replied.

'I'm sure you'll do very well Bethan, make sure you look after your fingers,' said Mrs Pugh.

Then the young lady got the two tickets out of her satchel.

She handed them to Mrs Pugh and said 'I would like you to be there, if it hadn't been for you I wouldn't be a harpist,' she said.

The teacher was thrilled and hugged the girl.

'Just you try stopping me,' she replied.

This kind gesture made the teacher's day; at last she felt vindicated for steering Bethan towards the harp.

On the evening of the concert Amser and Bethan decided to take a taxi to the Abbey. They'd been out shopping for new clothes and were feeling a little tired on their feet.

Mrs Jones had transported her harp to the venue using her estate car and harp trolley. It was very heavy and she needed to get a friend to help her lift the instrument into the vehicle and onto a pile of old bedsheets which she wrapped around it.

When she arrived at the venue help was needed once again and Mrs Jones called over two gentlemen who were sitting on a park bench.

She said 'I can see you've nothing to do, help me will you please.'

The men got to their feet and ambled their way to the vehicle.

'Come on, come on I haven't got all day,' she moaned.

The men hurried their step as if they were being paid to help her. One of them, a short fair-haired man in an old duffle coat, even apologised as he and his friend moved the harp out of the car and onto the trolley.

They wheeled the instrument into the Abbey with Mrs Jones following behind telling them to be careful at every turn. For once she looked very smart; she'd combed her hair and was wearing a new-looking, two-piece, pale-pink suit.

Mrs Jones spotted Bethan in the corner of her eye. The girl had arrived a few minutes before and was standing by a side entrance.

The lady called out 'Remember you're a harpist and a damn good one; enjoy your performance.'

Then the girl went to see the judges to register her attendance, leaving Amser to talk to Mrs Pugh who'd also arrived.

Mrs Pugh said 'I hope you don't mind but I've brought along my brother to see the concert as he adores classical music. He's gone to the restroom and will be back in a minute.'

Almost as soon as she'd spoken, a tall man with yellowish hair started walking towards her. Amser was looking in his direction at the time and when he came into closer view her eyes fixed upon him. He was wearing a light grey jacket with round silver buttons over a white shirt and a dark blue tie. He also wore dark blue trousers and black shoes.

The man looked very smart but there was something else about him that drew her attention. She couldn't quite place him but she did think he was vaguely familiar. The man also spotted Amser from a distance and couldn't take his eyes off her as he got nearer.

She was wearing a long satin maroon dress under a sheer white velvet jacket. They continued to stare at one another until they were no more than three yards apart.

Mrs Pugh sensed there was an attraction between them but reasoned 'Why shouldn't there be? They're two young people.'

Deciding to break the silence Mrs Pugh introduced her brother.

'This is Dickie,' she said to Amser.

Amser and Dickie were still looking straight into one another's eyes as Mrs Pugh mentioned his name.

Then she said to Dickie 'And this is Amser the lady I was telling you about whose daughter invited me to the concert.'

Dickie didn't take any notice and Mrs Pugh had to nudge his arm to get his attention.

'I'm talking to you,' she said.

Turning to look at his sister he replied 'Oh yes I'm sorry, she's going to play the harp isn't she, I'm looking forward to it.'

Then once again whilst gazing at Amser he remarked 'You must be very proud of her.'

She replied 'Right now perhaps you will forgive me if I seem a little nervous and anyway I think it's time we took our seats. The competition is due to start in ten minutes.'

The ticket numbers led them to row eight on the left side of the centre aisle. Extra seats had been added to the floor space for the concert so that as many people could be accommodated as possible.

A temporary stage had been erected three feet above the ground with steps attached, allowing access to both sides. At the front of this construction there were two large red curtains that could be closed or parted by pulling on a thick green nylon cord.

Amser sat down between Mrs Pugh and Dickie and they all had a good view of the event. On the stage many beautiful instruments could be seen, including the harp. Although they were safe with an ever-growing audience in front of them, Mrs Jones insisted on being close to her prized possession. She sat at the side of the stage out of sight.

St Johns Abbey was built in the fourteenth century and it imposed itself on Rowan. It could seat over one thousand people and was lit by twenty large golden chandeliers.

The ceiling was very high and in the middle there was a beautiful glass dome. The stone floor was littered with flat coloured grave stones and the few letters and numbers that remained confirmed the age of the building.

Outside, the abbey was surrounded by a graveyard. Four paths equal distance apart enabled access from the circular perimeter fence. As the focal point of this town both the inside and the outside of the abbey were maintained to a very high standard.

Many people gave up their time to make sure everything was neat, tidy and clean. Flowers were an important feature and the colours of the season were always in evidence.

This large building hosted many prestigious events and this evening was no exception. A visit to the abbey was special but this concert attracted entries from all over North Wales. There were to be performances on the piano, the clarinet, the cello, the violin, the trumpet, the flute and of course Bethan's harp.

The abbey was soon full and a small orchestra behind the stage began to play 'Mozart's Moonlight Sonata' by way of an introduction. This cover of music gave Dickie and Amser the chance to talk.

'Amser my darling, is it really you?' said Dickie.

He was trembling as he spoke, longing for the girl to answer.

'Yes,' said Amser.

'I can't believe it either I never thought I'd see you again.'

All sorts of questions were whispered which were masked from Mrs Pugh by the gentle sound of the piano.

Then Dickie said 'Can you ever forgive me for not turning up when we agreed to meet at the pier. I had to go back to Norfolk as my mother was taken ill. I'm sorry but there was no way I could let you know. I wanted to see you so much, I can't tell you how much.'

It was such a long time ago now and although memories of the past had faded Amser had carried the same guilt. For years after their meeting she had pictured Richard waiting for her and it had troubled her.

Amser was relieved; she sighed and said 'You've no idea how wonderful that is.'

He looked bemused. At first the girl couldn't understand why but then realised what she'd said.

'Oh I don't mean it like that. I couldn't make it either. My parents found out I'd gone to Amber Sands. They were furious and wouldn't let me go again. It was so hard because I wanted to see you as well.'

Then the music stopped and their conversation had to end.

There was stillness in the abbey in anticipation of the evening's entertainment as the red curtains were drawn closed across the stage. Amongst the audience were the parents, family and friends of all the musicians and they were all a little nervous.

Then an elderly lady arrived through a side door. She walked with a severe limp and was assisted by a man who'd been sitting motionless in a wheelchair to the left of the front row of seats. He was dressed in a dark woollen suit with a large red bow tie. The man surprised everyone by leaping to his feet and holding her arm as she climbed the three small steps on to the stage.

The lady called Christine Dunsdon was dressed in a shiny white blouse and black pleated skirt. Everybody waited for her to speak as she adjusted the height of her microphone and pushed her long black hair back behind her ears. Then without further ado she coughed as if she needed to attract people's attention and the noise from her mouth travelled around the abbey.

She started by saying 'Good evening, special guests, ladies and gentlemen, a very warm welcome to St Johns Abbey. There have been many events held in this beautiful building but the classical music contest for young people is one of my favourites. The performers you're about to see have worked hard to earn a place on this stage tonight. They've achieved remarkable standards and I know you'll be enthralled by their talent.'

She added 'The competition will be tough. It will test musical aptitude, musical ability and mental agility. At the end of the evening the performer considered to be the best by our judges will go forward to the National Finals in South Wales.'

In conclusion she said 'I would like to say good luck to all the contestants and thank them for all their hard work in reaching this stage of excellence. To you the audience, sit back and enjoy the wonderful music of the young people in North Wales.'

Enthusiastic applause rang out as the lady limped off the stage and this time she was helped down the steps by another gentleman in a dark blue suit who had been sitting in the front row. He rushed to her assistance and it soon became obvious they knew one another.

After taking her last step she pulled her arm away from his hand and remarked somewhat aggressively 'Where were you when I came in? I was so embarrassed. Do you realise I had to be assisted by a cripple?'

The man looked at her and replied 'I was in the gentlemen's toilet, you could have waited for me, I was only gone a minute.'

'I spend my life waiting for you,' she replied.

The argument continued with the man saying 'Well it's not my fault you fell out of that damn tree. You shouldn't have chased after that bloody cat. How many times did I tell you to leave it alone and now you couldn't chase a snail.'

Then in full sight of the people in the first few rows the woman responded by hitting him hard on the arm with her right hand before limping away in a huff and disappearing through the same door as she came in. The man calmed himself down and returned to his seat.

He didn't say a word but the lady next to him uttered 'She doesn't like cats then.'

'She doesn't like anything but she's my sister and you don't choose your family do you?' he replied.

Then he whispered under his breath 'More is the pity.'

Whilst this unpleasant scene was unfolding the performers were making their final preparations. All out of sight they heard every word the woman had said on her microphone.

It stirred mixed emotions in their minds, testing their confidence prior to demonstrating their ability. To add to the evening's excitement and the audience's anxiety, only the judges and the musicians knew what the running order was to be.

There was then a slight delay, making everyone involved even more nervous until the curtains were drawn apart. On the stage was a large man in a black dress suit, white shirt and sky blue bow tie. His name was Desmond Curly and he was the compere for the evening. He spoke with a very loud voice and didn't need the microphone in front of him.

His first task was to introduce the judges and he did so by inviting them to enter the arena one by one. First to be seen was

Mrs Caroline Wills, an internationally famed music teacher having worked in New York, Milan and London. This thirty six year old lady had long brown hair and was wearing a light blue two piece suit. Mrs Wills smiled at the audience before occupying the first of three chairs behind a small oblong table covered with a red cloth.

The second assessor was Mr Trevor Christian, a music critic for over twenty five years. This tall gentleman was wearing a white suit and open neck blue shirt but it was his short black hair that drew attention.

People could be heard laughing and saying things like 'Well if that's not a wig I don't know what is' and 'I bet he's as bald as a coot under that.'

He was employed by the *Daily Mercury,* the most read paper in North Wales. On hearing this unwelcome laughter he looked uncomfortable and made his way in large steps to the judges' table.

Finally Miss Georgina Smith entered the arena. She was in her early twenties but already a renowned international Welsh clarinet player and she received a very warm and enthusiastic greeting. This slim lady was wearing red shoes and a clingy red satin dress. She curtsied to the audience before taking the last vacant place at the table.

At last everything was ready and the first entry was announced. It was a nineteen year old male pianist and he was greeted with warm applause as he sat down in front of a grand piano.

He looked very smart in a black dress suit and black bow tie. For a few seconds Amser and Dickie had to stop talking as the audience waited in silence for the boy to begin.

His rendering was Grieg's Piano Concerto and the beautiful sound of his piano filled the abbey. The young man confidently exposed his talent and set a high standard for his fellow competitors.

Amser and Dickie asked more and more questions of each other. Having met so many miles away, they were intrigued as to why each other had turned up in Rowan. They'd so many stories to tell but in all the excitement their conversations flitted from one subject to another.

Dickie explained he was not called Richard these days, which disappointed Amser. This name was imprinted on her mind but in the present situation it suited her very well.

Other boys and girls entertained the audience and they all performed with such a command of their chosen instruments, it was going to be a difficult decision for the judges to make.

Bethan was the last competitor. She walked onto the stage dressed in a long dark blue flowing gown and was wearing a silver necklace. She looked very grown up and like all the other contestants received an enthusiastic applause.

Mrs Jones had already wheeled the harp into the centre of the stage and placed her bright red stool behind the instrument. Bethan was nervous and quite shaky having had to wait over two hours for her opportunity.

She smiled as people clapped and sat down in readiness to play. All of a sudden as the audience fell silent she felt unsure of herself but then spotted Mrs Jones looking at her.

The lady smiled and put her hands up to the sides of her face. She was reminding Bethan to forget the audience and the performances so far. The positioning of Mrs Jones' hands meant stay focused on what she'd been taught and that's what she did.

Bethan had chosen to perform the Welsh Lullaby 'Sou Gan'. It was one of her favourite pieces of music and she knew it would be well received in the abbey.

From the first note, the sound from every string she caressed with her fingers seemed to linger around this magnificent building. The audience was spellbound and Bethan was now oozing with confidence.

Dickie was very impressed and said 'Oh Amser she plays with a maturity beyond her years, you must be very proud of your daughter.'

Amser was overwhelmed and tears of joy ran down her cheeks. She'd longed for this moment. She'd had to cope on her own for such a long time and there had been many times when she needed Dickie.

She put her hand on his arm and then reached down a little to hold his hand and grasped his fingers. For a moment she looked away from Bethan and he could see the love in her eyes.

Then she sighed before saying 'I'm not sure this is the right time to tell you but she's your daughter too.'

For a moment Amser was fearful of Dickie's reaction. Bethan's music seemed to get louder and louder as he considered all the years they'd been apart.

Then he squeezed her hand and said 'Oh Amser, dear Amser, she's perfect. Is she really mine?'

Amser replied 'Oh Dickie my love, there's never been anyone else. It has been so hard at times but you've always been on my mind.'

Dickie found it too much to take in. Now not only had he found Amser; he had a beautiful daughter as well.

Watching Bethan's every movement he said 'I feel as though I love her already.'

Then Dickie said 'I'm sorry, so sorry I've not been with you.'

Amser looked at him and smiled 'Oh Dickie,' she whispered.

'Please don't be sorry it's not your fault. How could you have known?'

Now still holding hands, both parents sat there with their private thoughts. It was a time that Amser had never dared dream of. Now after all the years that had passed, Bethan at last had her father and Amser was comforted by him sitting beside her.

Bethan's performance drew to an end. The audience was very excited. People started applauding and rose to their feet all around the abbey. Bethan curtsied and walked off the stage but such was the applause she was asked to go back to acknowledge them once more.

On seeing Bethan again, this time there were cheers as well as clapping. Then, having grown so much in confidence, she pointed to the orchestra behind her. The musicians all stood up and there was even more applause. The conductor gave Bethan a kiss on the cheek before she walked off the stage again.

A brief interlude followed whilst the judges assessed all the performances. Coffee and tea were served at the back of the abbey and all around people were talking about Bethan. Amser and

Dickie both knew their daughter must have a good chance but they didn't dare think she might win.

Twenty minutes later the people in the audience were asked to take their seats once more. The judges were now ready and the results were handed to Mr Curly who had returned to the stage.

The top three performers were announced in ascending order and the pianist who had also been popular with the audience was placed third. Second place went to the cellist a young lady with long golden hair reaching down to the middle of her back.

It came to first place and everyone listened as Mr Curly prepared to speak again. Amser so much wanted her daughter to win but she was aware the competition was of a high quality. From the start she knew her daughter might not even be placed and in finding Dickie she'd already won one prize this evening.

Each second she and Dickie waited seemed to last that little bit longer and Amser had made up her mind it wasn't to be Bethan's night.

Then Mr Curly said 'I'm pleased to present the winning trophy to a young girl with music in her fingers and a big heart, or should I say big harp.'

The audience cheered and applauded before Bethan's name was announced. Amser was in tears and Dickie wanted to hug her as the young lady was invited back on to the stage to receive her award. It was a cheque for £250 together with a golden trophy in the shape of a treble clef.

Bethan was a popular winner and invited to play once more. At this moment a lady who'd been seated in the second row stepped onto the stage and spoke to a judge. There was a discussion between all the parties which resulted in Mr Curly talking to Bethan.

'Whatever is going on?' said Amser.

'Perhaps they want Bethan to play something different this time,' remarked Dickie.

Everybody wanted to know what was happening when they saw Bethan nod her approval. Then Mr Curly walked to the front of the stage and waited for silence.

When everyone was settled he said 'Special guests, ladies and gentlemen I'm delighted to say in our audience tonight we have Mrs Sandling who many of you will know is the leading mezzo soprano for the Welsh Grand Opera Company. She's asked Bethan if she could sing for her and the young lady has kindly agreed.'

This was a special and unexpected treat for everybody and an honour for Bethan. Mrs Sandling took off her long black coat to reveal a royal blue dress which complimented her dark blue shoes. She had short curly blonde hair and displayed a diamond necklace and matching ear rings.

Bethan started playing 'Sou Gan' again and although she was with a famous lady her nerves were gone. She'd a broad smile on her face and was enjoying herself. Mrs Sandling's voice and Bethan's harp lit up the abbey and this old building had never witnessed such an occasion. When this special performance came to an end Mrs Sandling, having taken one bow, stood back and allowed Bethan to receive her applause.

The evening drew to a close with the audience singing Hen Wlad Fy Nhadau. Then people started to make their way out of the building and the parents and friends of the young musicians waited for their children to join them.

Dickie was longing to meet his daughter. Now standing at the back of the Abbey with Amser, his eyes were fixed on the crowd of musicians who had assembled in the distance. Then a young lady started walking up the aisle towards them. He thought she was the most beautiful girl in the world.

Having been introduced, it was heart-breaking to watch Amser and Bethan embrace. The girl looked at him and smiled as one of the judges arrived to add his praise and she turned away. Mrs Jones had already congratulated Bethan and then Mrs Pugh arrived to take Dickie home.

There were many people who wanted to express their joy to Bethan. With all the attention being paid to the young lady, Dickie was able to place a small card in Amser's hand. She put it in her pocket without being seen. They wanted some time on their own but this was Bethan's night and the parents were to part with a handshake.

Chapter Twenty Seven

As she walked out of the abbey Amser's head was in a whirl. She was overjoyed with Bethan's success but ecstatic about finding her lost love. On arriving home Amser kept on kissing her daughter and congratulating her.

Bethan was calmer and although she knew she'd done very well she didn't understand why so much attention had been paid to her. Playing the harp had become as natural as riding a bike and what she'd achieved didn't seem that special.

Her mother's reactions seemed to be over the top and it wasn't until they were sitting in the lounge drinking hot chocolate that Amser relaxed. It was now 1.30am and they both went to bed.

However, once alone in her room Amser couldn't sleep. She kept thinking about the evening, her daughter's success and of course seeing Dickie. So many years had passed since she first saw him but in his company again she remembered what attracted her to him. His beautiful yellow hair, his vivid blue eyes and his softly spoken voice enchanted her once more. The card she was given contained his telephone number and she couldn't resist phoning him.

Just like for Amser, the day they spent together in Amber Sands was never far from Dickie's thoughts. He too hadn't had another relationship of any substance. He didn't know why but he didn't want to; it was as if he was waiting for Amser without realising it. People say there's no such thing as love at first sight but it seemed there was an unbreakable bond between them.

Dickie had immersed himself in his work as a structural engineer. Having qualified in Norfolk he was now a leader in his field of occupation. It was work that brought him to North Wales where he was able to stay with his sister. Now seeing Amser once again he was lying on his bed trying to convince himself it hadn't been a wonderful dream.

Dickie answered the telephone on the first ring. They chatted for ages about their lives, their heartaches, their pleasures and of course Bethan. It was exciting for them and they felt like teenagers again as they explored one another's thoughts and personalities.

They recalled their whole adventure on Amber Sands from the moment Dickie sat down beside Amser and dried her eyes to the moment they made love under the stars. They laughed about the fisherman that fell on his fish, the frosty pier attendant and they comforted each other over their anxiety at not seeing each other again. Now they wanted some time together alone and arranged to meet for dinner at a pub in the next village the following evening.

Whilst Amser was at school her head was in the clouds. She was known to be organised and efficient but on this day she was forgetful and indecisive. Children's questions were ignored and her intolerance of idle chatter was for once relaxed. All Amser could think about was Dickie; she was so excited about the evening that lay ahead.

When she got home from school Amser had a phone call from Mrs Jones. She'd a special surprise for Bethan. The young lady had been attending an after school club and when she got to her house she could see Mrs Jones's car parked on the drive.

'I wonder what she wants' thought Bethan as she opened the front door.

Mrs Jones and her mum were sitting in the lounge drinking coffee.

She greeted her teacher and then Amser said 'There's a surprise for you. Would you like to go into your bedroom?'

'What kind of surprise?' asked the girl.

'Go into your bedroom, will you please,' she replied.

Bethan ran upstairs and opened her door. She had a large room and in the middle was Mrs Jones' beautiful harp.

Bethan didn't understand 'I can't believe Mrs Jones wants to teach away from her own home' she thought.

On returning to the lounge the girl was a little reserved in her response. Mrs Jones had expected some excitement but the girl didn't know how to react.

She said 'Bethan you're the best pupil I've ever had. When

228

you play, the room is alive, the instrument becomes part of you. Remember all those things I said to you when you started having lessons?'

'Yes, Mrs Jones, I've never forgotten,' the girl replied.

'I know you haven't Bethan and that's why I want you to have the harp. I can't play so much now because of the arthritis in my fingers. I won't be teaching anymore. It's yours Bethan; you deserve it and I know you'll treasure it.'

Bethan hugged Mrs Jones.

'Now, now, you'll have me crying and that will never do,' she said.

In the evening Amser didn't tell Bethan she was going to be with Dickie. The pub was situated two miles away at the end of a single track road by the river. It was called Waters Retreat and the name could be seen in black capital letters on a board displaying two large fish. It swung in the wind from a post by the entrance to the property. The pub was very old, dating back to the 17th century. It had a slate roof, six chimneys and very small windows. The entrance was like a door to any house but the word 'welcome' in large white letters invited people in.

Dickie picked Amser up from around the corner to where she lived in his red five-seater hatchback. In the pub they were almost alone. One other customer could be seen sitting on the far side of the lounge bar and they'd a wonderful time chatting further about the past.

However, the main topic of discussion was Bethan. They agreed she must be told about her father but Bethan hadn't forgiven her mum for rejecting Russell. His name often cropped up in conversation and she missed him. They reasoned if Bethan was told the truth now she might reject him so they agreed to wait until Russell wasn't fixed in the girls mind.

Over the coming months Dickie enjoyed Amser's company more and more and they saw each other almost every day. Bethan got used to him being in the house and didn't have any reason to dislike him.

He was a kind and gentle man but this new relationship worried her. She'd been hurt before and was determined not to get close to her mother's friends again.

Not knowing who Dickie was, she was worried he might be rejected by her mum as well. With all these thoughts in her mind Bethan kept out of her father's way. Whenever he spoke to her she would reply with one word answers and never instigated any conversations with him. This behaviour upset Amser and she hoped things might improve over time.

Despite her concerns, life continued to be good for Bethan, as the harp played an even bigger part in her life. More exams were passed with Mrs Jones' continued support and grade eight status was achieved.

Sometimes however the sound of this instrument being played in the house got on Amser's nerves but she never complained. She was proud of her daughter and, with music always on Bethan's mind, Amser was able to develop her relationship with Dickie unhindered.

By now they'd been seeing each other for eight months. Their personalities gelled and they were always laughing in each other's company. It seemed so natural for them to be together and they felt like they'd known each other for a lifetime.

However, although they wanted to express their love more physically, it somehow didn't feel right for either of them until their daughter knew the truth. They agreed to keep sex on hold until their family was complete, with Bethan loving both of them.

The classical competition in Rowan had opened up another exciting opportunity for Bethan. As the winner of the regional competition she was automatically going to receive an entrance into the finals in the south of the country.

Music in Wales is very important and this competition was looked upon as one of the most prestigious events of the music world. This year it was to be held in the Farringdon University Concert Hall with the winner attaining a scholarship.

Bethan, having ignored her father for so long, now needed him. Somehow, she had to get to South Wales with her mother and take her harp with her.

'Do you think Dickie will take us?' Bethan enquired.

'I don't know,' replied Amser.

Of course Amser did know, she had already mentioned it to Dickie. He was willing to do what he could for his daughter. However, she was always reluctant to ask him for anything and whenever he tried to help her she always made an excuse. This time there wasn't any alternative. Dickie was her only hope and Amser decided she wouldn't make it easy for her.

'You'd better ask him, I'm sure he'll help you if he can,' said Amser.

'Can't you ask him for me, mum?' she pleaded.

'Look Bethan, he's always offering to help you and you always say no. I think you'd better ask him yourself, don't you?' Amser replied.

Bethan felt uncomfortable but that afternoon when Dickie came to the house for his tea she decided to make her move. Dickie had been forewarned and noticed Bethan was a little friendlier towards him than normal.

She said 'Hello' as soon as she saw him and offered a cup of tea. Amser was in the kitchen listening to the conversation.

Bethan sat down beside Dickie and said 'I need to ask you something but I expect you'll say no.'

'No then,' Dickie replied.

Bethan was upset. She got straight to her feet and called out to her mother 'There I told you didn't I?'

Then she stormed out of the room. Dickie regretted his unkind remark as soon as he said it but in view of Bethan's behaviour towards him over recent months she couldn't complain.

A few minutes later, Amser called out to Bethan who was now in her room with her head buried in a pillow.

'I've asked Dickie for you, he'd love to help. Come and say thank you, will you?'

Bethan was in no mood to be friendly. Although she'd got what she wanted, she'd now been humiliated and was summoned to come downstairs and tell Dickie how grateful she was.

It was over an hour later before Bethan surfaced from her

room. She'd wiped away the stubborn tears from her eyes and put on some makeup.

Walking into the lounge she said 'If we're going down south we'll have to stay over for two nights, what have you got planned?'

Dickie realised her comments were the closest he was going to get to an apology.

Amser was disgusted and frowned at her daughter.

He smiled and replied 'Oh, you leave it to me my girl.'

Bethan glared at him and snapped back 'I'm not your girl,' before leaving the room once more.

Amser remarked 'Oh dear things are still bad aren't they?'

Dickie was hurt but replied 'Patience my dear, all we can do is wait. Helping Bethan now is an opportunity to try and break the barriers down.'

Chapter Twenty Eight

The day before the concert they all set off on the journey with Bethan's treasured harp. Dickie struggled on his own to lift the instrument into the back of his car. Both Amser and Bethan watched as he eased it over a thick blanket into the boot. Bethan shouted at him to be careful but it was an awkward shape and he had to squeeze it into a confined space.

It was a long and tiring journey made worse by events along the way. The road south was narrow for long stretches and the traffic was slow moving. For over half an hour they had to contend with a farmer walking his sheep in front of Dickie's car.

On another quiet road they reached a 'closed' sign written in white paint. It prohibited access to their intended route. This caused them a major problem until an old lady sitting on an oak log close by approached the car. The woman looked dirty and untidy as if she'd been dragged through a hedge. Her long curly hair was matted and she'd mud over her shabby clothes and sandals.

'Problem for you is it?' she enquired looking at the sign.

The family had planned to complete their journey before it was dark.

Dickie replied 'Well it's a bit of a disaster, I don't know what to do.'

'There's another way, I can show you if you like,' said the lady.

'It's a gravel track but it will only take five minutes and will bring you back onto the road.'

Dickie wasn't keen and suggested they find another route. However Bethan and Amser were getting impatient and invited the lady into the car. She sat next to Bethan and smelt of body odour and manure.

The girl opened the windows but still had to hold a handkerchief over her mouth and nose.

The lady said 'It's only a bit of muck deary, nothing a good bath won't put right.'

Bethan looked at her and turned her head away in disgust.

Dickie was directed to reverse back a few yards and then turn left and drive up a steep hill. The road was full of pot holes and uneven surfaces. At one point the curvature of the surface tipped the car almost to a right angle on a dangerous ridge. Amser screamed when she looked out of the window to see the land dropping away beside her.

The lady said 'Don't look down deary, look straight ahead.'

Dickie went at a snail's pace until the road levelled out and the lady asked him to stop: 'I'll get out here if you don't mind' and told Dickie to continue along the track, down the hill and back onto the road.

Dickie thanked the woman but then, seeing an old caravan in the distance, realised he may have been conned.

'Do you know Amser I think we've been had. I wouldn't be surprised if she painted the sign herself. Didn't you think it was strange there weren't any other cars about and the sign did look tatty didn't it?'

Bethan started laughing and said 'You mean to tell me we've given the smelly old bag a lift.'

'It's your fault Bethan and your mother's. I was suspicious from the start.'

Amser replied 'Well you should have said something.'

Dickie looked at her aghast but knew there was no point in arguing - 'female logic' he thought.

The remainder of the journey was less arduous and they arrived at their destination as street lights were beginning to make their presence felt in the sky. Both Bethan and Amser had fallen asleep and Dickie had to wake them outside the hotel entrance.

It had been a long day and the girls were tired. A porter removed their cases from the car but, despite Bethan's concerns, the harp had to stay where it was. Being large and cumbersome Dickie didn't want to move it more than necessary. However the girl was comforted in the knowledge the hotel had a covered car park and an overnight security guard.

The party was greeted inside by Mrs Pinksmith the hotel manager. The lady lived up to her name by wearing a pink business suit and displaying pink painted finger nails. Talking with a slight stutter she asked the porter to take the cases to their rooms and offered complimentary tea and coffee.

The hotel, The Stables, looked attractive from the outside. Victorian looking lights exposed a cobbled road that wound its way up to the entrance. On either side there was a manicured lawn edged by all sorts of shrubs that came alive as the seasons unfolded.

Inside, the rooms were decorated in pastel shades brought to life during the day by the sun making its presence through the windows. The beds were soft and inviting and the en-suites boasted long deep oval baths. Amser and Bethan shared one facility and Dickie was located across the hall.

In the evening they dined together in the hotel restaurant and Amser believed this was a good opportunity for Bethan to start getting on with Dickie. However, despite her efforts to start conversations between them, the girl wouldn't look at him and didn't utter more than the odd word.

Dickie was upset and in a quiet moment when Bethan was in the wash room he remarked 'I don't think she'll ever accept me.'

Amser put her arm around him and replied 'I know Dickie it's hard but as you said to me before we have to be patient.'

When Bethan returned, further efforts were made to engage in conversation but to no avail. They were all getting tired and it was time for bed.

The following morning Amser was awoken by sunlight peeping through the bedroom curtains. Bethan stirred as her mother drew the drapes apart and buried her head under the covers. However she soon remembered why she was in a strange place. She bounced out of bed with enthusiasm for the biggest challenge of her life.

She joined her mother by the window and they both looked out over a beautiful castle and a winding river. It was ten o'clock and the sun was shining on the water. Dickie had been up for some time; he was washed, dressed and reading a newspaper on his bed.

They were too late for breakfast and went out for a stroll and a bite to eat in a local café. Conversation was still limited but the concert was getting closer by the minute and they all had butterflies in their stomachs.

It was beginning to dawn on them how important this competition was. It carried enormous credibility in the music world and the thought of participation scared them, especially Bethan.

Whilst she and her mum were making their own preparations, Dickie took the harp to the university venue. He was able to engage the services of a helpful middle-aged man who happened to be passing by. Together they removed the instrument from the car and onto the harp trolley. Then Dickie wheeled it into the university and onto the stage in readiness.

Bethan was reluctant to trust Dickie with her prized possession but, despite all her misgivings about his love for her mum, she knew he would look after it. However, with the harp in position he had to leave the university. He had to rely on people working close by on the lighting and the stage set to keep it safe.

Tickets had been issued to the performers for their families in a special allocated section close to the stage and also for friends in the middle of the concert hall. Amser had sent two invites to Rhonda.

For this special occasion Amser had bought her daughter a sparkling royal blue gown and, whilst Bethan was trying it on, she went to see Dickie. He was in his room and had been ready for the concert for some time.

Amser had never seen him looking so handsome standing in a black dress suit and matching bow tie. It wasn't long ago she'd never dared to imagine such an occasion and momentarily thought she must be dreaming.

Thinking she couldn't be happier when she returned to her room she was spellbound. On opening the door her daughter was standing by her bed facing her. Amser stood there motionless, looking at her with tears in her eyes. Her little girl had matured into a beautiful young woman.

Bethan said 'Whatever is the matter mum?'

Amser replied 'Oh, don't worry about me. It's a mother thing.'

Then Amser opened her handbag and took out a white double string of pearls.

Bethan said 'Oh my God mum they're gorgeous.'

'They belonged to your great grandmother,' said Amser.

She walked behind Bethan and fastened them around her neck.

Whilst doing this Amser said 'I want you to have them. I know she would have loved you so much and I've been waiting for the right moment to give them to you.'

Bethan turned around and kissed her on both cheeks.

'I love you mum and promise I won't let you down,' uttered the girl.

'I know you won't,' replied Amser. 'This is a very special day for both of us but I don't think I'll ever be more proud of you than I am tonight.'

Bethan looked at herself in the mirror.

'Oh mum,' she replied. 'They are so beautiful. I'll treasure them forever. Thank you, thank you.'

Needless to say there were more kisses and more tears.

Time was getting on and in all the excitement Amser hadn't even started getting herself ready. She'd purchased a new silk turquoise dress that she'd already laid out on her bed.

It complimented the colour of Bethan's gown and the girl said 'Oh mum it makes you look younger,' which Amser assumed was a compliment, and they embraced once more.

Outside the hotel it was raining and Dickie had gone to get his car. He drove his vehicle as close to the entrance as he could and waited for the girls to come out. The competition start time was getting closer and closer but the special moments mother and daughter shared together had put them behind. They needed a few extra minutes to put the final touches to their makeup before appearing in the hotel lobby.

As soon as Dickie saw them he shouted out 'Come on we will be late.'

However the ladies wouldn't be rushed despite the rain,

although Bethan covered herself with a large umbrella as she ambled towards the car. Time was now becoming a serious factor and Dickie sped along the road as fast as he could.

Bethan was frightened and asked him to slow down but in response Dickie said 'Look girl we have twenty minutes to get there. Let me drive, will you.'

Then whilst crossing some lights at amber Dickie needed all his driving skills to avoid hitting a van. It appeared in front of his car from the righthand turning and was being driven at high speed. Amser and Bethan screamed as Dickie put on the brakes and his car skidded to a halt on the wet road. The ladies breathed a sigh of relief and settled down for the remainder of the journey. It was now only a short distance to the university and with their stomachs churning all they could think about was the concert.

Dickie drove up to the covered entrance to allow Bethan and Amser to avoid the rain. They waited for him inside the main door whilst he parked his car a short distance away. Having left his umbrella with Amser, his coat was wet through and his hair was dripping when he returned.

Yet despite all he'd done for Bethan the girl laughed and remarked 'Perhaps you should have stayed in the car.'

Amser and Dickie made their way to their seats and watched as the large arena filled to capacity. People seemed to come in from all directions and the big red letters on the ends of each row made it easy for everybody to find their seats.

This venue was different to the Abbey in Rowan. It had a purpose-built stage and the musicians were already occupying a pitted area in front. Nevertheless the air of expectancy was just as apparent as families and friends discussed the competitors. The audience was noisy with so many whispers but it breathed excitement.

Meanwhile Bethan had gone back stage where the order of appearance was decided by ballot. Just as in Rowan the orchestra played some introductory music. However this was the famous 'Concord University Orchestra' and the sound of this large gathering of instruments playing the second movement of Rachmaninov's Second Piano Concerto lit up the hall.

Then the orchestra fell silent and the audience was told through a loudspeaker the competition would start in five minutes. During this time the last few people sat down and everybody waited until the first performer was announced. The order of participation was kept a secret to keep the audience in suspense.

The time crept up to 7.30pm and the curtains which had been drawn closed started to open. This prompted instant applause and whilst people were clapping Miss Tina Stevens a lady with grey wavy hair and wearing a long red dress walked onto the stage.

She waited for the din to subside as she stood in the centre behind a microphone on a tall stand. She smiled before greeting everybody and introducing the judges. Unlike in Rowan they were only announced by name and remained out of sight.

There was Miss Jayne Sommers, a celebrated American classical pianist and Egbert Bieber, a West German voice trainer. The respected assessor panel was completed by none other than Mrs Sandling, the Welsh Mezzo Soprano who had sung for Bethan.

'Do you think Mrs Sandling will help Bethan?' said Amser.

'I shouldn't think so and anyway our girl is good enough isn't she?' replied Dickie.

The lady went on to emphasise the status of the competition. She said 'The people you're about to see have excelled at regional level. They're outstanding individuals and all deserve your appreciation before they perform for you tonight.'

Applause rang out again from the audience and then without further delay she said 'The first contender for the Welsh National Prize and Musical Scholarship is harpist Miss Bethan Edwards.'

Amser and Dickie were startled to hear Bethan was to be first. They wanted to hear her perform but would also be pleased when her turn was over. However, they were mindful that sometimes it's not good to perform early on as you can easily be forgotten.

Bethan entered the arena whilst a short stocky man wheeled her harp into a central position and placed a blue stool behind it.

Bethan smiled nervously at the audience and acknowledged the large orchestra at the back of the stage with a nod of her head.

She couldn't see many faces in front of her because of the light's rays beaming down from above but she was conscious everybody in the hall could see her. It felt very warm with the heat of the lights and she felt intimidated by the surroundings.

People clapped but then the concert hall fell silent as Bethan took her seat. The stool was a little uncomfortable, she hadn't thought of taking her own and this one was a touch higher off the ground. Her seat at home was also softer but she knew it would have to do.

So this was it; the time for Bethan to demonstrate all her practising and hard work had been worthwhile. All the entrants had to perform two pieces of music, one solo and another with the orchestra.

Her first offering was Air et Variation from Handel's Concerto and was to be unaccompanied. Bethan took a deep breath and plucked her first strings. The sound of her harp filled the building and everybody was absorbed in this beautiful piece of music.

Bethan's nerves disappeared and her talent oozed out of her through the gentle touch of her fingers. The whole audience was in awe of her. When she finished Bethan stood up, looked out into the darkness in front of her and curtsied with a large grin on her face. She received much applause before seating herself once again.

This time Mr Tibbs the conductor stood up and took his applause before engaging the concentration of the orchestra with a tap of his baton. Mr Tibbs was bald-headed, had a large frame and was very animated. His dress suit seemed a trifle under-sized and he was only able to secure one button around his middle.

Bethan's second choice also from Handel's Concerto was Andante Allegro. Once more everybody was enthralled by Bethan's harp and the orchestra enhanced her performance with Mr Tibbs using the full length of his arms to conduct.

As soon as Bethan had finished she was relieved and received a marvellous reception from the audience who clapped and clapped. Bethan curtsied again and again, until she was ushered off the stage by a lady waving her arms about and beckoning her from the wings.

Now all Bethan could do was wait as other performers took their turn. Instruments to feature were to include the flute, piano, cello, violin, clarinet, horn and the trumpet. It was to be a long evening and after four artists had taken the stage there was a break, during which time people took the opportunity to stretch their legs, freshen up and enjoy a cup of tea.

There was chatter about the contestants who had performed so far but for some of the artists there was anxiety as they waited for their turn and for them it couldn't come quick enough.

The interval lasted forty minutes before the invited guests were asked to take their seats once more and the next contestant was introduced. It was violinist Miss Veronica Crisp and everyone realised she was nervous. She had to be called onto the stage a second time and entered in a bright yellow dress that was a little too long. It brushed the floor and the girl tripped over it causing her to drop her bow.

The audience provided its usual warm welcome and watched her as she sat down. The lady fidgeted in her seat; she couldn't get comfortable and dropped her bow again. Mr Tibbs became impatient and tapped his podium with his baton.

Miss Crisp was to perform her accompanied piece of music first but with all her anxiety she missed her introduction. The orchestra stopped playing and there was a silence in the audience. Everyone looked on as Miss Crisp broke down in tears.

The young lady's participation was over. She'd been intimidated by the ability of the other contestants and waiting so long had caused her distress. Miss Stevens came out to console her and led her off the stage to polite applause.

'I feel sorry for her,' said Amser.

'Yes sitting here, the pressure is enormous; I can't imagine what it's like for the artists. I'm pleased Bethan has had her turn,' Dickie replied.

The competition continued with the remaining performers

exposing their talent without any hitches and at 10.40pm the last note sounded in the hall. To the relief of everybody the competition was over and the judges had very difficult decisions to make.

They assessed choice of music, stage presence and playing ability. They also had to compare performances on such a wide range of instruments. The audience stayed seated until Miss Stevens walked onto the stage once more.

She said 'Well what a night it has been; the judges have asked me to tell you they've been amazed by the offerings of the wonderful contestants and have described them as all winners in their own right.'

Amser and Dickie waited along with the relatives and friends of the other performers for her to announce the prizes. Then for a moment Miss Stevens was silent as she opened the large red envelope she had in her possession.

There was tension, apprehension and expectation in the hall as she said 'As is customary I will announce the results in reverse order. In third place is flautist Mr Simon Bell.'

The young man came out to great applause to receive a certificate and a prize of £100 in music vouchers. He moved to the back of the stage with a big grin on his face and stood with his hands behind his back.

'In second place is harpist Miss Bethan Edwards.'

Bethan came out to both cheers and clapping and was given her certificate and vouchers of £250. She curtsied to the audience in appreciation before also moving to the back of the stage to join Simon and he kissed her on the cheek.

Then Miss Stevens smiled and said 'And the winner voted unanimously by the judges is cellist Miss Helen Reynolds.'

The young lady bounced onto the stage with such enthusiasm she nearly ran into the piano. She'd excelled and the audience had appreciated her performances.

They stood up, cheered and applauded and Amser and Dickie joined in. They were disappointed but realised their daughter couldn't always win. Miss Reynolds received her certificate, vouchers for £500 and most important was the announcement she'd won the scholarship.

She too curtsied and waved to the audience before joining the other winners. Photos were taken for the newspapers of Wales and they were also to appear in the media in England, Scotland and Ireland.

It was all over and Amser and Dickie made their way to the reception area for tea and cakes where Bethan would come and join them. A number of small round metal tables had been assembled, each surrounded by four matching chairs. The tables were covered with red rectangular cloths that drooped over the sides.

Amser spotted Rhonda standing at the far end of the hall.

'Look Dickie there's Rhon' and before he'd a chance to speak she rushed towards her friend.

Dickie hadn't seen her before except in a photo on the mantelpiece in Amser's lounge. She was dressed in a light pastel green blouse and white pencil skirt. The girls were excited to see one another and he looked on as they hugged and kissed. From the first moment they were crying, laughing and insulting one another as they always did when they were together.

Looking out of the corner of her eye Rhonda could see Dickie standing there like a lemon. Amser had told her a lot about him although for the sake of Bethan she hadn't told her they'd met before or who he was. She knew Rhonda couldn't keep a secret.

As they parted from their embrace Rhonda said 'Are you going to introduce me to your gorgeous friend then Ams?'

'This is Dickie,' she replied and he reached out to shake Rhonda's hand.

Rhonda ignored this gesture and put both arms around his neck before planting a kiss on his lips. He was a little embarrassed and felt even more uncomfortable as Rhonda took a step back and very deliberately looked him up and down.

'You're right Ams he's very sexy.'

Amser had said no such thing. She glared at her friend but then noticed something else was on her mind. Rhonda kept looking around behind where they were standing.

'Whatever is the matter Rhon, what is it?'

Very sheepishly she replied 'Oh its nothing, I'm pleased to see you and Bethan that's all. I miss you so much when we're apart.'

'Yes I know Rhon but there's something, I know you far too well; tell me what it is will you?'

Rhonda stayed silent and Amser was about to plead with her friend a little more when she heard a voice she hadn't heard for thirteen years.

Speaking in a quiet voice the words 'Amser my darling,' were uttered.

Her body shivered inside as she stood as still as a statue and the look on Rhonda's face turned from anxiety to fear.

She'd never seen so much intense emotion in Amser's face and it scared her. It was a moment Amser had always dreaded and as she pondered over what to do, further words were spoken.

'Amser, please let me see you, please let me look at you.'

Amser's mind was all over the place. She didn't want to turn around, she'd moved on. Her life was good now and, apart from her daughter's relationship with Dickie, everything was perfect.

Now her mother was once again to invade her space and Amser recalled how she looked the last time she saw her. She remembered her standing outside their home in Walwyn Gate dressed in her old clothes with untidy hair watching in tears as she and Bethan left to start their new life.

All of a sudden something inside gave Amser the desire to face her past. She turned around to see a woman dressed in an attractive turquoise suit. Her hair now turned from blonde to grey was groomed like it used to be when Amser was a child.

Rhonda seeing the two of them looking at one another was shaking wondering what she might have done but she could bear it no longer.

She said 'Ams I'm sorry but she misses you so much. When you sent me two tickets I had to bring her. Please forgive me.'

So much had happened since Amser walked out of her home in Walwyn Gate. It was the right thing to do at the time but she was only a young woman then. Now she was thirty four and her daughter was seventeen.

Amser could never forgive her mother for the neglect and heartache she suffered, even if she'd sent her a large amount of money to make her life more comfortable. However, Amser had carried a feeling of guilt for taking Bethan away and she realised this was the time for some reconciliation.

She reached out and touched her hands. Amser's mum was overwhelmed as she hadn't expected such a tender reaction. It sent a shudder through her body and lit up her eyes.

'I was going to go home straight after the concert Amser, I really was but Rhonda insisted I stay,' she said.

The feeling of her daughter holding her hands was more than she could bear as she tried to contain her emotions. She wanted Amser's arms around her. It was too much for Amser also. She too couldn't hide her feelings any longer.

Releasing her mum's hands, Amser put her arms around her shoulders and cuddled her. Then she kissed her all over her face. Rhonda was relieved as mother and daughter continued to embrace. Then they talked and talked with their arms almost glued around one another.

Nobody noticed Bethan who came out of a room at the back of the hall. She saw her mother embracing and as she got closer recognised the lady from the photograph her mother had given to her. She was very excited and moved into her eye line.

She said 'Grandma?'

'You are my grandma aren't you?' she quickly added.

'Come here,' she replied.

Bethan stepped forward.

'Let me look at you. Oh, you're so like my beautiful Amser. You have her eyes and her smile.'

The girl beamed and replied 'So do you grandma.'

Hugs and kisses followed and words of praise were uttered for Bethan's performance. Then it was time to leave as all the other patrons and guests had already departed. The tables had been cleared and packed away and a member of the university's staff wanted to lock the building. He stood by the door playing with his keys and coughing. It seemed he was in a hurry to go home.

Outside it was still raining and the street was awash with puddles. As they left the building Amser and her mother hugged once more.

Amser's mother said one last thing to her daughter.

'Promise me Amser you'll always look after Bethan. I know I made some terrible mistakes with you and I have to live with them every day.'

Amser pondered over this request. It was because of the way she'd been treated she'd never let her daughter down.

However, not wishing to open up old wounds, she replied 'Mum, Bethan means everything to me. I'll always be there for her.'

Then mother and daughter parted. They were never to see each other again but this meeting enabled both of them to draw a line under the past. They'd made their peace and it was to provide them with some comfort for the rest of their lives. Bethan also cuddled her grandma and, with her mother's blessing, said she would visit her in the summer.

Chapter Twenty Nine

Amongst all the excitement in Bethan's life she needed to find time to study as her A Level examinations were soon to be upon her. However the taste of success had provided her with a massive distraction. It had turned her head and now she didn't want to revise because she didn't think she had to. She even stopped playing her beloved harp. The girl was like most teenagers, she had an opinion about everything, liked pop music and was interested in boys.

The girl became grumpy and nothing was good enough. Her clothes didn't fit or didn't suit her. Her food was too hot or too cold. She became stressed and threatened not to take any of her exams. She wouldn't listen no matter what her mother said and even after all the celebration in South Wales she still rejected Dickie.

Mr and Mrs Peach rarely saw Bethan these days. Their only contact with the girl was a brief exchange of words in the front garden when arriving or leaving home. However, Amser had confided in Mrs Peach and told her how worried she was about her daughter.

Mrs Peach tried to re-assure her by saying 'She's a good girl, I'm sure everything will be alright.'

Amser replied 'The trouble is as soon as I open my mouth I get shouted at, I can't get close to her like I used to. I'm worried she's going to throw everything away.'

Mr Peach was also upset. He was very fond of the girl whom he'd come to love as much as any granddaughter he might have had. It was really none of his business but he decided to try and help. One afternoon, unknown to both Amser and Mrs Peach who were not expected home he made sure he was outside the front of his house when Bethan arrived back from school.

He realised if he didn't approach the matter with care Bethan would reject him in the same way she'd been rejecting her mother.

On seeing her he said 'Hello Bethan I've a problem, would you mind helping me please?'

She replied 'What is it Mr Peach, how can I help you?'

By this time he'd opened the front door and said 'Would you like to come in?'

Bethan didn't want to. She was in no frame of mind to help anyone. However, Bethan was very fond of the old man. She hadn't forgotten all the wonderful times they had spent together and made her way into the house.

'Tea and fruit cake for you Bethan?' said Mr Peach.

The girl was about to say no thank you when she spotted the refreshment laid out on the kitchen table. Looking around she could see the room was tidier than usual. Bethan was hungry after a day at school but usually waited for her dinner.

However the sight and smell of Mrs Peach's homemade cake was too inviting and she replied 'That would be lovely thank you.'

Having poured out tea and cut large slices of cake Mr Peach started reminiscing about the things he and Bethan used to do together. They chatted about the kite flying and Mr Peach's drawings. The old man wanted to know all about the harp and the last concert in South Wales.

An hour soon passed and Bethan was getting more and more intrigued about what Mr Peach wanted.

'You said you needed my help Mr Peach, what can I do for you?'

Mr Peach said 'Yes Bethan, there's something that's troubling me and I can't get it off my mind. I find I'm unable to sleep for worrying about it.'

'Whatever is it Mr Peach. Please tell me will you.'

He replied 'Well there's someone I know and love very much who's in danger of throwing their life away before it's even started.'

Bethan knew who he was talking about and got to her feet to leave.

She replied 'Oh Mr Peach, I suppose my mum asked you to talk to me, she'd no right, I have to go.'

Whilst making her way down the hall towards the front door

the old man said 'No she didn't but she's worried about you and was in tears the other day talking to Peachy.'

Bethan stopped and turned around. 'It's not my fault if my mum cries her eyes out,' she snapped.

'No, what in this world could possibly be your fault, you're a seventeen year old girl, I'm sure you're perfect,' he replied.

The old man had promised himself he wouldn't get annoyed but he cared about Bethan and she'd wound him up.

Speaking in a raised voice he added 'Look Bethan, you're such a lucky girl. You've everything you want and don't have to worry about a thing. It can't have been easy bringing you up on her own but I bet she's always put you first. I've no doubt you owe her a debt you could never repay although of course she would never expect you to.'

Bethan was standing still with her hands on her hips listening with her head bowed as Mr Peach added 'I'm a little disappointed in you. You think you're all grown up and can do what you like but with being a grown-up comes responsibility. Think how sad your grandma would be if she found out how you're behaving at the moment.'

Bethan didn't respond. Very rudely she turned her back on the man and walked out of the house. She made her way next door before running upstairs and into her room. She collapsed on her bed feeling agitated and annoyed.

Whilst lying on her back she spent time self-analysing her behaviour and didn't like what she found. The harsh words uttered by Mr Peach had brought her to her senses. When Amser came home that evening dreading another unsavoury confrontation with her daughter she was greeted on the door step with a hug and a kiss.

Her daughter said 'I've made some tea mum and will go and get the biscuit tin.'

Amser was stunned and speechless as Bethan removed her coat. Then she sat down in the lounge whilst her daughter waited on her. For the first time in a while life returned to normal.

When Amser tried to question her daughter's motives all

Bethan would say was 'It's alright mum, I promise everything is alright. I can't talk now anyway, I've some studying to do' and with a smile and a giggle she went to her room once more.

Amser was relieved although she never found out what happened. She cried as mums do in the knowledge that Bethan was contented once more and focused on her future.

Chapter Thirty

On the sixteenth of March it was Bethan's eighteenth birthday and Amser and Dickie wanted to give her something special. When the young lady came home from school she was already armed with an array of presents, cards and balloons.

'Goodness me, how did you manage to carry them all?' her mother asked.

'I didn't, I kept dropping them on the pavement,' replied Bethan as she giggled.

On closer examination Amser could see there were gifts of perfume, chocolates and various items of clothing. Bethan was very happy and looking forward to going out for a meal with her mum and some school friends that evening.

However she didn't know what else her parents had in store for her. A few days before, whilst Bethan was out, her mum had made the arrangements and no sooner had she changed out of her school clothes than there was a knock on the door.

'You'd better answer that Bethan,' called out her mum from the kitchen.

She skipped down the stairs and opened the door.

Standing on the welcome mat was a very large man with only a few strands of hair and an open neck blue shirt and black jeans.

'Bethan Edwards is it?' the man enquired.

'Yes,' replied Bethan thinking to herself 'what does he want with me?'

'I'll wait for you in the car,' he said.

Then he turned around and walked out of the front garden.

Bethan was shocked until her mum called out 'It's your first driving lesson, happy birthday darling.'

The girl was overwhelmed. So much attention had been paid to her already that day she didn't know what to say and went to hug her mum.

Amser gently pushed her away and said 'Oh go on will you, the man's waiting, you can thank me later.'

Once again Dickie had to disguise his feelings. His daughter's birthday present was from him and Amser but he could only watch as she embraced her mother that evening. It was very hard for him. He felt empty and helpless and was now getting upset on almost a daily basis.

It's a terrible thing to have a daughter and not know about it, but to have a child who doesn't know you are her father is heart breaking. To add to his misery Bethan continued to be cold towards him. Dickie was now desperate for her to know the truth. He couldn't sleep and was finding it difficult to focus on anything other than his daughter.

Amser and Dickie decided the burden of deceit was too much to bear any longer. They were intent on telling Bethan the truth and the following evening they went out to discuss it in a pub called The Lamb Stew in a nearby village.

The pub had a long dining room furnished with square oak tables and matching chairs. The couple were able to sit at the far end away from the ears and eyes of the other customers.

Amser was concerned about her daughter's likely reaction.

'Bethan should be pleased,' said Dickie.

'Yes I know but do you think she will be?' asked Amser.

'Forgive me Dickie but I know my own daughter. She'll feel betrayed and ask all sorts of questions. Most of all she'll want to know why we've waited so long to tell her.'

She said 'I know we have answers, but now all of a sudden they don't seem to be enough.'

Dickie tried hard to re-assure Amser. He could see how worried she was from her facial expressions and it was true he really didn't know her.

Gone was the warm smile he was used to seeing on her face and there was a look of fear in her eyes. She was also unusually quiet and when Dickie took hold of her hands he could feel they were sweaty and shaking. He was afraid she would try and persuade him to delay the revelation a little longer.

'Amser I can't imagine how hard this is for you but you know there'll never be a good time to tell her,' he said.

Dickie did feel guilty. He'd been pestering her for months and it seemed she'd given in to please him. However, although it was selfish he stuck to his guns.

Looking at Amser with his arms on her shoulders he said 'Look my love the deceit has gone on for long enough. You said yourself: Bethan will want to know why we hadn't told her before. Don't let's make it any worse. It's important we do it tonight and do it together.'

Amser found it hard to say the words and focusing her eyes on his, she nodded her agreement. For the next hour they prepared themselves for talking to Bethan and reached agreement on what would be said and by whom.

It was now ten o'clock and they made their way out of the pub. The journey back to Rowan was a little over five miles through a few country lanes and was to take no more than eight minutes.

During the evening rain had been falling and the roads were full of puddles and slippery with mud from farmers' tractors. The moon was hidden by heavy clouds and the night sky seemed even darker than usual.

Dickie took extra care to manoeuvre his vehicle down the winding roads as the rain increased in density. The journey was unpleasant and to make matters worse a strong gusting wind was rushing through the trees, causing the taller varieties to creak and sway.

As Dickie turned around a tight bend, a lone red deer appeared in front of the car. It had jumped from an adjacent field and seemed startled to see a car in its path. It stood motionless and Amser was scared half to death seeing the animal's eyes looking at her.

She put her hands over her face and screamed. Dickie, with only a split second to react, kept his calm. He swerved to the right and managed to avoid it. This was a quiet road but at this moment a car appeared from the opposite direction. It was travelling at high speed and got close to Dickie and Amser in the blink of an eye.

Dickie had to swerve again back towards the other side of the road. However, this time he wasn't so lucky and lost control on the muddy surface. On applying the brake the car skidded and there was an almighty smash.

The vehicle hit a tree and a large heavy branch fell from above crushing its top. Both the roof and the front of the car on the side where Amser was sitting caved in whilst the windscreen shattered into hundreds of tiny pieces leaving glass all over her.

Dickie had somehow avoided serious injury. He checked his body and found he only seemed to have cuts and bruises. The car had managed to snuggle itself into the forest undergrowth but Dickie, pushing with all his might, managed to open his door.

Amser, however, was unconscious; her head was wedged between her seat and the collapsed roof and her legs were trapped by the impact of the car with the tree. She was covered in blood but it was impossible for Dickie to see the full extent of her injuries.

The people in the speeding car didn't stop to help. They were gone in a flash and may not have realised what had happened. Dickie was in a panic. He knew how vital it was to get help but Amser was hardly breathing and he didn't want to leave her.

Getting out of the vehicle and looking all around he noticed a light in the gloom of the evening mist.

'It must be a farmhouse,' he thought.

'Amser I'm going to get help,' he said, not knowing if she could hear him.

It was a desperate situation and then for no apparent reason Dickie found himself looking into the sky. He wasn't a religious man, having given up believing in all 'that stuff' - as he used to call it - a long time ago. It was the sufferings that decent people had to endure, and things like the injuries to Amser on this night, that reinforced his view that there wasn't a God.

However, now faced with such an almighty challenge he found the need to pray. The faith he didn't think he had was being tested. Dickie knelt down on the sodden ground next to Amser's car door.

With his hand on the vehicle as close as he could get to his sweetheart and with tears running down his cheeks he pleaded 'Please God, I know I don't talk to you very often but I need your help. You know I've never asked you for anything before. I'm sorry but my dear Amser is very ill, please look after her. I need her so much and we have had so little time together. Please God, I'll do anything, anything at all, please help her.'

Dickie got to his feet and re-assured Amser he would get help. Then as he was about to run across the field towards the farmhouse a vehicle could be seen approaching from a distance. Two large bright lights at the front exposed the surface of the road and Dickie started waving for fear it would turn off at the junction beyond.

To his relief the vehicle kept coming and when Dickie saw it was an ambulance he couldn't believe it and stood in the road until it stopped inches in front of him.

One of paramedics said 'You're very lucky mate we were returning to the station on the top road but a tree has just fallen up there. We saw it come down in the distance so we've come this way.'

Dickie didn't feel lucky but he looked up to the sky again.

'Had his prayers been answered?' he thought.

It could never be proved, but it did make him wonder if there was a God after all.

The man asked questions about the accident as the other paramedic examined Amser. It soon became clear her condition was critical and she needed to be taken to hospital. However, as she was trapped by collapsed metal the fire brigade had to be called to cut her out of the car and as they waited the paramedics were getting more anxious about Amser's condition.

Time seemed to pass slowly until the red emergency vehicle could be seen flashing its light as it approached. Meanwhile Dickie comforted his beloved Amser as best he could by holding her hand and talking to her about the future.

Not having any idea if she could hear him he said 'They'll soon have you out of here. You'll soon be better and then we can take a holiday; we can go anywhere you like.'

It's very difficult to keep talking to someone when they can't speak and to see Amser with her eyes closed and looking so ill was almost too much for Dickie to bear. A paramedic had managed to fit an oxygen mask over her face to make her as comfortable as possible. All they could do was wait as Dickie continued to try and be positive and re-assure Amser everything was going to be alright.

When the fire brigade arrived one of the men assessed the situation and said removing the jagged metal would require a very delicate operation.

The waiting was getting all too much for Dickie.

He was a gentle man and rarely raised his voice but he was scared and called out 'Can't you hurry up,' as he walked up and down and around his car.

The firemen had been doing the best they could and it was wrong for Dickie to snap at them. However, they understood his worry and were used to this kind of outburst. Then a moment or two later Amser was released and lifted out of the car.

Whilst being trapped part of the car's exterior had rammed into her upper and lower body and the ambulance crew were worried about her condition. They were most concerned about her head injuries and her breathing.

From the time of the crash it took over two hours for Amser to reach hospital. Greenford General was over eighteen miles away and the journey seemed to take forever. With Amser's current state of health the vehicle had to be driven slowly over the bumpy country roads.

Dickie sat in the back and continued to comfort her although she was barely conscious. In all his anxiety he'd forgotten about Bethan until he remembered what he and Amser were going to tell her that evening. It was fortunate the ambulance driver was able to radio the hospital so that a telephone call could be made to their daughter.

The hospital staff were waiting for the arrival of the ambulance. As soon as it pulled up outside the entrance they opened the rear doors and assisted in the careful transportation of Amser onto a trolley before wheeling her inside.

Dickie followed and waited outside a closed door for some news. Whilst he was sitting on a long wooden bench Bethan arrived on the scene. Dickie saw her approach at some speed from the end of the corridor.

As soon as she could see him she started waving her arms and shouted out 'What have you done to my mum? Tell me will you, what have you done to her?'

Dickie looked at her, knowing how much she loved Amser.

He thought 'What can I say that will comfort her; what is there to say to a girl so stricken with grief and hate?'

Dickie ignored Bethan's questions but when she got closer to him he said 'She's very sick, they're doing all they can for her.'

The daughter was uncontrollable and started punching Dickie. Then on hearing the commotion a nurse came out of the treatment room. She was a small lady in her late twenties standing no more than five feet tall and was dressed in a smart blue uniform. Her badge said she was Staff Nurse Glenda Collins.

Bethan confronted the lady and exclaimed in a loud voice 'I want to see my mum I want to see her now.'

Not even waiting for a response she tried to enter the room and the nurse had to use all the weight in her arms to restrain the girl. Quite a struggle followed until Bethan stopped her aggression and sobbed in the nurse's arms.

'We're doing all we can for your mum. She's in good hands so please let us do our job,' pleaded the nurse.

Dickie looked on and sighed; how much he wanted to comfort Bethan. She needed his love more than ever and he was desperate for the love of his daughter.

Sitting on each side of the corridor they both waited in silence for some news. Dickie for the most part sat still, holding his head in his hands. Bethan's body however was on the move. The girl was fidgeting with her clothes, crossing and uncrossing her legs and playing with her fingers.

After a while the door of the treatment room opened and a tall male doctor with a long neck and thick wrists came out and introduced himself. He was a consultant called Doctor Ward.

He said 'I'm very worried about Miss Edwards; she's taken the brunt in an awful accident. The good news is she doesn't appear to have any broken bones but her body has taken a battering. Her breathing has been impaired by the pressure on her lungs and I'm sorry to say she's in a coma.'

'How long will she be in a coma for?' asked Bethan.

'We don't know, the condition is very unpredictable,' replied the doctor.

'It could be days, weeks, months or even more. We'll keep feeding her through drips and keep her body as healthy as we can.'

It was all too much for them to take in. It didn't seem possible such a terrible thing could have happened.

'Can I see her please?' said Bethan.

'Of course you can but I must warn you her body is attached to all sorts of equipment. Please try not to be put off by the drips and tubes, they're all helping her,' the doctor replied.

As Bethan entered she made it clear to the nursing staff and doctor she didn't want Dickie in the room with her. He was very upset but he was also exhausted and as much as he wanted to be by Amser's side, he didn't want to make things worse. He didn't argue and sat down again outside the room.

Bethan's first sight of her mother made her cry again. Most of the blood had been wiped from her head but she looked very ill. Nurse Glenda made it clear her mum would be monitored twenty four hours a day.

She said 'I promise you everything possible will be done to help make her better.'

She added 'Get close to her Bethan, as close as you can. You can talk to her as often as you like. We don't know if she can hear you but you never know. Hold her hand, stroke her face, she's your mum and she needs you now more than she's ever done.'

The nurse was used to seeing serious injuries but even she couldn't contain herself and had to move away to release her tears.

Bethan spent every moment she could at the hospital beside her mum and Dickie was either outside in the corridor or sleeping in the relative's room. Doctors examined Amser at regular intervals and there seemed to be no end to the different faces visiting her bedside.

Dickie and his daughter had been holding on to a glimmer of hope that things might improve. Bethan watched for the tiniest of movement and questioned the staff every time they assessed her condition. Father and daughter were exhausted and desperate for some news.

One day following his ward round Doctor Ward asked them both to join him in a private room adjacent to where Amser was being cared for. He invited them to sit down on some soft chairs and they feared the worst. All sorts of dreadful thoughts ran through Dickie's and Bethan's minds as the doctor prepared to speak.

Looking at Bethan he said 'You're aware how we've been nursing your mother. Her condition is stable but I've some sad news. I have to tell you our recent tests have confirmed your mum is paralysed from the waist down; I'm so sorry.'

Bethan and Dickie shed some heavy tears but this awful news was almost a relief. As hard as this disability would be for them to handle they felt they could cope with it.

Very naively they imagined this lack of mobility would be the extent of the long-term effects from the car crash. Dr Ward, judging their reaction, realised he needed to temper their expectations.

He added 'Now we must continue to be patient; we'll carry on looking after Amser but I have to tell you we still don't know how things will be if or when she comes out of her coma.'

Bethan's and Dickie's moment of satisfaction evaporated. Still not speaking to one another they resumed their dutiful positions and continued their wait, expecting to live their lives in this way for weeks to come. However, just twenty three days later Bethan saw Amser open her eyes.

She was excited and called out 'Nurse Glenda my mum's awake, look come and see.'

Nurse Glenda came straight over and on seeing Amser with her eyes open called for Doctor Ward. In less than ten minutes he arrived and Bethan was asked to move away from the bed whilst her mum was examined.

Several minutes passed as Bethan waited for the doctor's diagnosis. When he finished there wasn't a smile on his face. Bethan started to shake in the realisation she was to receive yet more bad news.

The girl was asked to sit down before the doctor said 'I'm pleased to say your mum will make a partial recovery. She's come out of her coma which is obviously a very good thing. However, you already know she's paralysed and has breathing difficulties. Now I have to tell you that your mum is blind.'

Bethan sobbed; since the accident her mum had been fighting so hard. It seemed unfair but now she'd lost the use of her legs and her eyes. The girl wanted her old mum back but she knew things would never be the same again.

Then whilst moving back towards the bed she saw the tiny movement in her mum's arms and she was trying to say something. It was very difficult for her to speak but with a great deal of effort she was able to whisper the name Dickie.

It became clear she wanted to see him. Bethan was amazed.

'Why did she want to see Dickie, perhaps she hadn't remembered what had happened, or the accident had changed her mind set?' she thought.

Bethan pretended she hadn't heard her mother But Amser mumbled his name over and over again and the girl knew she had to invite him in. With Bethan's reluctant blessing the nurse went outside to fetch Dickie and told him the news.

The girl had always remained positive but Dickie had feared the worst for some time. His heart was in bits but he was all cried out. As he entered the room he could see the hate in his daughter's eyes fixed upon him. She stayed silent and watched as he knelt down beside Amser's bed.

To Bethan's amazement her mum's face beamed when he took hold of her hand. He lent forward, kissed her on the cheek and cuddled her gently.

'I'm here now Amser,' he said.

Bethan could see the overwhelming joy Dickie's presence brought to her mother. No longer could she deny the love and affection they had for one another and for the sake of her mum she was prepared to share her with him.

Now they were both at Amser's bedside. At least they could take it in turns to stretch their legs, eat some food or get some sleep. Dickie felt they were at last a family, albeit in the most awful circumstances.

During this time Amser did get a little stronger. One by one the tubes were removed from her body until she was able to feed herself unaided. Her breathing and speech improved with each passing day until with some effort she could hold light conversation. However she quickly got tired and still required lots of rest.

With the help of a lady called Mrs Matilda Jennings she was able to start doing some exercises. This person had a large body frame and was quite elderly but she was a trained physiotherapist. She got Amser to move her arms and fingers. It was a very slow process but improvement could be seen after each session.

Amser hadn't been allowed any visitors apart from Dickie and Bethan until she came out of her coma. One afternoon Rhonda arrived and Dickie and Bethan saw her come into the room. She gestured with her hand over her lips for them to remain silent.

Amser could sense another person's presence and without any introduction Rhonda said 'Well honestly, what some people will do to get a room for the night.'

Coming from anyone else this would have been an awful thing to say but Amser laughed out loud. It was the first time she'd expressed this emotion since before the accident. She knew it was her best friend and opened her arms for a hug.

Rhonda rushed to get close to her and put her arms around Amser's body. She planted kisses on both her cheeks and Amser's face glowed with delight.

Rhonda suggested to Dickie and Bethan they take a well-earned rest.

'I can look after her for a while, please let me give her the Rhonda treatment.'

Having been left on their own the two ladies were soon chatting as if things were the same as they'd always been.

'Do you ever get out of this bed?' enquired Rhonda.

'You know I can't walk don't you,' replied Amser.

'Yes, Bethan told me but are you not able to get out of this bed at all?'

'I don't know, can I?' Amser replied.

'Well we'd better find out, I'm going to talk to the nurse,' she said and momentarily left the room.

Rhonda was never content: having only been in the hospital for a short while she was already intent on challenging Amser's daily routine.

Rhonda returned with Nurse Glenda and a wheelchair.

Amser heard the sound of tyres as it was pushed into her room and said 'Is that what I think it is?'

Nurse Glenda replied 'It's a beautiful day and your friend wants to take you outside. I don't think a ride in the sun is going to do you any harm.'

Turning to Rhonda she said 'Please stay in the hospital grounds will you and don't stay out longer than an hour.'

Nurse Glenda and Rhonda helped Amser into the chair and tucked her up in two warm blankets. Amser was excited but without her sight she realised for the first time how reliant she was going to be on others.

Rhonda pushed her out into the corridor and a passing doctor opened some double doors leading out into the hospital garden. It was warm and sunny but a rain shower earlier had ignited the aroma in the grass and the leaves on the trees. Amser had almost forgotten such wonders of nature having had to endure the clinical odours that filled her room inside.

Rhonda pushed her friend around the grounds until they reached the entrance gate. Across the road was a ladies hairdresser shop named Cutting Dreams. Rhonda hadn't planned this but she couldn't help noticing how long and untidy her friend's hair was.

The girls had already been out half an hour but without saying a word she pushed Amser over the road and towards the shop. It was 1pm on Saturday and a lady was locking the door.

'Are you closing?' Rhonda called out.

'Half day Saturday,' the lady replied.

Amser didn't know what was going on and enquired 'Where are we Rhon and what are you doing?'

'I was going to get your hair cut but it seems we are too late Amser.'

The lady was about to walk away from the shop.

She deliberated for a moment before turning around and asking 'Did you say Amser? It wouldn't be Amser Edwards would it?'

'Yes I'm Amser,' she replied.

Without further hesitation the lady re-opened her shop and invited Amser and Rhonda inside. She was upset seeing Amser severely incapacitated and small tears filled her eyes.

Rhonda didn't understand and remarked 'I thought you were closing.'

The lady introduced herself. Her name was Gladys Jewell and her grandson had been taught by Amser.

The lady had beautiful curly auburn hair and her nails were manicured to perfection and coloured brown. She wore a white cotton dress over a heavy body frame and stood about five feet three inches tall.

She replied 'I can't tell you how much your friend has done for my grandson, my shop will always be open for Amser Edwards.'

Amser reached out to hold Mrs Jewell's hand.

She said 'I remember, it was Martyn wasn't it, but I stopped him going on holiday. I seem to recall he'd been taking vegetables from an allotment.'

Mrs Jewell replied 'Yes and I was very upset at the time. Me and my husband could never have afforded such a holiday and we were worried how it might affect him. He'd always been a bit of a tearaway but to our amazement seeing other children get their prize made him realise reward comes from honest effort.'

She added 'He went back to the allotment as often as he could. The two men he stole from taught him everything they knew about vegetable gardening. I know they wouldn't have helped him at all if it hadn't been for your community project.'

Amser remarked 'You're too kind Mrs Jewell,' but the lady would have none of it.

'No, it's true and when Martyn left school he got himself a job at the Rowan Garden Centre. We are so proud of him,' she said.

Rhonda for once was speechless. She'd no idea what her friend had been up to and listened to every word.

'What do you think then Miss Edwards, a cut and blow dry for you is it?' asked Mrs Jewell.

'I think we've got to get back, it's getting late,' remarked Amser.

It was now almost an hour since Amser left her hospital room but Rhonda being Rhonda wasn't worried. Time was something she was never concerned about.

She shrugged her shoulders and said 'It will be alright Ams, you want to look nice for Dickie don't you?'

Carefully Mrs Jewell attended to her special customer whilst she stayed in her chair. Rhonda supported her friend's head when her hair was being washed and it was such a wonderful feeling for her to have water running through every strand. When it was done she looked like the old Amser and felt so much better.

She thanked Mrs Jewell before being wheeled out of the shop but the lady, still harping on about her grandson, was insistent it was her that should be thanking Amser. She offered free hair dressing and free manicuring whenever it was needed.

As Rhonda pushed the chair back across the road she asked her friend all about the school project but all Amser would say was 'It was something we did for the kids, that's all.'

On arriving back in the hospital they were greeted by Bethan and Dickie as soon as they entered her room. On seeing them pass her desk they were followed in by Nurse Glenda who had a stern look on her face.

'I think I said an hour didn't I? I wouldn't have let you take Amser out if I'd known you would ignore my instruction.'

Bethan too was angry, believing the exertion would have an adverse effect on her mum.

Knowing Rhonda's reputation from her mother she said 'Don't you ever do what you're told?'

Agitating Bethan further Rhonda replied 'No not really.'

Looking on, Dickie was the first to notice Amser's hair. Bethan and Nurse Glenda wouldn't stop moaning and after listening to them for a while he lost his patience.

'Will you both shut up for a moment,' he shouted.

'Look at Amser will you, she looks beautiful.'

Getting close to the bed he kissed her on the cheek and said 'I wish you could see yourself in a mirror darling.'

Then he turned to his daughter and the nurse and said 'Do you really think the outing did her any harm? I haven't seen her so happy for ages and look at her hair.'

The nurse was annoyed because her instruction had been ignored but she had to admit Amser hadn't come to any harm. Bethan too knew she'd over-reacted. They were both pleased Amser had a smile on her face and being pampered seemed to have done her the world of good.

After eight more weeks the doctors decided Amser was well enough to go home. This was exciting news but Bethan was concerned. She was going to require a great deal of nursing and didn't want Dickie in close attendance. However Dickie knew how much she wanted to go home. He welcomed the news and no matter how Bethan felt he was determined to look after her.

Bethan wasn't only concerned about her mother, she was also jealous of Dickie. It seemed Amser wanted Dickie close to her all the time and the bond between them that was getting ever stronger troubled Bethan.

Out of her mother's earshot she said 'Just because you feel guilty it doesn't mean you can play nursemaid all the time. I can never forgive you for the car crash and neither will my mum when she comes to her senses.'

Dickie replied 'Bethan I know you'll never believe me but it was an accident, a terrible accident. I re-live it every day and it will haunt me till I die but we were in the wrong place at the wrong time.'

Bethan had heard it all before and shrugged her shoulders. She remembered him driving on the way to South Wales for her concert appearance when he nearly hit a van. She was convinced he was driving too fast and nothing he said was going to change her mind.

'How will you be able to look after her anyway and what will you do about your work?' she enquired.

'I've already left my job in Elwy and nothing is more important than your mum. She has invited me to move into the house where I can be close to her all the time,' he replied.

Chapter Thirty One

B efore Amser's arrival at home Dickie brought her bed downstairs. It was placed in the dining room facing towards the back garden. She was wheeled from the ambulance up to her front door.

Dickie watched as Amser was about to be raised over the entrance step and said 'Wait, stop will you. I'll carry her' and with Amser's face beaming he lifted her into his arms and took her inside.

She no longer had her sight but Dickie had furnished her room with all the things she loved around her. Over the years she'd collected small soft toys and they'd all been placed on a shelf he'd erected on the left side of her bed. Also her light blue curtains had been hung at the window but most important of all was a wind chime that hung from the ceiling and tinkled with the slightest breeze.

Before the accident Amser often lay on her bed with her eyes closed and listened to the small pieces of metal caressing one another. She imagined they were playing all sorts of tunes and it was her way of relaxing when she had time to herself.

Dickie could see how weak his sweetheart was as she lay on the bed. The short journey by road and even being carried into the house had made her a little more breathless. She was very tired and soon fell into a deep sleep.

Iola and Mr and Mrs Peach were saddened to see Amser. Mrs Peach stood motionless on her first visit. It seemed inconceivable that a few months ago they were shopping together on a Saturday morning.

Mr Peach too was vexed. For once he didn't feel like laughing. He wanted to stay strong but, turning to Bethan, he broke down and cried in her arms.

Amser said to him 'Please don't cry, there are many people worse off. I have my daughter, I have Dickie, I have my friends and I have my wonderful neighbours. Despite everything I'm truly blessed.'

However, her neighbours didn't know Dickie was Bethan's father and they were concerned by the girl's animosity towards him.

Bethan became more and more agitated with Dickie because it was difficult for her to have a moment alone with her mum. His presence was overwhelming and it seemed she was being brushed aside. Dickie provided the eyes Amser didn't have and the love between them grew even stronger as he catered for her every need.

Every morning she was taken a cup of tea with a rose in a single vase. Amser was aware of its presence on her tray. She could smell the scent and always picked it up and held it to her nose. She would try and guess the colour and Dickie would often tease her by saying no every time as she went through all the possible options. It was a silly little thing but it made Amser laugh and that was all that mattered.

They chatted for ages each day about the news in the papers and the things going on in Rowan. The curtains were drawn apart as soon as it was light and when it was warm enough the window was opened.

Even though Amser couldn't see, she could hear the birds singing, the breeze racing through the trees and her wind chime that went into overdrive. She could also smell the scent from the flowers and Dickie would describe them in great detail when they came into bloom.

Mrs Jewell's grandson Martyn wasn't the only child who was helped by Amser. Her community project made such a difference to local people's lives and had been adopted by many schools. It was now known as the 'Edwards Foundation Project'.

When people became aware of what had happened to Amser the response was overwhelming. She received hundreds of cards and so many flowers she had to give most of them away.

Amser had many visitors but perhaps the greatest tribute was from the children of Selwyn College. For the school it was payback time. Children she'd taught in the past offered to do any jobs they could to help her.

Although Dickie was always around he realised how important it was to them. They got her shopping, cleaned the windows, weeded the garden, read her stories and talked about their life in the school. These visits gave Amser a lift but despite all this attention, she was reluctant to talk to Dickie about the project other than to say it was local kindness.

One morning there was a knock on the door and a slim young woman with long wavy jet black hair was invited in. Amser was sitting up in bed with her head leaning against some pillows. She was listening to some music when the person entered.

'You've a visitor Amser,' said Dickie.

The lady was upset to see Amser both blind and paralysed. However she'd been forewarned and was determined not to cry. Amser had been her teacher.

'Hello Miss Edwards. I don't suppose you remember me? My name is Holly, Holly Grande.'

Amser just smiled and nodded.

'You do remember me,' said the young lady with excitement in her voice.

Amser nodded again and reached out her hand for Holly to hold.

Then leaning forward towards the girl she whispered 'Cakes.'

Holly said 'Dear Miss Edwards I'll never forget the day you told us about the holiday. I started making cakes with my mum for the nursing home. I wanted that holiday so much I think I would have done anything.'

She went on 'You can't have any idea how much it meant to me.'

Amser of course did know from her childhood memories and smiled as Holly went on 'I've come to thank you, oh but not for the holiday.'

'Whatever is it then?' enquired Amser.

Holly laughed and said 'Well I'm still making cakes.'

'What for the nursing home?' enquired Amser.

The lady giggled and replied 'Well, yes but no if that makes sense. I make them for everybody now. I have my own shop in

Elwy called Holly's. I still make cakes for the nursing home and, if you don't mind, I would like to bring you a cake every week.'

Amser smiled and said 'You won't get another holiday.'

Holly giggled and replied 'No I don't suppose I will but I've never forgotten what you did for me.'

Holly brought a cake with her which Dickie cut up outside in the kitchen. He came into the room with three large slices on a plate.

Then Amser enquired 'How's Kitty?'

'Oh yes I'm glad you mentioned her. My mum is fine and she works for me now.'

Then putting her hand in her bag she said 'I nearly forgot, she gave me something for you.'

Holly took out an envelope and placed it in Amser's hand. Inside was a card and she could feel something else.

'Is that what I think it is? Is it a five pound note?' enquired Amser.

Holly said 'Yes but my mum wouldn't tell me why she wanted you to have it. I was asked to say thank you and God bless you.'

'I don't suppose you would care to tell me what the money is for,' said Holly.

Amser smiled and all she would say was 'Please give your mum a hug for me will you.'

When Holly had left the house Dickie brought the cake box into Amser's room.

He said 'My darling I purposely didn't tell you whilst the young lady was here but I think you should know what is written on the box.'

'What is it then, *love Holly* I suppose,' she replied.

Dickie said 'The box is red and printed in the middle in white large capital letters are the words *My Miss Amser Cake* and in the bottom righthand corner in smaller capital letters are the words *Inspired by My Teacher And Made With Love.* I wonder why she didn't tell you?'

Amser was touched by Holly's kindness.

She replied 'Some things are better left unsaid. I always told the children there is much more joy in giving than receiving and this is Holly's joy.'

Over the weeks ahead Amser got stronger. Her speech improved further and she was able to communicate in short periods without getting breathless.

Dickie was able to take her out in her wheelchair. He walked her for miles around the streets of Rowan and in the town park. How Amser loved to get out of the house. To hear the traffic was exciting and of course many people who knew her stopped to say hello. These outings gave her a new lease of life.

It was now mid August and A Level results were due. The post arrived as usual and amongst other items was a letter addressed to Bethan.

Dickie knew what the envelope contained and went and told Amser. They were both excited. Bethan, however, didn't share their enthusiasm and it lay unopened on the kitchen table.

'Aren't you going to open it Bethan?' Dickie asked.

The girl glared at him and shouted 'I don't care what the results are, it won't make any difference to me now,' she replied.

'What do you mean by that?' he enquired.

'I'm going to stay at home with mum. You don't think I'm going to leave her with you do you?' as she left the room slamming the door behind her.

Amser could hear what was being said. She could put up with her disabilities and the intrusions they made into her life. However she was dismayed by Bethan's hatred of her father and wondered if it would ever end.

Dickie too was becoming exhausted in his quest to get Bethan to accept him. It seemed they were now farther apart than ever.

Amser called out for her daughter to come into her room.

As soon as Bethan entered she scolded her 'So you think you can throw away your life do you. After all I've done for you, you selfish girl.'

Before Bethan could speak her mother commanded 'Go and get your results letter now.'

It had been a long time since Amser had been so stern with her daughter; Bethan was shocked but obeyed. When Bethan entered her room again Dickie was already present.

'Well open it then,' demanded Amser.

The girl didn't like being chastised and remarked 'I don't care about the results, your boyfriend can open it,' she replied.

Then whilst looking away, Bethan nonchalantly held out her hand for Dickie to take the envelope. He obliged and didn't waste any time in slitting the top open with his index finger. Inside was a single sheet of white paper folded in half. Opening it up, he had a moment to himself as he studied the results.

Amser was impatient and said 'Tell me will you.'

Bethan sitting at the end of her mum's bed continued to look disinterested as her Dad revealed the results.

'The grades are fantastic,' he remarked.

'An A distinction in Music, an A in Literature and a B in English Language.'

The girl still didn't show any emotion but Amser said 'Oh Bethan that's wonderful, I'm so proud of you.'

Bethan looked uncomfortable. She thought she'd done well but at that moment she wished she'd failed. These results meant Bethan could take her music degree but as hard as Amser and Dickie tried they couldn't persuade Bethan to contemplate living away from home. It caused them sadness because, despite their problems, Bethan's future was the one thing that had kept them going.

Bethan knew how upset they were but was unmoved and went to her bedroom. It was a desperate time for her parents but then an idea ran through Amser's mind. She reminded Dickie about the concert in Rowan Abbey.

'Do you remember the interest taken in Bethan by Mrs Sandling?' she asked.

'Yes darling, I seem to recall she made quite a fuss of Bethan,' he replied.

'She did Dickie, a lot of fuss; I know it's a long shot but I wonder if she might be willing to help.'

Dickie got out the telephone directory and, having found the number, contacted The Welsh Grand Opera Company. A lady with a squeaky voice answered his call but her greeting didn't sound very welcoming.

She said 'WGOC who's calling?'

Dickie felt intimidated and obliged to answer in a hurry causing him to mumble his words.

The lady became impatient but having got the gist of what Dickie had said replied 'I'm sorry it's not possible, Mrs Sandling is a very busy lady.'

By luck Mrs Sandling was in the building and happened to be walking past the telephonist's desk. She heard the name Bethan Edwards being repeated back to Dickie and it stopped her in her tracks.

'Did I hear you say Bethan Edwards?' she enquired.

'Yes, I've told the gentleman how busy you are,' replied the lady.

'Can I speak to him please,' said Mrs Sandling.

The telephonist handed her the phone. Dickie was relieved but felt even more intimidated now. Mrs Sandling was a star of the stage with worldwide commitments.

'Why should she want to talk to him,' he thought.

However, as soon as he mentioned the concert in Rowan and Bethan's harp the lady interrupted him.

She said 'How could I forget that wonderful evening? It's not often I am moved by a performance from someone so young but like all the other patrons I was privileged to witness something exceptional. In my opinion a new star was born that night.'

She went on 'I've often thought about Bethan and wondered how she was getting on. I read about her mother's accident in the newspaper; it was a terrible tragedy.'

Dickie expressed his appreciation.

'So what can I do for you, is it concert tickets for Bethan?' she said.

Dickie, now calm, replied 'Oh no, I wish it were that simple. It's Amser's burning desire and mine for Bethan to pursue her musical ambitions but she doesn't want to take up her degree in Liverpool.'

'Why ever not?' asked Mrs Sandling.

'It's because she doesn't want me to look after her mum. It's complicated,' he replied.

Dickie added 'There's nothing more important in Amser's life and we wondered if there's any way you can help please.'

Mrs Sandling had many reservations about interfering in personal matters but the family had endured so much pain so she was willing to assist if she could.

'I'll do what I can,' she replied.

It was the following morning that Mrs Sandling contacted the Edwards home and Bethan answered the telephone. She was surprised to get a call from this lady and wondered how it had come about.

Mrs Sandling said 'Ever since I saw you in Rowan Abbey you've been on my mind.'

'It was a horrible thing that happened to your mother and I've been meaning to telephone and see how you're getting on. How's your harp?' she asked.

Bethan replied 'I haven't had much time for it these past weeks, in fact I haven't played it at all.'

'How about your other studies Bethan?'

'I did take my A Levels,' she replied.

Bethan then told Mrs Sandling how her mum's accident had affected her and said she didn't feel able to take her music degree now.

Mrs Sandling said 'Oh luvvy I can't imagine what you've been going through, it must have been so hard for you.'

With all the attention paid to Amser this was the first time anyone had shown any sympathy towards Bethan. She wasn't selfish and had never looked for a shoulder to cry on but she'd been hurting too. Even when she saw Iola or Mr and Mrs Peach the conversation was always about Amser.

Mrs Sandling spoke with a soft compassionate voice and said 'Tell me Bethan, how much time has your mum spent helping you over the years?'

Bethan paused for a moment as she considered the question.

Then she replied 'My mum has always been there for me ever since I can remember.'

'Why do you think she's done that?' said Mrs Sandling.

'Because she wants the best for me I suppose,' Bethan replied.

'Then you have to go to Liverpool and fulfil your dream,' said the lady.

She added 'Don't you see it's your mother's dream as well? There must be someone who can look after your mum whilst you're away.'

Mrs Sandling knew full well Dickie would nurse her.

Bethan paused, and replied 'Well there is but I don't want to leave her.'

'I know luvvy but you have to,' said Mrs Sandling.

Bethan knew the lady was right but she'd needed someone else to tell her.

'Yes I do; thank you so much,' she replied.

Having said goodbye to Mrs Sandling and put down the telephone, Bethan burst into tears. All the stress that had built up inside her had been relieved. She went straight to her room and sat down by her harp. The instrument seemed like a stranger to her as she ran her fingers over the strings. With her eyes and cheeks still wet with emotion she pondered over what had been said.

Then with Mrs Sandling's words in her mind, she started to play 'Sou Gan'. In the next room Amser and Dickie could hear her music. They guessed what had happened and sitting close together held hands and Amser's face beamed.

She said 'Oh Dickie I think everything will be alright now. The noise of that bloody harp being played had almost driven me mad but right now it's the most beautiful sound in the world.'

Dickie put his arms around his sweetheart. He too was overjoyed and fortunately there was still a place at university available for Bethan.

Chapter Thirty Two

The next few weeks were frantic as Bethan tried to find somewhere to live. It seemed the better accommodation had been snapped up whilst she was resisting the change in her life.

One day however she received a telephone call from the university. They had a cancellation on campus of a room in a new four-storey building and she accepted it. At last everything seemed to be in place and there was nothing to stop Bethan now.

The day of her departure arrived and Bethan came downstairs dressed in her old jeans and a tatty old tee shirt and sandals. She'd made up her mind if she was to be a student she was going to dress like one.

She was already a little late and went straight to see her mother. It was a bright September day and Amser was sitting up in bed with a pillow behind her head. The window was open and as usual she was enjoying listening to the birds and smelling the scent of the garden. Bethan checked she was alright. She tucked in her bed covers and adjusted the curtain so the sun didn't shine on her.

'Stop fussing Bethan will you I'm all right; have you got everything ready?' she enquired.

'Yes I think so but I still don't have to go mum, I could stay here and look after you,' she replied.

Amser hugged her.

'Now, now we've been through all that. You're all grown-up and it's time for you to embrace the world.'

Dickie still unable to show his true feelings was also desperate to cuddle his daughter but, having said her goodbyes to her mother, she walked out of the house with no more than a forced smile in his direction. Bethan by this time had passed her driving test and was able to make the journey in a new car that her parents had bought for her.

Amser's injuries from the accident were so severe that,

although for a while it did seem she was she getting a little better, in Bethan's absence she began to deteriorate. Her breathlessness had become more apparent again and she was tired by midday. However, somehow, with Dickie's help, Amser was able to hide her poor health. She always managed to smile when the girl was in her presence. Amser was determined Bethan was going to get her degree.

Dickie did everything for Amser. He worked twenty four hours a day to make her as comfortable as possible tending to all her personal needs.

He washed her in the purest soap and dried her in the softest towels. He dressed her in clean, ironed, clothes and put on makeup and a little perfume. He helped feed her, read her stories and recited poems from the book given to her by Mrs Reece. He continued to describe the flowers as they came into bloom in the garden and talked about things that happened when he went shopping. He often made stories up and tried to make her laugh although he could see she was getting weaker by the day.

They loved one another very much and one evening when they were alone, sitting together holding hands on the bed right out of the blue she said 'You know Dickie, you don't realise how much you miss seeing and walking until it happens to you.'

Then she burst into tears and Dickie being so full of emotion had tears streaming down his face. He wanted to help his sweetheart so much. Holding her close all Dickie could do was promise he would be with her forever.

He went on to say 'If there's anything I can do for you I'm not doing now please tell me will you. I'll do anything.'

Amser deliberated for a moment. Although she couldn't see and was unable to write, her mind was still active. She'd spent days and even months lying on her bed in the hospital thinking about the past. Her life, although blessed with her daughter and many happy memories, had been tarnished with an unhappy childhood and much tragedy.

Recently she'd recalled the poem she started to write when she was living in Walwyn Gate. It related to the time she spent with

Dickie in Amber Sands and the words were never to leave her memory. Now the poem was on her mind even more and in her thoughts over the past few days she finished what she'd started.

Amser had never mentioned the poem to Dickie but decided she must make him understand what it meant to her.

'Will you really do anything?' she said.

'Yes Amser, anything, you know I will.'

'Then listen to me darling,' came the reply.

Dickie watched as Amser summoned up all her strength and started to recite. She could only speak softly but somehow she made the words flow from her mouth.

Sea shells on a silent beach
Dark skies almost in reach
Warm winds on a rushing tide
You lying by my side
Young hearts so wild and free
Embracing so tenderly
I felt the love inside of me
Oh how I wanted you

Amser stopped for a moment as her breathing became heavy and varied. Dickie was concerned but his beloved Amser was determined to continue. She went on:-

And how we've grown in many ways
Although so far apart
But through the years I've always known
That you were in my heart.
And now although I can't see you
I can feel your warm soft hands
And hear the sound of your sweet voice
and remember Amber Sands

Then whilst struggling more and more with her breathing she said 'Do you realise what I've been saying?'

'Yes my darling of course I do but you have to stop, the exertion is not good for you.'

Amser however wasn't to be deterred.

Trying to raise her voice as best she could she said 'Listen to me will you,' and went on to finish the poem.

So take me back once more my love
To where it all began
That treasure in my memory
Amber Sands oh Amber Sands

Amser had managed to complete her recital but her breathing was now almost choking her.

Dickie tried to calm her down; he took hold of Amser's hands and pleaded with her to relax.

Amser however was frustrated; her breathing had started to improve again and she moaned 'You don't understand what I've said to you, do you?'

Dickie hadn't realised there was a message in the words and she managed to repeat the last part of the poem again.

And now although I can't see you
I can feel your warm soft hands
And hear the sound of your sweet voice
and remember Amber Sands
So take me back once more my love
To where it all began
That treasure in my memory
Amber Sands oh Amber Sands

'What are you saying?' said Dickie.

Amser squeezed his hands.

'You mean you want to go back?' he said.

Amser nodded and said 'Yes my darling more than anything.'

'But you can't, you're too ill,' said Dickie.

Amser still struggling for oxygen, somehow replied 'Look at

me Dickie, you're always positive and talk about the good times ahead but we both know I'm not going to be here long. Let's not kid ourselves anymore I may only have days to live. Please my love, I have to go back, it's our destiny.'

Despite his concern Dickie agreed and now lying on the bed in each other's arms they felt so sorry for themselves, so cheated by life. They had so little time together but through all those years they had a wonderful daughter.

'We'll have to tell Bethan. If there's any chance I might be able to tell her the truth one day she has to be assured that this is your idea,' he said.

'I know,' replied Amser.

When the weekend arrived Bethan came home to see her mum. Amser once again summoned up all her strength to hide her failing health.

Whilst spending time together Amser said 'There's something I need to tell you.'

Bethan was worried. Her mum was unusually fidgety whilst sitting propped up in her bed.

'Whatever could it be?' she thought.

Amser said 'I know you won't be happy about his but I want to go to Amber Sands and Dickie has agreed to take me.'

Raising her voice the girl replied 'Amber Sands, why on earth would you want to go there?'

Not wishing to tell Bethan the whole truth Amser replied 'Because I have many happy memories there when I was a child.'

Bethan thought this was a very strange thing to do and questioned her mum's motive.

Without thinking she remarked 'What's the point, you won't be able to see Amber Sands will you?'

Amser replied 'Oh Bethan I don't need you to tell me that.'

Bethan felt awful and immediately apologised.

She'd now calmed down a little and said 'I'm sorry mum but I worry about you all the time. I can understand you must be fed up cooped up in this room but you aren't well enough to go anywhere and Amber Sands is miles away.'

However, as hard as Bethan tried to change her mum's mind, she wouldn't be moved and Bethan thought it must be Dickie's idea.

Getting more agitated by the minute she insisted 'I won't let that man take you.'

Amser tried to convince her daughter the trip was her idea but Bethan wouldn't believe her. She was very worried and if things had been difficult between her and Dickie in the past, they were at rock bottom now. She wouldn't speak to him or even look at him. Before returning to university Bethan tried once more to change her mother's mind.

'Please mum, don't listen to Dickie. Please don't go to Amber Sands, it's too much for you.'

Amser didn't answer but mother and daughter hugged and kissed as usual before Bethan embarked on her journey back to Liverpool. This time however, as Bethan left the bedroom, Amser called her back. She opened her arms and encouraged her daughter to hug her again. Bethan walked back to her mother's bed. Using every ounce of her strength Amser took hold of her daughter in her arms. She smiled and kissed her again realising it might be the last time she would see her.

Chapter Thirty Three

Dickie realised travelling to Amber Sands would distress his beloved Amser. He cared for her so much that despite the severity of her ill health, every day with her was special. Now she'd asked him to do this one last thing, how could he be selfish and deny her?

The journey was to commence the following morning. It was bright and sunny and Amser was feeling a little better having slept well. Dickie had already packed up the car with all the things she would need and then turned his attention to getting her ready. Washing and dressing Amser took a long time but as usual he attended to every detail. He helped her into her favourite black skirt and red blouse. He secured a gold pendant around her neck and put on her tiny heart-shaped gold earrings. Then he put some makeup and lipstick on her before combing her hair.

It was time to go and so he wheeled his sweetheart out of the house and to the door of the car. He lifted her out, sat her in the front seat and made sure she was comfortable before placing the chair in the boot.

Whilst travelling, just as at home, Dickie went about describing all the things and happenings around them. He wanted to make the long trip as interesting as he could and spoke about shops, people, flowers and the wildlife. It was difficult to keep up the commentary but Amser slept for a large part of the journey.

When they arrived in Amber Sands Dickie startled her by shouting out 'I can see the sea.'

The car had just turned a corner onto the sea front road and Amser smiled. Within a few minutes he'd parked close to the entrance to the pier.

Like Amser this was the first time he'd been back since the day they first met. It was winter and the only people to be seen were dog walkers and ramblers. The pier was closed and looked old and neglected. The puppet theatre had been demolished and the beach now had boulders on it to protect the cliffs behind. The whole place had a sorry look about it.

Amser was very excited as Dickie got her out of the car. She could hear the sound of the wind and the sea and the memories she had came flooding back to her. He carefully lifted her into her wheelchair. There was a chill in the air and Dickie wrapped a shawl around her head and shoulders just like he'd warmed her with his woolly jumper all those years ago.

Amser enquired 'What does it look like? Is it the same as when we were last here?'

Dickie paused; he didn't want to lie to her but he didn't want to tarnish her memory either.

He said 'I'm so pleased we are here; you're right: Amber Sands is a special place for both of us. The pier looks as if it has been repainted. The beach is beautiful and everything is the same as when we left it.'

'Walk me along the promenade Dickie,' said Amser.

Dickie pushed the wheelchair over the same ground they covered before as best he could remember until he reached the promenade's end.

Dickie said 'We can't go any further.'

Amser sensed where they were.

'Lift me out,' she said.

Dickie was worried and replied 'It would be better for you if you stay in the wheelchair.'

Amser was in a care free mood.

She said 'Oh come on Dickie just for a minute.'

Dickie obliged and whilst holding her in his arms she pleaded 'Carry me onto the beach.'

'I'm not sure I can; the sand is very soft and I'm frightened I might drop you,' he replied.

Amser was getting more and more excited.

'Please Dickie take me, will you,' she insisted.

'There's only one place I want to be. You know where it is.'

Dickie was scared but he knew he had to do this. Taking one slow step at a time he walked onto the beach, remembering where she had ran out in front of him and into the sea. His mind raced across the years. For a moment it seemed like ages ago and then in his next breath it felt like yesterday.

He couldn't take her to the spot where they made love because of the boulders that had been placed there but Amser didn't know and that was all that mattered. After a few moments he stopped walking and lowered Amser down onto the sand.

'Are we there, is this the spot?' asked Amser.

Dickie replied 'Yes my darling but the last time we were here it was dark and the moon sparkled in the sky. This time it's daylight and I can see the sun beaming down on us. It's a beautiful winter's day.'

Looking at Amser he could see she still had a beautiful face. It was difficult for him to comprehend what had happened and how ill she'd become. How Dickie wished she could see him but at least he was comforted in the knowledge she couldn't see Amber Sands.

'I think we should go now,' said Dickie but Amser didn't want to leave.

She replied 'Just a few more moments my darling. It feels so right to be here.'

Then she said 'Kiss me darling, kiss me like you did on that wonderful day.'

Amser put her arms around him and didn't want to let him go. In a few seconds however Amser was out of breath and their lips parted. Then Dickie lifted her up again and carried her back over the sand to where her chair was waiting.

It was getting colder now and Amser was even more tired than usual. As Dickie was pushing her back to his car he could see she was getting weaker and weaker. Clearly there was something very wrong.

There was a telephone box by the pier entrance and Dickie called for an ambulance. He also remembered to telephone Bethan but she was in Liverpool a long way away. Memories of the dreadful accident came flooding back to him as they waited for the emergency vehicle to arrive.

Although it seemed like ages, only three minutes passed before the ambulance could be seen speeding along the sea front. Within a few more seconds it was beside them and Amser was placed on a stretcher and lifted inside the vehicle. Dickie left his car and travelled with Amser to Amber Sands Hospital.

On arrival a man with a bald head and a grey bushy beard called Dr Thorne examined her in a private room whilst Dickie waited outside. He knew her remaining lifespan was short but never dared to imagine what it would be like without her. Now this dreadful thought might become a reality and he was shaking.

Then the doctor opened the door and confirmed Dickie's worst fears.

He said 'I'm so sorry but Miss Edwards is very poorly. I'm afraid there's nothing more we can do for her. Her heart is so weak and it is a matter of time before she passes away.'

Dickie sat down beside Amser and held her hand. He prayed Bethan would make the journey in time.

Still trying to stay positive he kept talking to his sweetheart 'Bethan is on her way to see you, I know you'd like her to be here,' he said.

Dickie could see Amser getting weaker; she was dying before his eyes. He was crying and she wasn't able to acknowledge him at all now. He knew there was very little time left and tried so hard not to break down but the emotional pain was more than he could bear.

Not knowing if she could hear him, he said 'My darling, darling Amser, I don't know how I'm going to live my life without you. You're everything to me and I love you so much. I would give anything to make you better. Dearest Amser I promise you somehow I'll make things right with our daughter.'

Then Bethan arrived and Dickie moved back a little so she could get close to her mother. She sat down and kissed her on the forehead but there wasn't any reaction in her mother's face.

Then she held her mother's hands and said 'It's Bethan.'

Dickie looked on, believing Amser couldn't respond, but to his amazement she softly squeezed her daughter's hand. Then Bethan told her she loved her before her mum gently passed away.

Bethan and Dickie left the room and sat in silence whilst a nurse made her look more comfortable. On returning to look at Amser, they saw her at peace. She wasn't in any pain now. No longer would she have to struggle with her life. She wasn't crippled or blind now and they had to believe she was going to a better place. They sat each side of the bed with their eyes fixed upon her.

There is a feeling of emptiness inside when someone you love dies and every emotion goes through your body. Since Amser's accident it had been a long hard road and both Dickie and Bethan were at their lowest ebb. Somehow, they were going to have to pick up their lives but Dickie knew Bethan would blame him for her mother's death.

In shedding his grief he'd promised Amser he would make things right with his daughter but he wondered if he would ever be able to do it.

When they left the hospital Bethan couldn't keep silent any longer.

'Why did you bring her here? Tell me why, will you?'

Without waiting for a response she added 'You killed her, you killed my mum.'

Dickie didn't answer; he was hurting as much as his daughter. They parted without another word and made their way back to North Wales, separately. Dickie still had a sister in Elwy and went and stayed there whilst Bethan returned to Rowan. They both felt empty and alone.

Amser's body was brought back to Rowan and the funeral was arranged from her home. Bethan invited her granny and Rhonda and the service was to take place in St Johns Abbey.

It was a cold winter's day and a car and hearse pulled up at the house at the stroke of 10am. Bethan had ordered special flowers and a pretty bright pink selection making up the word 'mum' could be seen on each side of the coffin. However, when Bethan opened the front door she was amazed to see the driveway covered in flowers. She wasn't prepared for all the bouquets, wreaths and messages of sympathy from local people.

As the vehicles made their way the short distance to the Abbey, Bethan, along with her granny and Rhonda, saw many people standing in their front gardens. Others had come out of shops and they were all bowing their heads in respect. Amser's mother and friend didn't have any idea of the impact she'd made on the town and were amazed.

As the cars got closer to the Abbey all the roads were packed with parked vehicles and on their arrival there were so many people outside it was more like a crowd for a concert than for a funeral. They'd all come to hear the service as best they could.

Walking down the aisle they could see every seat had been taken apart from the front row and, because of their love for Amser and out of respect, not a sound could be heard. It was going to be a very hard day for Bethan but this support from local people provided her with much comfort.

The service commenced with the singing of Love Divine All Loves Excelling. Then the Right Reverend David Hopkins invited Gerald Hinds to say a few words. He made his way slowly and solemnly to the pulpit and looked at Bethan and the congregation.

With a very loud voice he said 'When I first met Amser she said to me that she wanted donations from local business to send children on holiday. Well, it was a little more involved than that, but when I suggested she might not get the money she became very agitated.'

He went on 'She replied "the children will have their holiday with or without business". I'll never forget the look in her eyes. I knew then how serious she was and from that moment there wasn't a doubt in my mind she would be successful.'

He said 'Bethan, ladies and gentlemen, I can assure you all, Amser is alive in Rowan. The so aptly named Edwards Foundation is still flourishing today. It's created a partnership between our businesses and our schools and enabled our children to express themselves, to use their imagination and make their way in life.'

With much emotion in his voice he finished by saying 'Oh yes,

288

everybody in this abbey and outside knows it. Amser is every-where you look in our community.'

Mr Hinds left the pulpit in silence but on making his way back to his seat a man started clapping. Other people started joining in until the noise in the abbey and outside was deafening. Bethan was sobbing but with the arms of her granny and Rhonda around her she was very proud of her mother.

Then prayers were said and the congregation sang Cym Rhondda before the service was over. Dickie sat right at the back of the abbey with his own private thoughts and he too was overwhelmed by what he'd heard. Like Amser's granny and best friend he'd no any idea what impact Amser had made in the local community.

When it was all over, whilst Dickie stayed in the abbey, Bethan, her grandma and Rhonda made their way to the plot where Amser was to be buried. Rain started to teem down as they stood by the empty space and watched the coffin lowered into the ground. Amser was only thirty five and this final act was all too much for the party; every ounce of emotion was released from their bodies.

When they felt able to leave the grave they walked back to where their car was waiting. Turning to look towards the grave once more Bethan saw Dickie had arrived - she hadn't seen him in the abbey. He was kneeling on the ground beside her mother. She didn't want him to be there and was about to call out when her granny persuaded her not to.

'You've been upset enough today, we all have. Let's go home,' she pleaded.

Bethan's mother's friend Iola had stayed behind and had prepared some sandwiches for the family and friends. When the party arrived Bethan once again started to question her mother's trip back to West Wales.

Still filled with hate toward Dickie she enquired of her grandma 'Why did she have to go to Amber Sands? She might still be alive if he hadn't taken her to that dreadful place.'

Amser's grandma looked at Bethan; she wasn't sure how to reply. As soon as she knew where Dickie had taken her daughter she realised who the man was and pondered over whether to tell her. Rhonda, standing close by, overheard the conversation.

Amber Sands did seem a strange place to visit unless there was a special reason. She hadn't considered it before and cast her mind back to her childhood. It only took Rhonda a few seconds to realise what had happened and waited for the grandmother's response. The lady looked nervous and stayed silent whilst Bethan began to sob again. Rhonda knew her friend must be told.

Looking straight into the grandmother's eyes she said 'You know why Amser was taken to Amber Sands don't you?'

The lady still would not speak.

'I know you do,' Rhonda added.

Bethan didn't understand what was going on. 'What was so secret?' she thought.

'Will you tell me granny, what is it about Amber Sands?' she demanded to know.

'You have to tell her, she has to be told,' said Rhonda.

Two sets of eyes were now fixed on the grandmother. She knew Bethan had a right to know and reasoned there would never be a good time to tell her. She was also aware she'd done very little for her daughter whilst she was alive but she could do this one thing for her now she was dead.

Taking hold of her granddaughter's hands she looked at her and said 'Bethan my dear, Amber Sands is where you were conceived.'

Bethan thought about what she'd been told. It took a moment for it to sink in.

Then she stopped sobbing and dried her tears.

'Oh no, what have I done?' she said.

Her granny tried to comfort her once more.

'You weren't to know Bethan, how could you know?' she said.

For the first time in her life the girl felt sorry for Dickie.

'He's all alone,' she thought.

At last she realised how much he was hurting and, unlike her, he had no-one to lean on for support. Without another word Bethan left the house. She drove as fast as she could back to the abbey. On the short journey cars passed by, people were going about their business and a fire engine sped across the road at a junction.

Bethan didn't see anything or anybody as all her thoughts were focused on her dad. On entering the graveyard she could see him still kneeling by her mother's side. Ignoring the stone path and running towards him she stepped over old flower beds and ancient tomb stones. In her haste she almost tripped on the uneven ground but nothing was going to stop her now. She couldn't wait to get to her father.

Dickie's suit was saturated by the rain and water was dripping off his face. He was still crying as he looked down on the coffin.

Getting close, she heard him say 'My darling Amser I love you so much, so very, very, much. What will I do without you? Please help me Amser I feel so alone.'

Bethan knelt down beside him. Being so engrossed in his own emotion he didn't see her until she touched his hand. They looked towards each other and Dickie rubbed the rain and tears from his eyes. He thought Bethan had returned to be with her mother. Then for the first time in his life he was to receive the love of his daughter as she put her arms around him. They hugged one another and there were more tears.

Then Bethan said 'I know dad. I know all about Amber Sands.'

Bethan and Dickie had lost the most precious person in their lives but Amser's death had brought them together. Father and daughter had found each other at last. Now, having been strong for her dad, seeing the coffin in the ground upset Bethan once more.

She was still young and sobbed 'My mum wasn't supposed to die, she was only thirty five.'

More tears streamed down Bethan's face and it was her dad's turn to provide her with words of comfort.

'Bethan, it's so hard for both of us. Life will never be the same without her but always remember, you can talk to your mum whenever you like.'

He added 'You can ask her questions and she'll answer you because you know what she would say.'

He said 'She'll always be here, love her and she'll love you.'

At that moment, despite the dark clouds in the sky, the rain stopped. They both felt a strange feeling inside and hugged one another again.

'Do you think she has been listening to us?' said Bethan.

'Oh yes, she's heard everything she wants to hear. She's at rest now,' he replied.

Bethan and Dickie got to their feet, embraced once more before embarking on the journey home and, as they walked away, the rain started falling once again.

Acknowledgements

I would like to say a big thank you to my family and friends for their support throughout the writing of this book. It must have been tiresome hearing me talking about it at every opportunity and some may be relieved I have finally reached my goal. Nevertheless the help and advice they provided has been invaluable and will never be forgotten.

In particular I would like to mention Valerie Hinkin, Jenna Gould, Ann Neville and Deborah Younie. There were times when I doubted myself and was at a low ebb. It was their enthusiasm and words of encouragement that gave me the belief to carry on. They inspired me and I am truly grateful.

Printed by BoD™in Norderstedt, Germany